HAUNTED: DEVIL'S DOOR

LEE MOUNTFORD

FREE BOOK

1

JANUARY 1982.

'It's big,' Ray Pearson said, looking up at the house before him.

'And our home for the foreseeable future,' his wife Rita added, sounding almost hesitant. She stood beside him, and her brown eyes were squashed into a frown. 'Do you think we'll be able to handle it?'

'I hope so,' he replied.

It did seem an imposing task, but right now they were acting out of necessity.

'I like it,' their six-year-old daughter said. Chloe stood in front of her father, smiling, showing the two missing teeth from the top row. Ray's big and calloused hands rested gently on her shoulders. 'It's like a mansion,' she said.

Ray gave her shoulders a squeeze beneath the thick red coat she wore. Both he and his wife were well wrapped up, too, given the biting January cold. The clouds above were dark and threatened rain, and the gravel underfoot was wet from an earlier downpour. Their car—an old, burgundy Ford that had barely made the journey up here—was behind them, parked at the head of the long driveway the family now stood on.

Rita was right. The house, which was bigger than any Ray had seen, was to be their home now. The thought of living here was difficult to comprehend. He was used to small, terraced houses with families living practically on top of each other, where things were noisy and chaotic, yet warm. Here, they could live at different ends of the house and rarely see each other.

He didn't like the thought of that.

At the top of the walls in front of them—high above and over three stories up—were three distinct peaks cut into the roofline. They offered character to the front elevation of the building, and a symmetry Ray liked. The house was predominantly stone, but the craftsmanship of the stonemasonry was definitely something he could appreciate. The windows were taller than they were wide, with thin wooden frames and arched heads.

They sure didn't make them like this anymore.

'Suppose we knock?' Rita offered, which seemed the only reasonable course of action, given no one was coming out to welcome them. Ray had thought perhaps the noise of their car would have alerted the owner to their arrival. But, apparently not.

Rita took the lead, as she so often did, and started to walk up the steps before her, towards the front door. Whether she felt it or not, Rita never showed any signs of nerves or fear in social situations. Conversely, Ray wanted nothing more than to crawl back into his car and light up a smoke. And that was just at the thought of meeting the owner of Perron Manor.

Marcus Blackwater.

With his hands buried into his pockets, Ray traced a

nicotine-stained finger over his tobacco tin inside, feeling the pull. But he couldn't roll one up now. Rita had earlier warned him that first impressions counted, so he didn't want to have a rolled-up cigarette hanging out of his mouth for the first meeting with their new boss. Instead, he followed his wife, who was dressed in a smart, figure-hugging grey coat and matching wool beret. Beneath the long coat, legs wrapped in tight jeans poked out, and she had calf-high tanned boots on her feet.

Mid-way up the steps, Rita stopped and turned back to him.

'Well come on, then,' she said, quickly flapping her hand in a *come here* motion. He was dawdling... deliberately so.

Chloe skipped ahead and her long brown hair flowed behind her. The distinct red coat Chloe wore was as stylish as her mother's, and cost more than Ray had been comfortable paying. His own clothes—an old navy blue jacket, faded jeans, and boots—were simple but adequate in comparison. However, they did the same job and cost a fraction of the price.

He reached the top and stood by his girls, letting Rita take the lead. She was better at the social game than he was, and if first impressions did indeed count, then Rita would do well. To Ray, she was stunning, smart, and highly professional.

Ray held his breath. This was it: the first day of living in a mansion. And their job was to turn it into a hotel for the owner.

Rita used the brass door knocker—a lion's head, with a large ring hanging from its mouth—to signal their presence. After a few moments, Ray heard someone approach on the other side and saw a shape moving through the privacy glass set within the door. The door opened, and there stood Vincent Bell, Rita's older brother.

Ray had always found Vincent something of a flake, though he could be nothing but grateful to the man for casting Ray and his family a lifeline when they needed it most.

In truth, however, Ray didn't really understand the relationship between Vincent and Marcus, so he was interested to see what the situation here actually was.

'Sis!' Vincent exclaimed, wearing a big smile that showed his teeth. His thick, unkempt beard coupled with his long, slightly greasy hair, gave him a grungy sort of look. It was a shame, as even Ray could tell that under it all, Vincent could have been quite a good-looking man. Although, he looked a lot paler than Ray remembered, and much more gaunt.

Vincent's less-than-pristine appearance was completed by a frayed beige shirt, unbuttoned to the chest, corded blue trousers, and soft loafers.

He pulled Rita in for a hug, and Ray could tell his wife was a little surprised at the forwardness. It had been over seven years since they had last seen each other. It had been at their mother's funeral, and Ray didn't recall Vincent hugging Rita that day.

'How are you, Vinnie?' Rita said after pulling away. She wore a big smile as well, one that would have fooled most people.

Except for Ray.

He knew that it was, in fact, her business smile. It showed plenty of teeth, but to him seemed forced, and it wasn't nearly as warm or beautiful as her real one.

'I'm good, I'm good,' Vincent said. 'And I'm really glad you guys are all here. The house is amazing. You're going to love living here.'

Vincent then looked over to Ray and held out his hand.

'Nice to see you too, Ray. You're looking well.'

'Thanks,' he replied, 'you too.' Ray didn't exactly mean it, but didn't want to be rude. Besides, he knew that he wasn't exactly an oil painting either. 'Listen, Vincent, I want to thank you for this. For letting us stay here and helping out. We really appreciate it.'

'Ah, don't mention it,' he replied. 'Besides, it was Marcus who agreed to it all, I just put the idea forward. You're good with your hands, and Rita here has run a hotel before. You two are perfect. With your help, we'll have this place up and running in no time.'

'Thanks for the vote of confidence,' Rita said.

Vincent looked past them to their car on the driveway. Boxes were piled in the boot and back seat, which had forced Chloe to make the long drive up to Perron Manor riding on her mother's knee.

'You fit all your stuff in there?' Vincent asked.

'We travel light,' was all Rita said. 'So we won't take up too much room here.'

Vincent laughed. 'Room is one thing we have an abundance of.' He then stepped aside, revealing a grand entrance area inside, with a marble-tiled floor and wide oak stairs. 'Come on in and meet Marcus before you unpack.'

Ray and his family all walked into the foyer. It was double-storey space, with ceilings high up above giving a hugely grandiose feel to the entrance—which was no doubt what the original designers were shooting for. A plush carpet lined the centre section of the timber stair-treads, and the lower half of the walls had wooden panelling, which was the same dark oak as the stairs. The whole area had an odour of old wood and lingering varnish, which Ray appreciated.

Chloe started to click the heels of her shoes on the marble, giggling at the echoing sound. The smile on her face grew wider. Ray knew that the young girl was in love with the house already, and she'd barely seen any of it. To a six-year-old, this must have all seemed like one big adventure.

Vincent must have noticed the way they were all looking around in awe. 'Takes your breath away, doesn't it?' He then held his arms out to his side. 'Ladies and gentleman, I give you... Perron Manor. Or, as it will soon be known, the Black-water Hotel.'

Ray wasn't sure what Vincent expected them to do after the cheesy little announcement. No doubt Vincent had intended it to be significant and grandiose, but it only came off as... forced. Was a round of applause in order? Instead, Ray just gave a small smile and nod.

'So where is the owner?' Rita asked.

'He should be along shortly,' Vincent replied, and then as if on cue Ray heard a door open to one of the walkways above. He heard footsteps move along the gantry until a figure appeared above them as it turned onto the stairs.

While Vincent's appearance was rather grungy, Marcus was the polar opposite. He had dark, brushed-back hair with no signs of grey, blue eyes beneath dark brows, a slight tan to his skin, trimmed stubble, and wore what looked to be an expensive black shirt and pressed dark trousers. To Ray, the man reeked of money and confidence, and he wore a charming grin, likely to show off his perfect white teeth.

'Ah,' Marcus said, his voice deep. 'The hired help!'

Ray assumed that was supposed to be a joke, even if it was mostly true, so he offered a polite chuckle. But Marcus

Blackwater had yet to even look at Ray. His gaze had been focused purely on Rita and there was a wolfish, almost predatory look in those bright blue eyes.

Marcus started to descend the steps slowly, taking his time. He still wore the smile that had at first been charming, though now it seemed just a little off to Ray.

First impressions count, Rita had told him. Whether it was just Ray's own insecurities clouding things or not, his first impression of their host wasn't a great one.

Though he did like the fact that Marcus was much shorter than him, looking about five-foot-seven at best. Given Ray himself was six-foot-two, it offered him a little comfort to be able to tower over Marcus as the man stepped out onto the marble floor to join them.

Marcus walked straight over to Rita, keeping his eyes on her. He took a hand that wasn't offered before planting a slow kiss on it.

'Pleasure to meet you all,' Marcus said, keeping his unblinking gaze fixed on her.

Rita quickly pulled her hand away and gave a forced smile. 'You as well, Mr. Blackwater,' she replied. She then turned and held an arm out to Ray. 'This is my husband.'

It was only then that Marcus finally turned his attentions away from Rita. 'Ah yes... Raymond, am I right?' He held out his hand. Ray shook. Marcus' grip was strong and tight.

'Just Ray,' he replied.

Marcus nodded, still smiling. 'Of course.' Then he turned and looked down to Ray's daughter. 'And you must be Chloe?'

Chloe giggled. 'Yes, sir. Pleased to meet you.'

Marcus gently ruffled her hair. 'You too.' He then looked back to Rita, but appeared to address them all. 'Now, I'm sure you are tired after your long drive, so how about we get you settled into your rooms first? Then we can go about getting you all fed. How does that sound?'

Rita nodded. 'Sounds good to me.'

'Excellent,' Marcus replied, clapping his hands together. 'Well, let's get your belongings from the car.'

They all walked out to the car, Ray staying by Rita's side the whole way.

2

'WHAT DO YOU THINK?' Rita asked as she hung one of her blouses inside the wardrobe.

Unpacking their essentials was taking a while, but it was a job she wanted done quickly—one less thing to worry about later.

'Think about what?' Ray asked. 'The house, or our host?'

Rita smiled. She'd seen Ray tense up the moment he'd laid eyes on Marcus. But, in fairness, their new boss *had* been a little singular in his attentions while he blatantly focused on Rita. She hoped it wouldn't develop into a problem.

'Let's start with the house,' Rita said.

'It's beautiful,' Ray replied. 'And huge.'

'*I* love it!' Chloe added from her position on the bed, her legs dangling off the edge and swinging to-and-fro. Rita was glad about her enthusiasm, as Chloe not acclimatising to her new environment had been a big concern. Chloe had her large stuffed doll on her lap. The doll had button eyes and red, stringy hair. Chloe had named it Emma, and it was by far her favourite, even though it was starting to show its age and fraying at the edges a little.

After meeting with Vincent and Marcus earlier, they'd all gone back to the car to retrieve the family's belongings. Then the four of them—with Chloe helping where she could—had carried everything over to the two rooms designated for Rita, Ray, and Chloe.

The whole time, Marcus had not been shy at looking Rita over, though she didn't think Ray had noticed, thankfully.

Her husband tended to be a little insecure at times, though not to a degree where it was ever an issue. She just wished he could see his own worth and his own attractiveness. He was a large and broad-shouldered man, with a square jaw, cleft chin, and dark eyes under thick black hair which was always worn in a simple side-parting. And he had a kind smile that lit up his whole face.

The family had been put towards the back of the house, on the middle floor, and both rooms were on one of the protruding wings that ran out into the rear grounds. Chloe's room was set at the end of a short corridor, with Rita and Ray's just next to it. Those were the only two rooms in the short corridor.

Both bedrooms were nice and very traditional in their décor, befitting a manor such as this one. Rita and Ray's room had a dull but thick brown carpet, pale green walls, black cast-iron radiators, and high ceilings with ornate coving and chandelier lighting. The furniture was dark oak —a theme that seemed to run through the house—but the centrepiece was, without doubt, the four-poster bed. The frame was dark wood, with cream fabric hanging down from the canopy, and the sheets and pillows were a mix of reds and whites. Rita had never slept in a four-poster bed, and none of the previous hotels she'd worked at had ever had them.

Very fancy.

Chloe's room was similar in style and layout, but the carpet had a checkered pattern to it, and the walls were a plain white, which made the room feel lighter. Chloe had a four-poster bed as well, and upon seeing it her eyes had lit up.

Rita continued to unpack, but she felt Ray's eyes on her.

'Do you think we'll be able to do what they're asking?' Ray questioned. 'I mean, just the four of us to run a hotel... surely we need more hands.'

Rita shrugged. 'I honestly don't know. Depends on how quickly business picks up, I guess. Suppose we won't know until we try.'

She was trying to be optimistic but could understand Ray's reservations. The deal was that they come and live here and help get the hotel ready for launch, then help run it for as long as the Pearson family wanted to stay. How long that would be, exactly, Rita was unsure, but the offer had come at a time when they'd needed it most.

Ray's work as a labourer and handyman had been inter-mittent at best recently, and Rita had lost her job as a hotel manager after a recent takeover. They had no actual income, and the little bit of savings they did have squirrelled away was fast running out.

And then, out of the blue, Vincent had gotten in touch with an offer of a job. The stars had aligned, and there was no way they could refuse.

Negotiating pay had been a quick process: Marcus had a figure in mind that he would pay them both and wouldn't budge from it, even though Rita—through Vincent—had tried to haggle for more. However, their combined wage meant they would actually be making more in total than they had in a long while. That, plus the fact that they didn't have to pay for their housing, made it an easy decision.

At the very least, Perron Manor was a place where they could get back on their feet, even if things didn't work out long term. They made the leap, as well as the long drive up to the far north, to the outskirts of a town called Alnmouth.

'Well,' Ray went on, 'let's hope for the best. At least we have a roof over our heads for now.'

They eventually finished unpacking and setting up both rooms, with the task taking close to two hours in the end. Chloe had helped with arranging her own room, taking great pride in setting out her scores of books. When done, Rita felt ravenous and was looking forward to some food. They had arranged to meet Marcus and Vincent in the great hall at four-thirty, which gave them just over half an hour to kill.

'Why don't we go explore?' Chloe asked. 'We've hardly seen anything of the house so far.'

'Not yet, hun,' Rita told her. 'I think we should wait until we've been shown 'round first. It's only polite. You'll have plenty of chance to run around here later.'

Chloe made a face and continued to play with Emma's stringy hair.

'Can't hurt to have a little look around,' Ray cut in. 'Nothing else to do. And besides, we live here now. We can't be prisoners in our rooms the whole time.'

Rita mulled it over for a few moments. Ray did have a point, and it couldn't do any harm as long as they didn't go snooping anywhere they shouldn't.

'Fine,' Rita eventually said, getting a cheer from her daughter. 'How about we throw on our coats and have a quick walk around outside, see the gardens?'

'Sounds great!' Chloe said, hopping down from the bed. 'I'm gonna go get my coat.'

After putting on their shoes and cold-weather wear, the family walked along the mid-floor corridors before making their way down the stairs and into the entrance lobby. They then stepped out onto the paved area beyond the front door, and Rita breathed in air. It had rained recently and she could smell the wet grass. Rita could also see the tall house behind her in the puddles on the ground.

Though the skies above were grey and the air was cold, the house felt so private and remote that Rita was filled with a sense of peace. It was a sharp contrast to the terraced streets she was used to, packed with cars and neighbours chatting out on the pavements. She was now surrounded with dew-lined lawns, bushes, shrubbery, and even some plants that were enduring the winter. The many trees, on the other hand, had all lost their leaves, and the naked branches clawed at the air like spindly, skeletal fingers.

'This way!' Chloe called out and hopped down the steps before them. Ray linked arms with Rita, and they followed their daughter down before making their way along a pathway around the side of the house.

The rain had caused a light mist to crawl across the ground. That, plus the onset of dusk, lent their surroundings a serene quality.

Everything was so *quiet*.

'I could get used to this,' Rita said. 'Walking the grounds of our home every day.' She leaned her head onto Ray's shoulder. 'It's lovely.'

'It is,' Ray agreed. 'And it'll be even better in summer, with nicer weather.'

That was probably true, but Rita had always liked the winter. The bite of the cold made her feel more awake and alert, and the world resetting itself for the bloom of spring had a unique beauty to it.

At the rear of the house, the ground dropped away from the external courtyard in tiers until it met the back garden, where there were lawns, lines of hedges, planters, and even a fountain: a stone woman with a water jug on her shoulder. Nothing ran from the fountain at the moment, but the rain had filled the circular base with dirty, stagnant water.

Rita and Ray stood at the top of the tiered steps and watched Chloe as she excitedly explored her new surroundings. She seemed happy, enthralled at the new adventure. Rita then turned to glance over at the courtyard, which sat between the two rear prongs of the house behind them. The ground there was paved with cobbled stone, and around the edges sat a line of planters. Other than that, however, the area was pretty plain. There was certainly an opportunity to liven it up and make it more of a feature.

After sensing movement in her peripheral vision, she glanced up at one of the top-floor overlooking windows. It was, like most others in the house, taller than it was wide with thin white frames.

Behind the glass, Rita saw a figure looking out at them.

Since she was three stories down, it was difficult to make out much of the person, other than their general form. Whoever the person was, they quickly stepped from view.

Rita could only think that perhaps it was Marcus or Vincent up there, looking out on her family. Her initial instinct had been the person was female, though, given their rather thin frame and wider hips.

They all stayed outside for a little while longer, until the sound of a cough behind drew their attention.

Rita turned, her attention drawn to the rear glazed door of the house. It was open, and Marcus stood outside, smiling. He had changed into something a little less formal, wearing a dark sweater—rolled up to the elbows—and grey trousers.

'Enjoying the grounds?' he asked, calling over to them. 'Quite something, aren't they?'

'They are indeed,' Rita agreed. 'Sorry, we got finished unpacking early and Chloe wanted to explore a little.'

Marcus waved a hand dismissively, and even from this distance, Rita could see the blue glint of his eyes. 'Don't apologise,' he said. 'This is your home now. You can all explore most places here at your leisure.'

'Most places?' Ray asked.

Marcus just nodded. 'We'll get to that later. But for now, if you're hungry, come inside. I've fixed us up something to eat.'

He didn't wait for a response, and instead just turned and walked back into the great hall, leaving the door behind him open.

'I guess we're going to eat,' Ray said.

3

THOUGH RAY WAS a little loath to admit it, the food was delicious, and every mouthful was packed full of flavour.

They were all seated at the long table placed within the great hall. Since there were only five of them, and the table seated twelve, they had all clustered at one end, with Ray seated next to Chloe, Vincent and Rita opposite, and Marcus at the head of the table.

The atmosphere felt formal, almost like a job interview, and Ray kept looking over to Rita for reassurance, mimicking her movements as best he could: taking a sip of wine as she did and keeping his mouthfuls of food small when all he wanted to do was shovel the food in until his cheeks bulged.

He continued to put on a front, remembering what Rita had told him about impressions counting. Rita always handled herself so well, with an endless amount of class. She was from a working-class background, the same as Ray, but hid it so much better.

Her makeup—light lipstick and a touch of eyeshadow—was always subtly applied and used only to accentuate her already beautiful, angular features. Her long, wavy hair was currently worn down, and there was a sweep of fringe coming close to her left eye. But, as beautiful as Ray thought she was, Rita always seemed to carry a frown of concern, as if she were constantly bearing the weight of the world.

The great hall they were in certainly lived up to the name, with a deep green wallpaper covered by twisting golden patterns, a stone-tiled floor, and four square support columns spaced evenly around the room that ran up to an ornate plaster ceiling. A variety of expensive-looking paintings hung on the walls: portraits, landscapes, even some biblical imagery, as well as a large, gold-framed mirror.

The meal was served in a bowl and consisted of large chunks of chicken—still with the skin—marinated in a delicious sauce which had hints of garlic and wine. Marcus had announced it was a French dish, called *coq au vin*, which Ray had never heard of before. However, he agreed that it certainly *sounded* French. Chopped mushrooms and tomatoes floated in the brown sauce, and they only accentuated the flavours.

'Hope it's to your liking,' he said as everyone devoured their food.

'It's delicious,' Rita replied, dabbing her mouth with a napkin. She then took a sip from her glass of red wine. In truth, Ray wasn't much of a wine enthusiast, and this one didn't do much to change his mind on that front. A good beer would definitely have been preferred. The other three certainly seemed to enjoy it, and Chloe was clearly happy with her lemonade.

Marcus then turned to Ray, with eyebrows raised, seemingly waiting for his approval as well.

'I love it,' Ray replied, not knowing what else to say.

'Excellent,' he said in reply. 'So, everyone is happy with the arrangements here, I assume?'

'We are,' Rita said. 'It will be a lot of work, though, given a skeleton staff of just the four of us.'

Marcus nodded and took a slow sip of his wine. 'I understand that. And, to make matters worse, I'm going to be honest and say I won't be contributing a whole lot. I have other matters that will keep me busy.'

'Oh.'

'You can call on your brother as you need to, of course,' Marcus added.

Ray turned to Rita and squinted his eyes in confusion. Rita went on, 'Well, that is your choice, obviously, but running a hotel is a huge undertaking. We need bodies so we can stay on top of things.'

'The way I see it,' Marcus said, 'is that we just start small. There will likely only be a few guests while we build things up. Things should be manageable that way. If it gets out of hand, then we can look at pulling in more help. The thing is, while I want this venture to work, I don't have an endless pot of money to throw at it.'

Ray again looked to Rita, who was chewing the side of her mouth. 'Fair enough,' she eventually said. 'We can see how it goes. But, we'll need to set up a reception area close to the entrance lobby. And I'll need a space for an office.'

'Done and done,' Marcus replied. 'You have the run of this place, for the most part, so use whichever rooms you see fit. I have no issue with that. See, Rita, the thing is... I want you to take ownership of this project. The hotel is now your baby. Grow it and make a success of it, and I promise you will reap the benefits. As far as the business side of things go, you are in charge... until I see a reason for you not to be.'

Ray didn't consider himself the smartest man in the

world, but he knew that Marcus had just issued his wife a pretty clear challenge. And, given what had happened at Rita's previous hotel—where she had been discarded without a second thought despite still being the best person for the job—he knew it would be a challenge she would relish.

'There won't ever be a reason,' she replied confidently. 'I guarantee it.'

'Excellent,' Marcus exclaimed, and a wolfish grin spread over his face.

'But what about supplies?' Rita asked. 'I understand you want to keep costs down, but there are still things we'll need.'

'There is a business bank account set up, with a deposit of money in to get you going. You will have access to that account. All the money we make goes in, and it is up to you to manage everything from there. You will pay yourselves the agreed wage, I will get a dividend, and you will also manage the stock and inventory. Like I say, this is your place to run.'

Rita widened her eyes in surprise. 'That's a lot of responsibility,' she said. 'Don't get me wrong, I'm up to it. But it should also have had a bearing on my wage.'

'And it will. Eventually,' Marcus told her. 'If this place does well, then so will you. The only ceiling to your success would be your own failings.'

Ray felt a little lost, like he was just going along for the ride, but he certainly saw a fire in Rita's eyes. This wasn't just a stop-gap lifeline to her anymore; it was a chance to prove herself again.

But, to Ray, something about the whole thing seemed... off. However, he couldn't put his finger on why. He hated feeling like things were just happening without his involvement. So, he spoke up, if only for the sake of speaking.

'What kind of improvements do you want to make to the building before opening?'

Marcus was slow to take his eyes off Rita, but eventually looked over to Ray and shrugged. 'I don't think we need to do an awful lot in that regard. A few tweaks and a freshen up. It would be good to get the gardens into a nicer state to suitably impress the guests. But have a good look around the place and see what you think needs to be addressed. This is your project too, Ray.'

'Okay, no problem,' Ray responded. It was all he could think to say in reply.

'And when are you looking to get the hotel open for business?' Rita asked.

'As soon as possible. I think a couple of months should give us plenty of time to be ready. Do you think that's feasible?'

Rita nodded. 'Yes. I think we can do that. But we should start putting the word out now, and also try and get a little coverage in the local press.'

'That shouldn't be hard to do,' Vincent cut in. 'This house has something of a history and is well known in the area. I'm sure if people found out it was opening up to the public that would create a buzz of its own.'

'History?' Ray asked. 'What do you mean by that?'

'We can go over that another time,' Marcus said, again waving a dismissive hand. 'Trust me, we'd be here for hours. But, Vincent is right. I believe it should be quite straightforward to generate interest. However, one thing to note, and something that is quite important: the top storey is strictly off-limits. Both for guests and also yourselves, at least for the time being.'

'Wait, are you serious?' Rita asked, frowning. 'Why?'

'Because I said so,' was all Marcus offered in reply, grinning playfully.

'But that is cutting off how many rooms we can rent out,' she shot back. 'Do we really have to lose a *whole* floor?'

'Not permanently,' Marcus answered. 'But there are two rooms in particular that I will be using on a permanent basis up there. We can look at blocking that area off in time, which would then open up the rest of the floor.'

'The sooner, the better,' Rita argued. 'Given our own bedrooms are out of use anyway, cutting off the top storey as well will only hurt our revenue.'

'Noted. But that is how things stand for now.'

Ray could tell his wife was not completely happy with that arrangement, but she relented. 'Fair enough. But what's up there that is so private?'

'Another time,' Marcus said, and he then finished the rest of his wine. 'Why don't you enjoy the house? Explore. Make yourselves at home and feel free to indulge in any food or drink in the kitchen that tickles your fancy. For now, however, I have business to attend to.' Marcus then dabbed his mouth with his napkin and stood up. 'Leave your plates and glasses. Vincent here will clean everything up.'

And with that, he gave a small, courteous nod and walked from the room. Ray couldn't quite believe it. He turned to his wife, eyebrows raised. *Is he for real?*

Rita, in response, just gave a shrug of her shoulders. Even Chloe watched on with a confused frown.

'We'll clean up after ourselves, Vinnie,' Rita said. 'It's no trouble.'

'Oh, it's fine,' Vincent replied, getting to his feet. He then began to stack the dishes. 'You do as Marcus suggests and have a look around the house; get acquainted with your new home. There's lots to see, but just be careful down in the basement. The light switch is at the bottom of the stairs, which can be a pain. The furnace is down there as well. Ray, you might want to familiarise yourself with it.'

'Will do,' Ray told him.

Vincent picked up the pile of plates he'd gathered and smiled at the others. 'Then I'll bid you goodnight. I have to assist Marcus as well, so I may not see you again until morning. But just enjoy yourself. Tomorrow we can start planning how to make this place a success.'

He then walked off, leaving the great hall via a side door to what Ray assumed was the kitchen. Ray and Rita looked to each other.

'Thoughts?' she asked him.

He shrugged and shook his head, unsure what he was feeling about the whole thing. 'Honestly, hun, I have no idea. I guess we just have to roll with it for now. It isn't like we have any other options, right?'

'I guess not,' she replied. 'But I think there is an opportunity here, if Marcus was being honest. I can make this place a success, Ray, I know it.'

He smiled. 'I know you can too. I don't doubt it for a second.'

'So what are we going to do now?' Chloe asked.

'I don't know, sweetie.' Rita said to her daughter. 'What do you want to do?'

'I want to explore some more!'

Rita chuckled. 'Not a bad idea. Can't hurt to start getting used to the new house.'

4

'Well,' Rita began. 'This is as creepy as all hell.'

Ray couldn't help but agree. Their first port-of-call had been to walk down to the basement, because Ray was keen to see what kind of heating system he would be dealing with in the house.

'Do you think it's haunted?' Chloe asked, a sense of excited wonder in her voice.

'I don't think so,' Ray replied. 'No such thing as ghosts.'

'And how do you know?' Chloe asked, putting her hands behind her back and making a smug face. 'You can't say for certain, can you?'

'I'm certain enough,' was his reply. Ray then moved over to the large, metallic structure of the furnace. It was tall and quite deep: a mix of ribbed iron and sprouting pipework, almost gothic in its architecture and design. Rita hated it as soon as she saw it.

'What do you think?' Rita asked, nodding to the huge appliance.

'Out of my league,' he replied. 'Hopefully it works okay. If not, we'll need to call somebody in.'

Ray saw Rita hug herself. It was certainly cold in the basement, and smelled of damp and coal. He didn't foresee Rita spending much time in the basement if she could help it.

The walls around them were bare stone, and streaked watermarks ran down to the uneven floor. A dull orange hue from the light fittings in the ceiling above was not strong enough to illuminate the whole area, leaving pockets of shadows. Piles of coal and wood were dotted around the space, and the only other feature of note was the line of what appeared to be old cells against a far wall. All were open to the front, and some were full of more fuel for the furnace.

It was dirty and horrible down there, and certainly no place for Chloe.

'How about you come back down here later?' Rita suggested. 'I'm sure there are nicer places for us to explore tonight. Vincent or Marcus can show you how to work *that* thing another time,' she nodded towards the nightmarish furnace.

'Yeah,' Ray agreed. 'Besides, we need to get out of here before the *ghosts* get us!' He then widened his eyes and zombie-walked over towards his daughter, groaning as he did. Chloe squealed and giggled, then quickly ran away from him.

'Careful you don't fall,' Rita admonished, but was unable to keep her tone serious as Ray grabbed his daughter and scooped her up.

They made their way back to the stairs, with Chloe going first, followed by Rita. Ray was last, so he hit the switch, killing the lights. Rita looked back down at him just as Ray placed a foot on the first step. As he did, he quickly turned his head back to stare into the dark.

What the hell was that?

'Everything okay?' Rita asked him.

'I... yeah, I guess,' he said, though he shook his head in confusion. 'Thought I heard someone whispering.' He then chuckled and turned back to her, then waggled his eyebrows. 'Maybe Chloe was right.'

They moved on and looked around the rest of the ground floor, taking in all the rooms, including the large kitchen—which had a large cupboard full of wines, whiskeys, and rums—a dining room, living room, and even a library.

'There are so many books!' Chloe exclaimed while inside. And it was true. Ray wasn't much of a reader, but even he was impressed with the space. It had dark wooden bookshelves along two of the four walls, all filled with leather or cloth-bound books. There must have been hundreds of tomes in there.

'I'm going to read them all,' Chloe said, smiling, eyes lost in the treasures before her.

'Well, we're going to have to vet them first,' Rita replied. 'Some of them might not be suitable for you.'

Chloe made a face and stuck out her tongue.

The floor of the library was polished hardwood, and there was an ornate recliner with pale green cloth and golden edging sitting near to the window. Given the room was to the front of the building, it provided nice views out over the long driveway, front lawns, and the boundary gate in the distance.

There was a musty smell of old wood and paper, and the single chandelier lit the space: golden with elegant and intricate patterns to it.

The room was impressive, and Ray could certainly see why Chloe would be so enamoured with it.

'This would be good for the hotel,' Rita said, taking everything in. 'A nice, peaceful reading room for those who want it. Lends the place a lot of class.'

'So you don't want me to rip the bookcases out?' Ray asked with a smile.

'God no!' she replied. 'This definitely stays as it is. Maybe a few more chairs or something, make it a little more cosy. But that's about it.'

The library was accessed both directly off the entrance lobby and also from an adjoining corridor, and even Ray saw that it could become a nice focal point for guests. It even had a fireplace, and he could imagine some of the higher-ups in society in here at night, reading by firelight with a glass of scotch or port.

Rita turned to leave. 'So far, so good. I can really do something with this place, Ray. I just know it.'

Shortly after, they made their way up to the floor above. That one consisted mostly of bedrooms, as well as some toilets and storage rooms. The bedrooms, while decorated in slightly different ways, all had a similar feel to them, with grand four-poster beds, classically patterned wallpaper, and thick carpets.

Including the four bedrooms on the ground floor, Ray counted a total of sixteen rooms, not including any on the storey above. If they took away the rooms already allocated for those that lived in Perron Manor—the Pearsons, Vincent, and Marcus—that left twelve available to guests.

Ray mentioned that point to Rita as they ventured down a corridor at the back of the house. He then asked, 'Do you think that's manageable for us?'

'Probably,' she replied after giving it a few moments of thought. 'At capacity we might be stretched, but we need to get the bedrooms upstairs in use as well. That is just going to hold us back.'

They approached a flight of stairs that ran up to the top-floor. Ray could hear very faint voices, which he recognised as Marcus and Vincent. 'Speaking of which, what do you think is going on up there?' he asked, pointing a finger to the stairs.

Rita shook her head and rolled her eyes. 'No idea.'

Ray looked up and saw that the small section of the hallway up there seemed identical in decoration to the one they were in, with pale green wallpaper above wooden panelling, and a high, decorative plastered ceiling. There was no obvious reason Ray could see why the floor above could not be used for guests. That meant Marcus had something up there he didn't want people to see, or know about.

'I'm sure we'll find out in good time,' he said.

'We better,' Rita added. 'I don't like working with one hand tied behind my back.'

The family of three then made their way back to their own rooms to change for the evening. Ray had a mental list of things he could start working on the next day, and after slipping into a thick but comfortable chequered shirt and a fresh pair of jeans he scribbled the items down onto a scrap of paper. It consisted of small tasks, mainly, like changing the odd fitting or bulb, and making some adjustments to stiff or squeaky doors. He'd consult Rita on some of the bigger jobs, however, so that they were on the same page and his work would fit in with any plans she was formulating.

For tonight, however, they planned simply to relax. The lounge on the ground floor looked cosy and had a television in there that Ray thought may have been a colour set. They all headed down together, and Ray got the fire going with fresh logs that had been stacked on the fireplace, ready for use.

Rita switched on the television. It had wooden veneer surround and two large knobs on the front—one that controlled the channel and one for volume. After quickly adjusting the aerial, a picture emerged from the static, and Rita cycled through the three available channels, settling on the BBC station. It was showing a talk show that she liked.

Rita then took a seat next to Ray on the sofa that sat against the far wall, and Chloe took her place on the other one in the room, which ran perpendicular. Their daughter snuggled under a blanket with Emma and one of her books, one that featured a kind-hearted giant.

With the heat and flickering light of the fire, Ray felt extremely relaxed. He concentrated on the skies outside more than the television, watching the already dark blues turn to black. Clouds blocked out any stars that may have shone through, but it was still nice to look out into the dark and see a little of the grounds that were close by. The peace and quiet was far removed from anything he was used to, and something he could certainly enjoy. However, he did consider one problem: if the rooms here were all to be used by guests when the hotel was up and running, then what were they supposed to do with their free time? They couldn't stay barricaded in their own rooms all the time when off duty, and Chloe would need to be able to roam and play. He considered bringing it up with Rita, but decided against it for the moment. It could be sorted out later, and he just wanted to enjoy the feeling of calm and warmth. All that was missing was a glass of scotch.

I can fix that.

'I'm going to go to the kitchen and get us a drink. Red wine?'

'That sounds fantastic,' Rita said, leaning over to kiss him on the cheek.

'Any brand in particular?' he asked.

'Just see what is there,' she said, with a shrug. 'Dealers choice.'

Ray turned to Chloe. 'Do you want anything?' He already knew what the answer would be.

'A cup of hot chocolate!' she exclaimed with a big grin.

Ray got to his feet with a groan and ruffled her hair. 'I'll see if they have any. If not, I can fix you some warm milk.'

'Thanks, Daddy,' she replied. Ray realised that she hadn't stopped smiling since they arrived at Perron Manor. The place certainly met with her approval. Considering the two-bedroom, rented council house they had come from, he was pleased to see it—even if he was a little worried she would develop a taste for the finer things in life he would scarcely be able to provide.

Still, it was an adventure for her, and he decided it wouldn't hurt to try and look at things the same way.

Ray left his two girls and navigated through to the kitchen, cutting through the great hall on his way. The echoing of his footsteps on the tiled floor was unsettling in the otherwise dead silence, especially since he was used to the soft patter of carpet.

The kitchen—vastly larger than any he had owned before—was quite something. Though the shade of yellow paint on the walls wasn't to his liking, the abundance of cupboards was impressive. There was also an honest-to-God larder. The floor slabs underfoot were a rustic stone with splashes of natural browns and yellows mixed in with a dark grey. An old, strong-looking wooden table sat central to the room, and there was a cast iron cooker against the far wall, with eight burners, which looked like it could feed a platoon.

This will come in handy when we have the hotel up and running.

Ray dug through the cupboards and kitchen units, looking for the one that housed the alcohol. When he eventually found the double-height unit flanked by a fully stocked wine rack, he was amazed at the choice inside.

There were scores of bottles. And the colours of the liquids inside ranged from ambers to browns to clear, and even purples. Thankfully, they were all categorised into the alcohol types, and he quickly found the scotches, selecting an already-open eighteen-year-old blend. After pouring himself a drink and selecting a random red wine for Rita, he managed to find a tin of powdered hot chocolate.

Perfect.

Ray gathered up the drinks and made his way towards the door that led from the kitchen to the great hall. He then crossed the main hall. En-route, he stopped at the glazed rear door. Movement in his peripheral vision, from outside, had drawn his attention. However, when staring out into the night, he could see nothing. Whatever movement he had registered had only been fleeting, likely a bat or something whizzing past the glass.

Thinking no more of it, he set off again—but halted immediately when he heard a quick and light rapping sound on the door. Again, he looked outside but was met with the same result.

Nothing.

He walked closer, bringing his face close to the glass, though he could only see the reflected image of the great hall behind him mixed in with the black of the night outside.

He shook his head and then turned away, satisfied that it was nothing of importance. Just an old house making strange noises. Or even bugs hitting the glass—certainly no cause for concern.

Ray headed back to his family, ready to enjoy a cosy night in front of the fire.

5

Rita had awakened early, a little before six, and padded through to the en-suite to bathe, letting Ray sleep a little longer.

She was an early riser anyway, but today she felt especially motivated. Marcus' speech last night had certainly lit a fire, and Rita no longer saw the work ahead as just a stopgap to keep the family afloat.

While she didn't really know Marcus or his motivations, if he was true to his word, then they could really make something of the hotel. And make some good money themselves while doing it.

The water in the bath was close to scalding—at least that's what Ray would have told her. But it was to her liking. She enjoyed showers the same way: to the point of turning her pale skin red. It helped burn away any leftover morning grogginess. Not that there were any showers to enjoy in Perron Manor: it was a bath or nothing.

Today she hoped the red-hot water would also scrub away completely the already fading memory of last night's dream—one where she was being dragged down through a

hole in the earth while awful moaning and screaming
sounded around her.

It was very strange, especially since Rita wasn't usually
one for nightmares.

She slipped into the water, wincing a little, but then let
the water settle around her. Her mind was alive with ideas:
coming up with endless lists of tasks and trying to sort them
by importance. The reception desk and office area would be
two of the first things to focus on, as they couldn't run a
hotel without either.

She didn't want to set anything up in the entrance lobby:
it was a magnificent space, so preserving its original
aesthetic and grandeur would be important. However, the
reception area would still need to be close to the entrance,
as asking guests to travel too far before being welcomed
would run the risk of them getting lost and confused.

First impressions count.

Two rooms were accessed directly from the entrance
lobby that could be used as a reception area. First, there was
the library. But just like that lobby, it would need to be left as
it was. Even if it ended up being rarely used, the fact it was
there added a great deal to the building, lending an authen-
ticity to its original roots as a manor. Rita would make sure
every guest saw it on their initial tour, knowing it would be a
great area to follow up with after the entrance lobby. And
then, with the great hall to follow, she had no doubt the
patrons would be sufficiently wowed.

The other room was a study and was directly opposite
the library. It currently contained some seating, a writing
desk, and a half-full bookshelf. That space didn't really add
anything to the house, so it would be the perfect choice.
They would just need to add in a reception counter to the
front of the room, and the area behind could be used as the

office. It would be easy enough for Ray to add in a wall to separate the two areas and hide away the office, Rita assumed. Then, all that would be needed was some signage out in the lobby to point guests the right way.

Perfect. One decision made.

Next was sourcing the supplies they would need. To do that, Rita would need to find reputable and dependable retailers. She would require sheets, towels, plates, glasses, bathmats, toiletries, and food, at least, and getting supply-chains in place was critical.

Rita felt that the rough deadline of two months' time was eminently achievable. That meant she also needed to think about how to start getting the word out and build a little bit of buzz about the opening. The thought of getting started with the PR side of things excited her.

She hadn't felt this motivated since being promoted to manager at the last hotel she'd worked at—The Fenton.

Rita's mood soured as she remembered how that had turned out. She began to scrub her hair and scalp hard with shampoo. All her best-laid plans and efforts had been wiped away by the new owners, ones who had their own man in mind for the role of manager.

So Rita was gone without ever being given a proper chance to prove herself, and her previous sterling work had been ignored completely.

Thanks and goodbye.

But this would be different. Though she couldn't say she trusted Marcus completely—after all, Rita barely knew him —he simply had no reason to bring anyone else in now to replace her. At least not yet.

She had an opportunity. One that she planned to seize.

After finishing with her bath, Rita dried off and walked back into the bedroom, with only towels wrapped around her. Ray had woken and was sitting up in bed, hands clasped together behind his head as he stared out of the window.

'Did I wake you?' she asked.

He yawned and shook his head. 'Not at all, hun.'

'Good. The bath is free.'

'Isn't there anywhere to get a shower around here?'

'Not that I know of.'

Ray had never been one for taking a bath, preferring the in-and-out speed of a shower. She smiled. 'We could put some bubbles in and get you a rubber ducky if it helps?'

Ray laughed and got out of bed. 'Soap and water will be just fine.' He then walked into the bathroom, leaving Rita to ready herself for the day.

Given the cold weather outside—and even *inside*—she slipped on a pair of nylons over her legs and covered them with black trousers. She then put on a tan blouse and gathered up her hair into a neat bun. Subtle lipstick, concealer, eyeshadow, and some heels completed the look: professional and all business.

Rita then strode out into the corridor and rapped on Chloe's door, hearing her daughter yell, 'Come in,' in response.

Rita entered and saw that her daughter was wide awake. The young girl was lying on her bed and reading one of her books.

'Been awake long?' Rita asked.

Chloe shrugged. 'A little while.'

'Hungry?'

'Very!' Chloe replied with a nod of her head.

Rita smiled. 'Come on then. I'll give you a bath, and then we will go down for food.'

Once the family were all ready, they made their way

down to the kitchen to figure out what to eat. The cupboards were well stocked, and since Marcus had told them to treat the house as their own, Rita set to work making a breakfast of crispy bacon, poached eggs, and French toast. She and Ray both had coffee to accompany it, and Chloe slurped down an orange juice. Though the great hall was just next door, they decided to stay in the kitchen to eat. The hall was impressive, but it lacked intimacy and warmth.

Halfway through breakfast, they were joined by Marcus and Vincent.

'Why are you hidden away in the kitchen?' Marcus asked as he entered wearing a dark polo-neck jumper, and jeans with flared bottoms. Rita had to keep from bristling, thinking that the look which was so obviously meant to be stylish just seemed pretentious.

Vincent, in contrast, was in a simple, light-blue shirt—again, open to the chest—with the beginnings of sweat patches beneath each arm, dark blue cord trousers, and scruffy trainers.

'It's a little cosier in here,' Rita replied. 'There are some eggs and bacon ready if you want some.'

Marcus looked over to the remaining food keeping warm on the stove, and his nose wrinkled up. 'Thanks, but I'll fix something else a little later.'

Rita could not stop herself from growing annoyed a second time, but made no comment. Vincent, however, stepped forward and grabbed a plate. 'Don't mind if I do,' he said, heaping on rashers of bacon and spoonfuls of eggs. He took a seat next to Ray, and then poured himself a coffee.

'Have fun,' Marcus said. 'Take a few days to get your thoughts together on this place, and how you intend to take it forward. I'm sure you both have some ideas already, but we can sit down soon enough and get a plan of action together. For now, I need to head out for a few hours.'

Marcus didn't wait for a response before he left, but he did make a point of meeting eyes with Rita. His gaze was a hungry one. She didn't like it at all.

Ray took a long sip of his coffee, then turned to Vincent, who had a mouth full of food, some of which had dripped onto his bushy beard. 'Your friend is a little... different,' Ray said. 'If you don't mind me saying so.'

Vincent chuckled, nodding his head in agreement. 'I guess so. He's eccentric... but he's also very intelligent. Even brilliant, in some ways.'

Hearing her brother speak about Marcus that way, almost in reverence, didn't sit well with Rita. She hadn't seen Vincent in a number of years prior to coming here—they weren't exactly close—but even so, Rita still cared for him. However, she got the impression that Marcus only saw him as a lackey.

'So, what is he to you?' she asked her brother. 'Like... a friend? Or a boss?'

'What do you mean?' Vincent asked, tilting his head.

'Well, it's pretty clear he calls the shots.'

'Of course he does. This is *his* house.'

Rita shook her head. 'I know that, but what do *you* get out of the arrangement between you two?'

'Other than living rent-free in an amazing building?' he asked as if that should be answer enough.

But it wasn't. 'Yes,' Rita stated. 'Other than that.'

Vincent paused and frowned, but continued to loudly chew his food. 'We're friends,' he eventually said. 'We share interests. And we have the same outlook on life. So why *wouldn't* I take him up on his offer to live here?'

'Fair enough,' Rita replied, holding her hands up. She

didn't want to upset him and rock the boat so soon after moving in.

'So,' Ray said, picking up the conversation for her. 'How did you meet him?'

'We've known each other since university,' Vincent replied. 'We shared a class and got to talking. Hit it off from there.'

'So... friends for a long time?'

'Yeah,' Vincent confirmed.

Ray nodded. 'Fair enough.' He then added, 'Vincent, I still want you to know we appreciate you getting us in here. I promise that we won't let you down.'

A big smile broke over Vincent's face. 'We know you won't,' was all he said in reply.

6

IT WAS a little after lunchtime and Chloe was relaxing in the library. She was reading one of her own books since her mother had told her not to take one from the bookshelves until they had all been fully approved. She might have only been six, but Chloe fancied she could read any of the thick books in there, though they did look *quite* dull and boring.

The house still excited her, and the sense of adventure was still fresh. However, she knew there was a wrinkle waiting in the wings to put a damper on all the fun. Before the move, her parents had found Chloe a place in the local school, and she was due to start next week. She wasn't against going to school at all—it was something Chloe usually enjoyed—but being the new girl wasn't something to look forward to.

However, that was next week's problem. A lifetime away.

An approaching car drew her attention, and Chloe sat up from the lounge-chair she was sprawled out on to look out of the nearby window.

The car that rolled down the gravel driveway looked like an expensive one. It was black, with a long front and high grille, which had two headlights on either side, giving four in total—something she hadn't seen before. Light bounced off the polished body and silver trims.

It looked like Mr. Blackwater had returned.

The car made its way to a covered carport and pulled to a stop. Her father's car was also in there, but tucked away at the back and out of sight.

Mr. Blackwater got out and walked towards the front door, wearing a long, black, wool coat. He had a small pack of books tucked under one arm, about four in total, and they all had dark brown, leather bindings. They looked old and well worn. Mr. Blackwater then disappeared from view, and Chloe heard the front door open.

She was intrigued by the owner of Perron Manor, though she hadn't seen a whole lot of him since moving in. Granted, Chloe and her parents had only arrived the previous day, but even so, Marcus Blackwater always seemed to be hidden away on the top storey of the house. She then heard dull footsteps on the stairs and knew instantly that was where he was going again.

Her curiosity was piqued. And while she knew she shouldn't, Chloe had a strange desire to sneak upstairs and see what held Marcus and Vincent's attention so much.

A moment's trepidation held her, because Chloe was not normally one to do something she knew could get her into trouble. However, the excitement of the new adventure was still coursing through her, pushing her to be more daring. Chloe set her book down and got up to her socked feet. She padded over the hardwood floor of the library, satisfied with how quiet she was being. She was confident she could be stealthy enough to get upstairs without being heard, and then maybe she could see a little of the upper floor.

But did she dare?

With a smile, Chloe decided that she did indeed dare, and she left the library to make her way to the foot of the stairs. She listened, hearing no movement above. Satisfied that no one was close—and knowing her parents were busy in the dining room, she placed a foot on the bottom step and pushed herself up. The stairs were strong and sturdy, and none of them creaked under her steps. Perhaps an adult would have made more noise—Marcus certainly had—but Chloe moved almost silently.

Once on the mid-floor, Chloe snuck around the corridors until she reached the stairs that led up to the top storey. As before, she waited at the bottom and listened. She could just make out muted voices, but only barely. With a tingle of excitement at doing something she knew she shouldn't, Chloe moved up to the first step. Then the next. And then, confident she would not be caught, she silently moved to the top. The hallway she found herself in was decorated just like the ones below it: wooden panelling on the lower half of the walls, pale green wallpaper above, and ornate plaster ceilings that had a woven pattern to it—like plaited hair—running around the edges.

The stairs had led up to the back of the house, where a window in the wall before her gave fantastic views out over the courtyard and even beyond the boundary wall. She listened again, detecting the voices coming from somewhere towards the front.

Chloe felt like she was on forbidden ground, but was surprised to find there was a certain thrill that came with it. That thrill pushed her forward along the hallway, tiptoeing as she went. Chloe then discovered that both Mr. Blackwater and Vincent were gathered in one of the corner rooms to the front of the building.

The door to the room was ajar, but only a little, so she

couldn't see much of what was inside. Chloe kept her distance and pressed herself flat against the wall at an angle where she was confident she was safely hidden from view. Unless, of course, someone came walking out. Holding her breath, Chloe tried to tune in to the conversation taking place. Given Mr. Blackwater had the deeper voice, she was easily able to distinguish between the two men.

'I agree,' she heard Mr. Blackwater say, but Chloe was unsure what he was agreeing with. 'But I'm not sure they'll reveal anything we didn't already know.'

'May... may I read them?'

That sounds like Uncle Vincent.

'When I'm done,' Mr. Blackwater replied. 'For now, I'm going back to the translations. Leave me alone for a while.'

'Okay,' Vincent replied after a pause. He sounded a little disappointed. 'But I'm not sure why you don't trust your grandfather's work.'

'Latin is a difficult language, and translation is not a straightforward process. Things can often be open to inter-pretation, and I can't let that—'

A noise cut him off, and it also made Chloe jump. It had come from the corridor she was standing in. A door close to her which had been open had somehow been blown closed.

But there is no breeze up here.

However, the sound had obviously caught the attention of Marcus and Vincent. She heard footsteps coming from their room, and panic seized her. Without thinking, she quickly turned and ran, trying to be as quiet as possible while she headed back towards the stairs again. She was completely out of sight before she heard the door creak open and was confident she hadn't been spotted. But she needed to keep going, so she quickly descended the stairs, her heart beating rapidly.

Chloe didn't stop until she was back in the library, where she jumped into the lounge chair again and snatched up her book. She was breathing heavily and felt a film of sweat develop on her forehead.

Maybe the whole thing hadn't been such a good idea. Chloe expected the owner of the house to burst into the library at any moment, to point to her and yell, 'You were spying on us!'

But that didn't happen.

Ten minutes passed, then twenty, then an hour. And eventually, Chloe was satisfied that she'd gotten away with the whole thing. The relief she felt was palpable, as was the returning excitement.

Sneaking about had been fun.

7

'RAY, WAKE UP!'

The sound of his wife's voice pulled him from sleep. He blinked a few times, feeling a little disoriented, but he quickly got his bearings. Ray then rolled over to see his wife sitting on their bed—on top of the covers—leaning over him and pressing a hand onto his shoulder. She had gone to bed wearing just a black nightie but was now covered with a light blue dressing gown.

His first thought was that he'd slept in. However, given it was still dark, he knew that wasn't the case.

'What is it?' he whispered back before glancing at the bedside clock that sat on the nightstand. He had to squint to read the two black hands in the dark but saw that it was close to three-thirty in the morning. He felt Rita shake him, and he turned back to her.

'Listen!' she insisted, bringing a finger up to her mouth, signalling for him to be quiet. He did as instructed. He didn't hear anything at first.

Then quick and heavy footsteps passed by the door to their room from the hallway outside.

Ray sat up.

They were too heavy to be Chloe's.

Then, abruptly, the footsteps stopped.

'Who the hell is that?' he said, pulling back the covers and swinging his legs from the bed. Ray suddenly stopped as the noise repeated, sounding like it was coming back the other way. A few quick, heavy steps... then silence once again.

Ray stood up, but Rita tugged on the shoulder of his white t-shirt.

'I already checked,' she whispered. 'But there was no one out there.'

He turned to her with a frown. 'You should have woken me up right away,' he replied, 'not checked yourself.'

'Well, you're awake now, so what does it matter?'

Ray shook his head, but then made his way over to the door anyway. The chill was only slightly warded off by the thin t-shirt and long pyjama bottoms he wore, and he felt goosebumps form on his bare forearms. All Ray could think was that perhaps Marcus or Vincent were pacing around outside, though he couldn't even begin to guess why.

He took hold of the door-handle and turned, pulling it open. Ray then poked his head out, looking both left then right, and saw a dark yet quite empty hallway.

Strange.

After a few more moments of staring into the shadows, he stepped back fully into his room and pushed the door shut. Rita had one eyebrow raised.

'No one there?' she asked, though it was close to being less of a question and more a statement.

'No,' he replied, shaking his head in confusion.

'I heard it three times before I checked,' she went on.

'But I didn't see anyone either. After I came back to bed, I heard it again. That's when I woke you.'

Ray then looked up to the ceiling. 'Maybe someone is moving around upstairs,' he offered. 'Thin ceilings, no insulation between the separating floor... the sound could travel and make it seem like the footsteps were outside.'

Rita shrugged but looked less than convinced. 'I guess.'

Ray considered his own suggestion. He knew he was grasping at straws. However, while unlikely, it *was* a possibility. In truth, it was the only explanation they had.

But, then again... those footsteps had sounded like they were *right* outside. Ray moved back over to his wife and sat on the bed with her. 'Something to remember for the to-do-list,' he told her.

'What do you mean?'

'If the noise travels like that, it's going to disturb the guests.' He chuckled. 'Can you imagine how people would react if they heard other guests getting it on? I don't suppose it would go down too well with the stuffy, well-to-do types.'

Rita laughed. 'Fair point. I guess we need to do something about it.'

'Insulation between the floor joists should help,' Ray said. 'We'll go in from above, take the floorboards up. Don't want to ruin the ceiling-work by going in from underneath. I'd never be able to replicate the detailing they have.'

Rita looked up at the ceiling. She nodded. 'Good point.' She then lowered her head and stared into his eyes.

'Tell me,' she started, 'do you think we're being crazy by coming here?'

He shook his head. 'We're doing what we need to.'

'I know that, but... you really think we can make the hotel work?'

He took her hands in his and caressed the backs with his

thumbs. 'With you leading the charge, I *know* we'll make it work. Trust me, this is going to be the most popular hotel for miles around.'

She smiled. Even though her big brown eyes looked a little tired, Ray couldn't help but appreciate just how beautiful she was. 'Thank you,' she said, and placed a gentle, lingering kiss on his lips.

As she pulled away, he felt something stir. He then brought a hand up to the back of her head and kissed her again. Passionately. His tongue found hers. Rita pulled away a little, but only so she could again look into his eyes. There was a hunger there, an intensity that excited him more.

She gave him a coy smile. 'Should we? I mean, I don't want to wake everyone in the house. Especially if the sound travels—'

Ray brought a finger up to her lips. 'Then we'll be quiet,' he whispered. Rita giggled, and the sound was the sweetest Ray had ever known. She fell into him as they rolled onto the bed.

8

2 DAYS LATER.

Rita, Ray, Vincent, and Marcus had all gathered in the great hall and were seated around the table there. It was a little before midday, and though it was cold out, a strong winter sun shone brightly, melting away a morning frost sprinkled over the grass outside.

For Rita and Ray, the past couple of days had been spent acquainting themselves more with the house. Especially for Ray, as he wanted to figure out how much manual work lay ahead of him. A recent trip down to the basement had proven eventful, where Vincent had shown both Rita and Ray how to start up the furnace and heat the building. The noise that the huge metallic unit had given off when starting up had been... surprising, to say the least.

Rita, for her part, had been formulating and coming up with her plan of action, and she now took the time to relay it to the owner of the house.

Marcus had before him a leather-bound notepad and an elegant fountain pen in hand, scribbling down notes as Rita went over her ideas and plans for Perron Manor—a place that would soon be known as the Blackwater Hotel.

In one sense, Rita was surprised how much interest Marcus was taking during this briefing. He had been aloof at best since their arrival, always hidden away up on that top floor. It was something of a concern that he hadn't taken a great deal of interest in what Rita's plans were. She had suspected the whole endeavour was something of a game for him: a whim, with no real drive to see it succeed.

But he was now listening intently and making extensive notes, which gave her confidence.

Rita finished her ideas and let Ray chip in on the maintenance and repair side of things. Then they waited for Marcus' response. He finished scribbling down the last of his notes, then set down his pen, clasped his hands together, and made direct eye contact with Rita. His face was unreadable, at first, but he soon broke into a large grin.

'Excellent!' he exclaimed. 'I love what I'm hearing. And, I'm on board with it all.'

He then reached into the pocket of the smart black jacket he wore and pulled out an envelope, which he then slid over to Rita.

'These are the details of the business bank account so you can start withdrawing money and placing your orders. Time to make it all happen, Rita.'

She couldn't contain her smile. Marcus' comments felt like validation. 'Thank you,' she replied, picking up the thick envelope. Her already high motivation was suddenly supercharged.

'And if you agree,' Marcus went on, 'I think we can look to open in March.' His eyebrows were raised, waiting for confirmation.

'Yes, we can definitely achieve that.'

Marcus clapped his hands together. 'Then let's get to it!' With that, he stood to his feet.

Meeting over, Rita assumed, and she stood up as well, along with Ray and Vincent. Marcus' lingering smile was tight-lipped, and he walked with the others as they moved out of the room. Rita felt a gentle hand tug at her elbow, and she turned to see him motioning for her to stop, with Vincent and Ray still a few steps ahead.

'I want you to know,' he said in a low, soft voice, 'that I am extremely impressed.'

'Thank you,' Rita said again. 'I'm glad to hear that.' Ray stopped up ahead and turned to face them as well. But Marcus then leaned in so only she could hear him speak.

'If you stick with someone like me, I think you could go far.' The smile he wore was not a happy or pleased one, anymore, but something else entirely. Something more predatory. She felt his thumb, still on her elbow, begin to caress the skin through the silk material of her blouse.

The revulsion and anger that overcame Rita was hard to keep under control. Her skin crawled at his touch, and at his self-assured grin. She had a sudden impulse to slap him hard across the cheek.

She didn't. Instead, she quickly moved her arm away and gave him a humourless smile while she kept her eyes serious. When she replied, her voice was low, ensuring her words were only for him. 'While I'll carry on with the job at hand, Marcus, I need you to know that I'll be sticking with my family and my husband. I trust that's clear?'

His expression didn't change, which infuriated her even more. But, he at least nodded his head in confirmation. 'Of course.'

'Good,' Rita stated, then turned and walked away, keeping the envelope tucked tightly under her arm.

Ray was frowning in confusion as she passed him. 'Everything okay?' he asked.

'Fine,' was all Rita said in response.

9

3 Days Later.

Chloe's heart was racing. A slight sweat had formed on her brow, and she tried to subtly dab it with the back of her hand. Her chest felt tight.

She wanted to be away from this place—to be anywhere but here.

But she was trapped. And *that* moment was coming.

'And,' Mrs. Taylor began, from the front of the class. 'We have a new student today.'

Here it is. Chloe wanted the ground to swallow her up in that moment.

'Chloe Pearson,' Mrs. Taylor announced with a big smile. The older woman had frizzy brown hair and glasses that dangled from a chain down over a heaving chest hidden beneath a thick cardigan. 'Would you please stand up?'

Chloe's face flushed a shade of red so deep she could have been mistaken for a tomato. Nevertheless, she did as instructed and timidly stood to her feet. Chloe could feel the eyes of all the other students on her.

She didn't like the classroom she had been assigned to. Not the people, necessarily, as she didn't really know anyone yet, more the room itself. The flaky paint on the walls was a sickly yellow covered in lots of areas with large swathes of black sugar paper. That paper, in turn, was mounted with drawings from her new classmates. The floor was a beige, sticky vinyl, and the ceiling was lined with square tiles, some with evident water stains. The only windows in the room were high up—close to the ceiling— and were long and thin, making the room feel dark, dank, and oppressive.

The students were all seated at tables that faced towards the front of the room, and the chairs were hard plastic and not very comfortable. Chloe, thankfully, was seated towards the back and shared a table with two other children—a boy and a girl—though she didn't know their names yet.

'Why don't you tell us a little about yourself, Chloe?' Mrs. Taylor asked, though it was clear it was a command, not a question.

No! Chloe thought. *How about I don't!*

But she took a breath, slow and steady, and tried to force away the nerves she was feeling. 'I'm Chloe,' she started, her voice cracking as she began. She coughed and pushed on. 'I'm six, and I like to read. I just moved here and don't know many people yet.' She paused. 'And that's all I can think to say.'

'Very good, Chloe,' the teacher said. She then looked around the room, hands held out wide. 'Now, does anyone have any questions for their new classmate?'

Chloe sincerely hoped they did not. To her disappointment, however, a hand went up from the little girl seated next to her.

'Yes, Alice,' Mrs. Taylor said. 'What is your question?'

Alice, who had long, dirty blond hair, with a narrow black headband wrapped over the top, looked up to Chloe.

'Do you live in that scary house?'

Chloe frowned, confused at the question. The teacher cut in. 'That isn't the type of question I meant, Alice. Does anyone have any specific questions for Chloe that are about *her*.'

Another hand went up, this one belonging to a boy across the room.

'Andrew, go ahead.'

'Have you seen a ghost there?' he asked.

A small ripple of giggles permeated through the class, making Chloe feel like she was outside of a shared joke. The kids obviously knew about the house she lived in and had a certain opinion on it.

'It isn't haunted,' she snapped.

'Alright,' Mrs. Taylor said, bringing up her index finger to her lips. 'That's enough. If no one has any *real* questions, then we can move on. Chloe,' the teacher said, looking over to her, 'you may take your seat.'

Chloe sat, and her face felt hot and flushed. Mrs. Taylor went on with the lesson, holding court to a less-than-rapt class while she taught some basic division. The girl next to Chloe, Alice, leaned over.

'I didn't mean to make you angry,' the little girl whispered.

'You didn't,' Chloe lied, not looking back at her. She kept her voice low.

'It's just *everyone* says Perron Manor is haunted.'

'It isn't,' Chloe said flatly.

Alice paused, then nodded. 'Okay,' was all she said, seemingly happy with Chloe's answer.

Chloe tried to concentrate on what Mrs. Taylor was

saying, but struggled to focus. She was not happy with how her school life at Alnmouth Primary School had started. If all the kids here thought her house was weird, that would probably make them think less of her, in turn. And all without even getting to know her.

Just after ten o'clock, the class broke to allow the children out into the large playground. Kids from all different age groups and classes could mingle, but with no circle of friends to gravitate to, Chloe kept to the edges of the yard. She leaned against the metal boundary fencing, her hands tucked deep into the pockets of her red, wool coat. She stared down at her black, shiny shoes, feeling utterly alone. Chloe didn't remember her first day of school back home being like this.

Until today, the move to Perron Manor had been exciting for her. An adventure to be enjoyed. Now, however, the realisation of all she had left behind—her friends and her old way of life—was beginning to sink in. It had been brought into sharp focus today as she now stood alone while other kids laughed and played.

A football bounced off the fence near to her, causing Chloe to jump. A short boy with shaggy black hair ran over to retrieve it.

'Sorry,' he said earnestly, and punted the ball back over to his friends. He then jogged away.

In truth, Chloe would have preferred to have been back inside her classroom. At least there she had a place to sit and a lesson to concentrate on. Out here, she felt lost and exposed.

'Hi,' a voice said, approaching from her left. Chloe looked up and saw Alice walking towards her. She had on a dark blue coat that was similar in style to Chloe's.

'Hi,' Chloe replied, not wanting to be rude. At least

someone was talking to her, which would stop her from looking like a loner to everyone else.

'Are you okay?' the little girl asked. 'Not nice being the new girl, is it?'

Chloe got the impression that Alice was speaking from experience. She shrugged. 'I'm okay,' she lied once again.

'I just started a little while ago, too,' the girl went on to say, confirming Chloe's suspicions. 'Haven't made many friends yet.' Alice then offered Chloe a smile, and she noticed the girl was missing the same two top teeth as Chloe was.

Chloe smiled in return, not really sure what else to do. Then, a question came to her, one she really wanted to know the answer to.

'Why does everyone say the house I live in is scary?'

Perron Manor had never been scary to Chloe, not in the short time she had been there. It had been *amazing*.

Alice shrugged. 'I've only heard other kids talk about it, but that's what they say. Might just be because it's old and creepy.'

'It isn't creepy,' Chloe stated defensively.

'But it's *definitely* old,' Alice replied with a big grin.

Chloe smiled too. 'Yeah. It's old. I just don't get why the others would say it's haunted when they don't even know.'

'Well, I've heard them tell stories about it. One of them was about an old man who killed a load of kids up there.'

'That didn't happen!' Chloe snapped. 'It's probably just a stupid story.' Chloe had no way of knowing for sure, but refused to believe that could ever happen in her perfect new home.

Alice just shrugged. 'Just what I heard.'

'When was it supposed to have happened?' Chloe challenged.

'Dunno. A lot of years ago, I think.'

'Well... *I* don't believe it.'

'Okay,' was all Alice said in reply.

The bell then sounded, bringing an end to their break-time. Chloe made her way back inside and Alice walked beside her. 'I hope we get to read now,' the girl said. 'I love reading.'

'Me too,' said Chloe, feeling like she was at least starting to make a friend.

10

'DON'T LISTEN TO THEM, HONEY,' Ray told his daughter. He was trying to placate her, but something about what she'd said didn't sit well with him.

'So they were just lying?' Chloe asked.

'Well,' Rita began, 'it's just kids telling scary stories, that's all. And because this house is kind of out of the way, and big and old, it's probably a bit of a mystery to the kids in your school. That's why they make up stories about it. We used to do it, too.'

Chloe considered that for a moment. 'But I don't like it,' she said, her face full of sadness.

The family of three were in the library. Chloe had run straight to it after getting home from school. Ray and Rita had followed her in, knowing something was wrong, and she had told them both what the other kids had been saying about Perron Manor.

Initially, Ray assumed it was just kids being kids. But that story about the old man killing children here seemed a little too... specific. Though maybe he was reading too much into it.

'I know,' Rita went on. 'but it'll pass when they get to know you. And then you can just tell them all about how great the house is.'

'Can I get them to come over?' Chloe asked hopefully.

'Maybe,' Rita replied. 'We'd have to just check with Mr. Blackwater. But I don't see why not.'

That seemed to satisfy Chloe, but Ray had his doubts. Other guests wouldn't exactly be happy with an army of kids running around. He again considered if Perron Manor was going to be good for Chloe, or if it would restrict and isolate her.

Not that there was any choice in the matter. They had come here out of necessity.

Ray and Rita both gave Chloe a hug. 'Are you okay?' he asked her, laying a gentle hand on her shoulder.

She smiled and nodded. 'Yeah, I'll be okay, Daddy.'

'Good,' Rita said. 'You can go up and read your books for a little bit if you want, and I'll call you when it's time to eat.'

Chloe grinned, then grabbed up her school bag, walked from the library, and headed upstairs to her room. He was happy to see there was more of a bounce in her step than when she had first come home.

Ray and Rita then walked back to the study opposite the library, the one that was going to be converted into an office and reception. The jobs he'd done so far had all been small, but the task ahead felt like the first semi-substantial project, one he could really sink his teeth into.

Once inside, he turned to Rita. 'What did you make of all that?'

Rita shrugged her shoulders. 'Just kids being kids.'

'Yeah, but... the thing about children being killed here? That seemed a little more graphic than the standard ghost story to me.'

Rita laughed. 'Kids are different than when we were young, Ray. They're exposed to a lot more. I wouldn't worry.'

'I'm just saying, we don't really know anything about this house. And most stories and legends are based on some kind of fact, aren't they?'

'I'm sure it's nothing, honey,' his wife said, laying a hand onto his arm. She was probably right, but even so...

The sound of the front door opening drew their attention, and Ray poked his head out into the entrance lobby to see Vincent standing inside with a shopping bag in each hand. He was wrapped up in an old, green polyester coat and his cheeks burned red from the biting cold outside. He saw Ray and raised his eyebrows in greeting.

'Just been out to get a few things,' he said, raising up the plastic bags. Then, with a frown, he added, 'You didn't want anything, did you?'

Bit late to be asked now, Ray thought. But he answered with, 'No, we're fine.'

Vincent nodded, then started to walk forward, but Ray stepped out of the study. 'Hey, Vincent,' he began, 'let me ask you something.'

'What's that?' Vincent replied. He stopped and turned round to face Ray. Ray could see the handles of the plastic bags digging into the skin of Vincent's fingers, turning them red, so he tried to be quick.

'Chloe heard a story today at school,' he started. Rita quickly stepped out beside him.

'Come on, Ray,' she said. 'We don't need to go over that. It was just a story.'

'And I'm only asking a question,' Ray told her. He then turned back to Vincent. 'She heard that an old man killed a bunch of kids up here a while back. Any truth to that?'

Vincent didn't answer immediately, but his slightly shocked expression was all the answer Ray needed.

'Well...' Vincent began, but then trailed off, clearly searching for the words.

'Oh my God!' Rita exclaimed. 'It's true?!'

Vincent took a step back, shrinking away. 'It's an old house,' he eventually said. 'Lots of things have happened here. But it's nothing to worry about.'

'Jesus, Vinnie!' Rita spat. 'Why did you never mention it to us?'

'Would it have made a difference?' a voice asked from the top of the stairs.

Marcus started to descend to the half-landing. Today, he was dressed in a pair of dark-brown loafers, black, pressed trousers, and a black, thin jumper with sleeves rolled up to the elbows. He definitely had a preferred colour palette when it came to his clothing.

'Well,' Ray replied, 'it would have been nice to know. Might have made a difference when making our initial decision to come up here.'

Marcus cocked his head and smiled, showing no warmth in his eyes. 'Is that so?' He then looked to Rita. 'So, if you knew that the house had a history, as most old houses do, then you would have... what? Become homeless instead of travelling up here?'

Ray felt a swell of anger. More so because the man had a point. That knowledge wouldn't have changed anything, because Ray and his family had been desperate.

Marcus continued down the remaining flight of stairs and stepped out into the lobby, then walked over to them. 'Consider a house that has stood for centuries will have seen war and famine, and a plethora of other tragedies. None like this stand without having some kind of death attached to them.'

'Yes, but there's a difference,' Ray shot back. 'Most others won't have had a man kill little children in them.'

Marcus just stared at Ray with a less-than-impressed expression. 'But they may have had other equally despicable acts carried out there. And to think otherwise is just naïve.'

'So what else has happened here that we aren't aware of?' Ray challenged. He felt Rita's arm on his shoulder, and knew her intent. *Leave it alone before you get angry.* But Ray just wanted a straight answer.

Marcus let out a small chuckle. 'Where to start? The house was built in the twelve-hundreds, so the number of souls it has seen come and go boggle the mind. I could give you *scores* of stories, if not hundreds. But, again, I have to ask... does it matter?'

Ray took a breath and eventually shook his head. 'Probably not,' he admitted. 'But I'd still be interested to know.'

'Then you can!' Marcus replied, with surprising enthusiasm. 'I'd be more than happy to tell you. Both of you.' He looked at Rita now as well. 'The house does have a bit of a local reputation, but the history is long and fascinating, far beyond what most people realise. If you are both genuinely interested in hearing about it, how about we have dinner tonight in the great hall. All of us. I can tell you a little more then.'

'Is it something Chloe can hear?' Ray asked.

Marcus paused. 'Good point. Caution might be the best way forward there. After all, we don't want the poor girl scared of her own home. How about we have drinks after she is in bed, then? We can gather in the dining hall at the front of the house instead. Somewhere a bit more intimate.'

Ray would have suggested the living room, since it was a

little more comfortable and informal, but regardless, he was interested to hear just what Marcus had to say. He looked to Rita to see what she was thinking, and his wife gave him a subtle nod.

'Fair enough,' Ray told him. 'We'll meet for a few drinks. Sounds good.'

'Excellent!' Marcus exclaimed with a clap of his hands. He then looked over to Vincent. 'Put those away would you?' he said, nodding towards the bags Vincent was struggling with. 'Then fix some dinner. I'm ravenous.'

Vincent nodded then trotted off like a dutiful dog. Ray frowned at Rita. Marcus and Vincent certainly had a curious relationship.

Marcus gave them both a polite smile and started to walk through to the kitchen after Vincent.

'Don't let me keep you,' he called back. 'I'm sure you have lots to be getting on with.'

11

MARCUS TOPPED up Ray's glass of whiskey, and Ray did not protest, despite already feeling lightheaded.

They were all seated around the polished, rectangular dining room table, and in its centre was a silver tray that held bottles of scotch, spiced rum, and red wine.

Ray and Marcus were sharing the delicious whiskey, which had a smoky finish. Vincent enjoyed the rum, and Rita was on her second glass of wine.

The family hadn't spent much time in this room since moving in. Not that Ray didn't like it, of course, it was just that the living room was a little more comfortable, and a little more... *them.*

While it wasn't as grand as the great hall, the dining room was certainly impressive, and quite formal. The walls had a dark oak covering, giving the room a slightly heavy and oppressive feel to it. The plush red carpet underfoot only added to the traditionalist style, and the room smelled of sandalwood, which was given off by the scented candles Marcus had lit before starting. He obviously preferred to set the mood with them rather than using the electric chande-lier overhead.

Whenever their drinks had run low, Marcus had taken it upon himself to refill them, which surprised Ray. He'd assumed that was just something he would have tasked Vincent to do, as it seemed to be the case with everything else. However, Marcus was clearly making an effort as host tonight and took great relish in telling his stories about the house's long history.

Ray had to admit, it was all very impressive to hear. If a little disturbing.

There seemed to have been—from what they'd been told—a disproportionate amount of death inside these walls. But, as Marcus had put it, they had only been discussing it for a little while, and the history spanned *centuries*. Was it really so strange? Of *course* it was going to sound a lot when condensed into such a small time-frame.

Even so, the very first story, where Marcus recounted the time when the building was a monastery, had creeped Ray out a little. All of the monks that lived here were, apparently, slain by one of their brothers, someone Marcus referred to only as 'the Mad Monk.'

But there were other tales of slaughter and murder as well—such as in the thirteen-hundreds, when the building was known as Grey House and was under the stewardship of Edward Grey. That man had constructed the basement level used back then as a jail. He'd captured prisoners from the war with Scotland, and those prisoners were taken down-stairs to be tortured. Grey eventually went mad, it was said, and killed all the prisoners before then taking his own life.

Marcus then went on to tell them that it was in the fifteen-hundreds that the building had gained the name of Perron Manor, when it was taken over by the illustrious

Perron Family. Again, however, a similar tale was weaved, where almost a century later the last surviving heir passed away. There were stories of Robert Perron's devotion to the 'Dark Arts,' and when the house was investigated after his death, a horrific scene was uncovered: scores of dead bodies strewn about the house, many strung up, while others looked like they had been used in some kind of occult rituals.

In addition, the building had also been used as a sick house, as well as an orphanage, and other strange events had supposedly taken place during those periods as well.

Marcus had been talking for close to an hour and a half before he finally got to the story Chloe had heard at school: in 1936, a vagrant had been found in the house after killing six children. He was arrested, of course, but always maintained he was being controlled. As he had killed the children he had sung nursery rhymes to them, to both try to soothe their fears, and also to block out their screaming.

'Well,' Rita said after Marcus had drawn his storytelling to a close, 'that is certainly a lot to take in.'

'I'll say,' Ray added in agreement, and took another long sip from his whiskey. The pleasant burning sensation was soothing, and Ray was well aware he'd hit the point where the alcohol was wrapping his mind in a nice, comforting fuzz. Marcus had divulged a lot, but Ray was certain their host had only scratched the surface.

'Now, just to be clear,' Marcus went on. 'The reason none of this was brought to your attention earlier was because I simply didn't think it was relevant to your decision. As you can see, I have absolutely no qualms telling you anything you need to know about Perron Manor. I certainly don't want this to be an issue.'

Ray supposed he could see that point of view, as much as he didn't really want to admit it.

'Okay,' Rita said. 'Like you said, it isn't going to make a difference. But it would have been good to know, so we could have thought about how it would affect Chloe. If this house has a reputation locally, then it stands to reason that would get back to our daughter.'

Marcus considered her words, cocking his head to one side. Then he nodded. 'Understood,' he replied. 'That was not something I had considered. But, any other questions you have, just ask. Please. I'd be happy to answer them.'

Then, before Ray's filter could kick in, he blurted out the question that had been on his mind for a while.

'Why is the top floor out of bounds, then? What are you two doing up there all the time?'

In his peripheral vision, Ray saw Rita's eyes go wide, as if that line of questioning was taboo. Maybe it was, but Marcus had just said they could ask anything.

Their host just smiled and ran a finger around the rim of his whiskey glass. 'Fair enough,' he said, 'I suppose I do owe you an explanation on that one.' He then took a few moments before continuing on. 'I conduct my business up there. And I need a private area to do so.'

'What *is* your business?' Ray asked, genuinely curious.

'I have carried on in my grandfather's footsteps. He was a trader of rare and valuable artefacts, and I have continued his legacy. So, as you can imagine, I have quite a few items up there I need to keep secured.'

'You could have told us that from the beginning,' Ray said.

'Forgive me,' Marcus rebutted, 'but I did not know you or your family at all. Vincent had spoken highly of you, especially Rita, and it made sense to invite you up here given my plans with the hotel. However, I am not in the habit of broadcasting what I do or what kind of things I keep in my possession. As you can imagine, it would be quite the temptation for someone to try to—'

'Hold on,' Ray interrupted. 'You thought we might *steal* your stuff?'

'I didn't know one way or the other,' Marcus replied firmly. 'So, I held off from telling you. Quite frankly, it was none of your business, anyway. This is *my* house, after all.'

'He didn't mean anything by it,' Rita cut in. 'But I can promise you, Marcus, we would never snoop or steal any of your belongings.'

Ray thought that point should have been obvious. He and his family weren't rich, but they certainly weren't *thieves*.

'No, I understand that,' Marcus eventually replied. 'Which is why I am happy to share that information now. Even though you've only been here a little while, I trust you all.'

Ray looked over to Rita and saw her frowning at him. He took another drink, feeling it best to keep his mouth shut for a little while.

'Can I ask?' Rita began. 'If your business is trading, then why the desire to turn Perron Manor into a hotel?'

'A good question,' Marcus replied. 'The simple answer is... why not? Perron Manor is a big place. Far bigger than I need. I have my space and privacy to attend to my personal affairs, but the rest of the house feels like it is going to waste. If we can get the hotel up and running, and make it the success I know you can, the extra revenue will be most welcome to me. Of course, you will get a share of that as well.'

'So this whole endeavour is a serious venture, then?' Rita

asked. 'Bit late to ask, of course, but I need to know you won't throw the whole thing away on a whim.'

'It is serious,' Marcus confirmed. 'I can promise you that. The only way things will change is if the hotel fails and I cannot financially support the endeavour any longer.'

'Then let's make sure we keep the money coming in,' Rita said with a smile, raising her glass. The others joined her as well, though Ray was a little slow on the uptake. He felt warmth in his cheeks and realised he might have had a little too much of the beautiful amber liquid, which was starting to have more and more of an effect. But then again, what did it matter? Ray didn't drink a whole lot, other than the odd glass at night, and he couldn't remember the last time he'd gotten even a little tipsy, let alone drunk.

'If the locals all know of the house,' Ray said, hearing his own words slur ever-so-slightly, 'do you think they'll even come and stay here?'

Marcus shrugged. 'Maybe. Maybe not. Depends on how well we market it.'

'Well, I think we also need to target people farther afield,' Rita offered. 'We also need to make it clear that the hotel is a perfect relaxing getaway. We are going to be targeting a certain level of clientele, I think: those that enjoy weekend breaks to country manors. This place would be perfect for them.'

'I like it,' Marcus said, grinning. 'Clearly something you've thought about.'

'Of course,' Rita said. 'If we do that, the history of the house won't be an issue.'

'Or,' Ray cut in, 'you could make the history a focus.' He then took another drink. When he lifted his head, all three of the others were looking at him, and Rita had one eyebrow raised in confusion.

'What do you mean by that?' Marcus asked, curiosity evident in his voice.

'Well, you know... Chloe said all her friends thought the house was haunted and that grisly things have happened here. Play up to that.'

Rita shook her head. 'I think you've had too much whiskey, dear,' she said, curtly. 'We are *not* turning this place into some kind of cheesy haunted-house attraction.'

Ray shrugged. 'Fair enough. Just an idea. You're the expert on these things. But, imagine how much interest you could generate if you... I don't know... had a big event over, say, Halloween. The place would be jam-packed with people who are into ghosts and that type of thing. It could be huge.'

'Thank you for the input, darling,' Rita said, letting out a chuckle that bordered on condescension, 'but leave the planning and marketing to me, okay?'

'No, wait,' Marcus said as he held up his hand. 'You might be on to something there, Ray.'

Ray lifted his eyebrows in surprise, then turned and shot a smug grin over to his wife.

Rita rolled her eyes and shook her head. 'I don't think that is fitting for a place like this,' she said. 'You want to exude class, not use cheap, corny tactics.'

'But as a one-off-event, Ray is right. It could be huge. Trust me, *everyone* has at least some interest in the darker things in life—especially the upper classes, from what I have seen. An event like that could draw great interest. Imagine the number of bodies we could pack in here over that weekend.' He then cast a glance to Vincent, who had remained pretty much silent the whole night. Marcus rubbed his chin. 'Something to think about.'

'How about we use that as a fallback plan,' Rita argued.

'If we aren't filling this place up week-in, week-out, then we could consider it.'

Marcus pondered for a while. 'Let me think about it. Like you say, something to keep in the back pocket, at least. Great idea, Ray.'

Ray smiled, even though he was perfectly aware Rita was currently scowling at him. He took another drink, enjoying it.

This whole marketing thing was easier than he'd thought.

12

RITA PEERED through the dark at the ticking clock on her nightstand.

Three-twenty-seven.

She rolled over to her back again and looked up to the ceiling, letting out a sigh.

Another broken night of sleep.

It was becoming a common thing, and something she could do without. Her eyes felt tired and itchy, and rubbing them only made the sensation worse—as if tiny granules of sand were lining the fleshy orb.

The side of her face felt cold, specifically her inner ear, as if an icy breeze had been flowing over her while she slept.

It was again a certain dream that had woken her—one of being dragged down into the earth as she fought and screamed against an unseeable thing that pulled her down against her will. The tight hole she was sinking into had at first been made up of earth and rock, but that eventually gave way to a different kind of material that reminded her of flesh and skin. Rita caught glimpses of eyes and mouths within the constricting walls; her own screams were lost, overpowered by those that bellowed around her from an unknown origin.

Through it all, she had still been able to make out a strange whispering, one that seemed to burrow into her skull. It repeated the same thing over and over. However, Rita was unable to properly understand the word, given it was definitely not English. It sounded more like gibberish, concocted from her own tired subconscious.

Dede!

Rita had never been one for such visceral nightmares before, nor had she ever suffered from such a constant stretch of broken sleep, at least not since Chloe was a baby. Back then, she'd been woken by the cries of her daughter, whereas this was all the doing of her own mind.

She could only assume it was because of the self-imposed pressure she was under to make things work at Perron Manor. Once again, Rita felt she had to prove herself, to know for sure she was as capable as she thought.

Being let go from her last position, even though Rita felt it unwarranted, had certainly made her question her own abilities.

What if they were right?

She closed her eyes again and waited, listening to Ray's snoring. She hoped the exhaustion that throbbed behind her eyes would soon seep into her mind, quiet it, and allow her to get some sleep. But after over ten minutes of lying with her eyes closed and feeling nothing but agitated, Rita quietly got out of bed.

Rita could think of nothing but the hotel and the work ahead. That, and Ray's stupid idea which he'd floated earlier —one that threatened to turn the hotel into some kind of ridiculous haunted-house attraction.

That idea was something she planned to derail. Quickly.

She padded quietly to the desk in the corner of the room and picked up a pen and her planning binder. She then threw on her dressing gown and headed out into the hallway outside, quietly closing the door behind her. It was cold, and the unreliable heating system had obviously ground to a halt. Rita headed down to the kitchen, where she fixed herself a cup of warm milk before moving on to the living room. It was a place she could sit in comfort and work for a while. If she grew tired, Rita figured, then all the better, she could just return to bed. If not... then tomorrow was going to be a very long day. But at least that night would have been productive.

Given the chill in the air, Rita decided to get the fire going. There looked to be enough coal in the fireplace, and the warmth might help relax her again.

Once the fire was lit, a pleasant smokey smell began to fill the room. Rita took a seat at the small, circular table close to the window and set down her pad. She was facing the television, which was positioned in the corner of the room, as well the fireplace, and the crackling flames in her peripheral vision were soothing. The thick, royal-green curtains were pulled closed across the window, and they helped ward off the cold that seeped through the single-glazed glass panes.

Picking one of the more simple tasks to focus on, Rita started to think of any signage she may need, such as direction plaques, room numbers, reception sign, a welcome sign outside the front door and also at the boundary gates. Given there may be long timescales for delivery to consider, Rita wanted to get a handle on the signage quickly.

After listing down her items, she set the pen down and took a drink, cupping her hands around the warm mug. She then let her eyes wander around the room. Her gaze passed over the television set, then to the fire... and then back to the television, where something seemed out of place.

It was an instinctive glance back, with her mind not quite sure what had felt wrong. Rita focused on the blank screen, and it only showed a somewhat dulled reflection of the room she sat in. In it, Rita could see herself, holding her cup, as well as the table. She could also see the sofas in the room, even the pictures on the wall.

But why is the reflection so troubling?

And then she noticed it, and immediately drew in a quick breath.

Her vision locked on to the reflection of the doorway. While the door itself was open, the space was filled by the shadowy form of a person.

The outline was too blurry to make out too much clearly, but Rita could certainly distinguish the shape of a head, arms, torso, then hips and legs. The figure also seemed to be naked, from what she could tell.

Rita instantly whipped her head around in fright... but saw nothing out of the ordinary.

She then turned her head back to the television set, half-expecting to see the doorway clear this time.

The figure was still there, face blank—or at least too blurry to be readable—and standing absolutely motionless. Rita felt a cold, creeping sensation, like icy fingers crawling their way up her spine.

She quickly stood, and the chair beneath her screeched as she pushed it back. However, when she looked over to the door, it once again did not match the reflection in the television. It was empty. Rita felt her heartbeat start to quicken.

Get a grip; it's probably nothing. She braced herself while turning her head back to the reflection in the televisions screen, only this time the strange form had gone.

Whipping her head back and forth, like she was watching a live game of tennis, Rita repeatedly checked the doorway and the television set. Whatever it was she had seen was no longer there.

Still, that feeling of foreboding hung in the air, like a heavy cloud had descended over her. Suddenly, Rita wanted to be back in her room and in bed with her husband.

Had she really seen anything? Whatever the truth was, she could admit to herself that she was scared. She felt on edge and jumpy, like at any moment she expected *something* to happen.

So Rita got up and quickly placed the solid-iron fire-guard over the opening of the fireplace to cut off the air supply. She didn't plan to wait around and watch the fire die out, and instead gathered up her binder, then trotted from the room while casting another look into the television screen.

Thankfully, the coast was clear.

As she stepped out ·of the living room, a chill ran through her, like she had stepped into a refrigerator. Rita broke into a run, feeling rising goosebumps pinprick her skin. She moved, and the temperature around her normalised, but she pushed on, not daring to look back. Rita made her way through into the entrance lobby, then took the stairs up two at a time.

Rita hurried upwards, feeling anxious. The house around her seemed oppressive. She kept having to look back over her shoulder, for some reason fully expecting to see someone behind her.

Stop it, the rational part of her brain admonished. *You're freaking yourself out over nothing.*

When Rita was close to her room she happened to glance out of one of the windows. As she looked, something hit the glass with an awful bang, making her jump and cry out in shock. However, even though it had initially surprised her, Rita had seen enough of the object to know what had happened. She'd even heard the tiny squeak after impact.

It was a bat, and it had swooped full speed into the glass pane. Though much of the motion had been a blur, Rita did see the animal drop after impact and fall to the ground below.

She now stood motionless, breathing heavily, clutching her binder to her chest for protection.

Calm down, it was nothing to panic about, she told herself. *Just a bat. You saw it yourself.*

Regardless of that being true, Rita's anxiety level shot up a hundred-fold. Then, another sound startled her, this one the opening of a door. She breathed a sigh of relief as Ray poked his head out from their bedroom, eyes still half-closed and his hair a wild mess.

'What is it?' he asked in a groggy voice, squinting at her. 'Did you shout or something?'

'I... a bat hit the window,' Rita said, pointing to the point of impact. When she looked closer she saw a small crack in the windowpane.

Ray frowned, then stepped out into the corridor to look at the glass. His sleepy eyes widened. 'Strange, don't often hear of bats colliding with things. Don't they have sonar or something?'

Rita had no idea if that was the case or not, but this one certainly had suffered a mishap. So she just shrugged. Ray ran a finger over the crack.

'This will have to be repaired,' he said, then turned to her. 'What are you doing up, anyway?'

'Couldn't sleep, so I went downstairs to do a little more work.' Rita then held up the binder.

Ray looked at the folder, then back to Rita. 'Get much done?'

'A little,' she replied.

'The bat thing scare you?' he asked. 'You look as white as a sheet.'

Rita considered telling her husband what she had seen —or what she *thought* she had seen. But, it sounded crazy even in *her* head, so she had no idea how Ray would react to such a fantastical tale.

'It made me jump a little,' she finally said. 'But I'm okay.'

He held out a hand, and she gratefully took it. 'Come back to bed,' he told her. 'Try and get some sleep.'

She did, eventually managing to drift off after another half-hour of lying awake and staring at the shadows in the corner of her room.

13

March.

Today was the day—the grand opening of the Black-water Hotel.

'Grand' wasn't exactly an apt term. After all, only three rooms had been booked out.

Ray knew it wasn't the start Rita had been hoping for. Despite her best efforts to get the word out—even garnering some press coverage in the local paper—the buzz hadn't really taken hold. Rita had been dismayed to read the newspaper report she had worked so hard on actually focus on the notoriety of the building, instead of keeping the story on the upcoming opening.

The reporter had even used the phrase, 'the purportedly haunted building,' which enraged Rita further, causing her to toss the newspaper into the bin and label it a tabloid rag.

The hotel certainly looked the part, and Ray was pleased with how he'd managed to convert the old study into the office and reception area. The separating wall he'd constructed was basic, but he'd managed to make it look fairly seamless, save for the break in the original's ornate coving, something he was not able to replicate.

That day, Ray was dressed in a smart suit that Rita had bought for him, but he thought it made him look like a butler. Maybe that was the point, but he hated it. He also hated that he had to pretend to be something he was not.

But Rita needed the opening day to be perfect, regardless of the low guest count, and Ray didn't want to get in the way of that. So, he went along with it in the hopes that the first impressions to the guests would be good ones. Rita's aim was that despite the low numbers the guests would at least pass on good recommendations to their friends.

From their position in the office, adjacent to the entrance lobby, both Ray and Rita heard the rumble of a car engine approaching the house.

'They're here,' Rita said, her voice full of nervous energy. She strode from the room, waving Ray after her, and headed out into the entrance lobby. Rita suddenly turned to Ray and straightened out his collar, then brushed off his shoulders, even though Ray knew they were clean—mainly because she had been brushing them off intermittently for the last half an hour.

He took hold of her by the elbows. 'Rita... stop fussing. Everything will be fine. You'll be charming, I'll carry the bags, and the guests will have an amazing time.'

His wife took a deep breath, but he could feel her shake slightly in his grasp. She eventually nodded. 'It will. It will all be great.'

She sounded like she was trying to convince herself, rather than really believing it, but Ray didn't doubt her. All of the nervous energy would dissipate the instant she needed it to, and Rita would transform into the consummate professional with a kind smile and courteous demeanour.

Rita led Ray outside to stand at the top of the steps out front of the house. The weather was crisp and clear, with the beginnings of spring starting to show: shoots of new yellow and white flowers had begun to bloom, and the green nubs of leaves had started to appear on the formerly bare trees.

The couple watched with big, forced smiles as the car drove over to the carport. After it was parked, Rita and Ray trotted over as the visitors inside disembarked. The couple were fairly advanced in years.

'Welcome,' Rita said, sounding calm, polite, and professional, just as Ray knew she would. 'I hope your drive up here was pleasant?'

The lady was small with angular facial features, and had dark, curly hair without a grey in sight, meaning it was probably dyed. The guest smiled at Rita. Her lips were decorated in bright red lipstick, and they pulled back into a smile that revealed gleaming white dentures. Thick makeup covering her sagging skin and a heavy layer of blue eyeshadow completed the look of someone desperately fighting against the never-ending march of age. She wore a tan shawl over a smart white and black tartan jacket, and black trousers beneath.

'Oh yes, it was indeed, dear,' she replied in a light Irish accent. 'Very tranquil.'

'This is a lovely area,' the gentleman added, with the same accent as his wife. If Ray were to guess, he'd say the man was a bit older than his wife, due to the bald head that was smattered with liver spots. He also bore a trimmed, white moustache that hung under a rather pointed nose, and his eyes were a pale, dulled blue. The man wore a tan dinner jacket, white shirt, and cream trousers, a look that

Ray found gaudy, though he assumed was the norm for people of wealth. The couple were quite obviously wealthy, and their car was a clear indicator of that: a pristine, oil-blue Bentley convertible which gleamed in the daylight. Ray felt a pang of jealousy looking at the sleek automobile.

Oh how the other half live.

The old man was holding a hand to his lower back and gave a wince of pain, and Ray noted the gentleman hadn't quite fully straightened up yet. 'Bit of a drive, though, not good on the old back.'

'Then let me get your bags,' Ray said, stepping forward.

'Thank you,' the man replied, and popped open the boot of the car. There were three suitcases inside, which Ray after a bit of adjustment managed to gather up in one go. He held a bag in each hand, and the smallest was tucked under his right arm.

'So, Mr. And Mrs. Lancaster,' Rita began. 'If you would care to follow me, we will get you checked in and then settled into your room, which I am sure you will love.'

Rita then led the couple up towards the house. Ray had read the arrivals for the day but had no idea how Rita knew these were Mr. and Mrs. Lancaster. All guests were able to check-in from 2 o'clock onwards, so it could have been any of them, given all three rooms were booked out to couples.

'Lovely building,' the man said, staring up at the hotel.

'It is,' Rita agreed as she began up the front steps, guiding the guests while Ray brought up the rear. The bags Ray was carrying were heavy, though manageable. Rita went on, 'It was built in the twelve-hundreds, believe it or not, and was first used as a monastery.'

Ray couldn't help but smirk, given Rita hadn't been exactly thrilled when she'd heard the history of the house, though she was now happy using it to impress the guests.

He also noted that she conveniently left out the part about the 'Mad Monk' going on to kill all of his brothers.

'Fascinating,' the lady said as they entered the great hall. 'This is quite something.'

Ray could see Rita allow herself a small smile—the two guests were suitably impressed. An excellent start to their stay.

'Now,' Rita began, motioning towards the door that led to the newly formed reception area. 'If you please come this way, we'll get you checked in. My husband Ray will take your bags up while we deal with the formalities. Then we can give you a tour of the building if you'd like.'

'Sounds wonderful, dear,' Mrs. Lancaster said. Rita gave Ray a look—his indication to scuttle off with the suitcases. He already had the key to their room, which was one that overlooked the front of the property. Ray gave them both a polite smile, which he hoped didn't look as awkward and forced as it felt, and climbed the stairs. As he did, he felt the solid plastic handles of the cases start to chafe his fingers.

Once he got to the room, Ray set the cases down and unlocked the door, nudging it open with his foot. He then carried everything inside and set the luggage down next to the bed, which he'd made up only that morning. Ray then double-checked the bathroom to make sure the towels and other toiletries were all present and correct, and when he was happy everything was ship-shape he headed back downstairs.

Rita was just finishing off with the checking-in process, and after that was complete the four of them began the tour. Rita led the way and used some tidbits of the house's history that Marcus had divulged. Again, the more morbid and controversial details were obviously left out.

The stairs to the top floor were also pointed out to the

guests, though only to clarify that they were currently out of bounds. There was also now a red rope across the opening to the stairs, with a 'no entry' sign. Rita used the excuse that the floor above was still being renovated and wasn't fit for the public to see just yet. That seemed to be enough to satisfy the guests' curiosity.

Once Mr. and Mrs. Lancaster were settled into their room, Ray and Rita made their way back down to the office area. When Ray checked the time, he saw that he had just over an hour before he needed to go pick Chloe up from school, and he hoped the other guests would be checked in by then—otherwise Rita would be carrying the bags up herself.

'How did you know which couple they were?' he asked his wife. 'Did they give their car registration or something?'

Rita shook her head. 'I recognised Mrs. Lancaster's voice from when she made the booking,' Rita replied, impressing Ray with her attention to detail.

'Well, I think they were suitably charmed, hun. First ones down, two more to go.'

As if on cue, they heard another car approaching. Rita and Ray walked outside to see this couple were younger than the last—in their mid-to-late thirties—but clearly still quite well off. The husband had brushed-back, dark brown hair, and the woman—dressed in a tight-fitting dress that showed off her curves—had long blonde hair that looked to have been expensively styled.

The last of the guests arrived shortly after as well. These were the oldest pair of the three, with the husband being a retired Royal Infantry veteran. In fact, Rita had to pull Ray away and scold him for talking the guest's ear off and asking about the man's old war stories.

Everything went perfectly that day. All the guests made

use of the facilities to relax: reading in the library, walking the gardens and grounds outside, and drinking coffee in the great hall while looking out over the courtyard. In the evening, Rita and Ray prepared the meals, and the guests seemed to enjoy the food—Ray even received a few compliments on his friendly service when dishing out the food. The last to retire for the night was the younger couple, who got a little tipsy on the cocktails Rita served. However, they caused no trouble, and Ray and Rita managed to climb into bed a little before midnight.

The couple had even managed to carve out time to spend with Chloe; each had taken turns to deal with any guest requests that came up. Making sure Chloe wasn't starved of attention was something of a concern for Ray. But, so far, it all seemed to be working.

It wasn't until the next morning that the perfect start hit something of a snag.

Mr. and Mrs. Lancaster, the first guests to check in, were also the first to check out, deciding to skip breakfast. Ray arrived at the reception desk at six in the morning, prompt. The two guests came down—fully packed and suitcases in hand—by six-ten.

They immediately demanded to speak with Rita, who came down as quickly as she could.

'Check us out immediately,' the lady snapped, slamming her key down into the reception desk. Rita looked stunned.

'Of course,' Rita replied, maintaining her calm. 'Is everything alright?'

'It most certainly is not,' the husband answered. 'I don't know what kind of place you are running here, but if it is a place where people are allowed to run around in the nip, that should have been made known.'

'The nip?' Rita asked from behind the desk. Ray stood next to his wife, just as confused as she clearly was.

'You know... *nude*. Is this some kind of swingers resort? It is not what we expected.'

Ray hadn't heard that colloquialism, which was possibly an Irish thing, but he was confused at the accusation about the hotel. Even Rita—normally unflappable—struggled to find her words. 'Sir... I... I'm not quite sure what you mean. This isn't that kind of establishment at all.'

'Well,' the man replied haughtily, 'you might want to tell your *other* guests that.'

'What happened?' Ray asked, unable to keep quiet.

'I'll tell you,' the woman took over, jabbing an angry finger at Ray. 'I was woken up in the middle of the bloody night by one of the other guests. I don't know how, but he'd managed to get our door open. Probably picked the lock. And he just stood there in the doorway, watching us sleep, naked as the day he was born!'

Ray heard a small gasp from Rita. 'Oh my lord,' she said, bringing a hand up to her mouth. 'I'm... I am so sorry about that. We really had no idea. I can promise you, though, this is not that kind of place. Do you know which guest it was? I will, of course, speak to them and—'

The husband just held up his palm. 'No need,' he snapped. 'We don't want to hear excuses. And no, we don't know which one it was, so don't ask. But now I can't get the image of his pale bloody body out of my mind. It was quite disturbing, being watched like that. I told him to scram, but the pervert just stood there, watching. He didn't vanish until I turned on the light and got out of bed. He was quick on his feet then, I can tell you. I didn't even see him move. He was just gone. Probably afraid of what I was about to do. So, as you can imagine, we've seen enough of what the Blackwater Hotel has to offer and will be taking our leave now.'

'How about I deduct some money from your bill,' Rita suggested. 'For your distress. It's the least we can do.'

The two guests did not seem interested, however, and were already gathering up their cases.

'Deduct money?' the man said with a scoff. 'I'm not paying a single red cent. Not after that fiasco.'

Ray felt a small pang of anger. He had previously suggested that all guests pay upfront, but Rita argued that it was better for them to pay on check-out, to show confidence in the services.

Ray opened his mouth to speak, feeling their stance was grossly unfair, but Rita raised a hand and placed it on his chest.

'I understand,' she said to the couple.

Ray didn't like it. After all, it wasn't *their* fault one of the guests had a penchant for naked strolls in the night. He also had no clue how the guest had managed to pick the lock.

No more than ten minutes later, Mr. and Mrs. Lancaster had driven away in anger, leaving Ray and his wife dumbfounded.

'Who the hell was watching them sleep?' Ray asked, but Rita shook her head.

'I have no idea. Maybe the younger guy?'

It seemed a logical guess, given the brief description, and Ray doubted it was the veteran. But then, the younger man was hardly pale in Ray's estimation, which went against what Mr. Lancaster had said. 'So... do we confront him?' Ray asked.

Rita shrugged. 'I don't see how we can. Without knowing for certain who it was, we can't level something like that at him. It's not like Mr. Lancaster is still here to identify the guy.'

'Jesus fucking Christ,' Ray said with a sigh. 'What a start. And how the hell did he get the door open?'

Neither had an answer, so Ray went up to check. However, he couldn't find anything wrong with the lock, or any sign of forced entry. In fact, something sprang to mind that he should have mentioned earlier. The doors all had pull-chains across, and if that was on its latch, there was no way someone from the outside could have gotten the door open. So what the hell had happened?

Perhaps the Lancasters were just spinning a lie in order to get out of paying, which only angered Ray more.

While Rita maintained her impeccable air of profession-alism for the rest of the day, Ray could tell the less-than-stellar experience of their first guests was bothering her.

The opening of the Blackwater Hotel had been rocky, to say the least, and Ray just hoped for Rita's sake things wouldn't continue that way.

14

APRIL.

Rita watched the young couple she had just checked in follow Ray as he led them up to their rooms. He would then carry out the tour on his own.

Only two rooms had been booked for the whole weekend, which simply wasn't good enough. Rita rubbed her tired and sore eyes. The dull headache, which was turning into a constant annoyance, threatened to blossom into something much worse. She needed sleep. But every night, Rita's own body worked against her, waking her in the dead of night like clockwork.

She retreated to the closed-off office and took a seat, leaning herself back and letting out a sigh before propping her feet up on the neat and orderly desk before her.

They were a month in, and though there had been guests in that time, the stream had been underwhelming—more like a trickle at best.

That had meant adjusting to their new life here had been relatively easy in some respects, as balancing time with Chloe hadn't been too much of an issue. On the other hand, the stage of needing to bring in more staff seemed to be a million miles away.

To make matters worse, when Marcus had gone over their recent progress he'd once again raised Ray's idiotic idea for an event in October as something to think about. Unfortunately, Rita couldn't really afford to look down her nose at the idea anymore, considering her own efforts had been lukewarm.

And yet, try as she might, that elusive 'ah-ha' brainwave or spark of inspiration that would transform their fortunes had simply not come. The more Rita focused on the problem, the more it festered and ate at her. It seemed impossible to overcome.

On top of all that, spending so much time inside the house seemed to be getting to her as well, and she felt like cabin fever was setting in. Rita always had the sense of being watched, and she was often uneasy late at night, though she'd never had another incident like the one two months ago where Rita had thought she'd seen something in the television's reflection.

Looking back on it, she knew it was only her mind playing tricks on her.

Rita had half an idea to nap for an hour or so, but a knock on the door to the office startled her. She looked up to see Marcus standing in the doorway, dressed in a dark blue wool sweater, blue jeans, and suede loafers.

'You look exhausted,' he said.

'I'm fine,' she replied, swinging her feet from the table. She felt slightly embarrassed that he'd seen her laid back like that. Though Rita had always worked hard for him—for them all—she hated the idea that anyone may think she was lounging around.

'If you say so,' Marcus shot back, smiling as he entered

the room. 'How are things going? Not many guests so far this weekend, I've noticed.'

'No,' she admitted and got to her feet. 'Bit of a quiet one.'

'They all seem quiet ones, don't you think?'

Rita paused, feeling like she was under a spotlight. 'Maybe,' she admitted. 'But you have to build to success. It doesn't just happen overnight.' That was an excuse. She knew it was. While the statement was true enough, Rita had still been expecting far better of herself.

'Fair point, I suppose,' Marcus went on. 'Have you given any more thought to the event in October?'

This again. 'Not really,' she replied. That wasn't necessarily true. Rita had thought about it *a lot*, but purely in terms of how to avoid it.

'Well, I think we start making plans for it,' Marcus stated. It wasn't a suggestion.

Rita felt her defences go up. 'I really don't think that's a good idea. We are building something here, Marcus. An establishment that screams class, not cheap gimmicks and parlour-room tricks. It won't help us, believe me.'

'Well, I think we try it,' Marcus insisted. 'I have little doubt we could fill this place up for the weekend if we did, and the word of mouth would help.'

'I understand what you're saying, but—'

Marcus held up a hand, stopping Rita in her tracks. 'I appreciate your point of view, Rita,' he said. 'I do. But we aren't screaming 'class' at the minute, are we? We are screaming 'empty.' So please, indulge me. We move ahead with this. I'll speak to you later this evening about how we go about it. Plenty of time to get things prepared.'

Rita clenched her teeth together. 'Well, we can't very well fill this place up when the top storey is *still* off-limits, can we?'

She then took a breath. She'd thrown that point up in pure frustration, and while it was true, they hadn't even come close to needing those extra rooms. Still, if he wanted this event on Halloween to fill up the hotel, then the top floor would indeed be needed.

'That is another good point' Marcus said. 'And something I intend to rectify. The top storey will soon be opened up for use. I will need to keep two rooms back, so I want to speak to Ray about a conversion that will help. But the rest of that floor will be available to the public.' He then smirked and added, 'If you even need them, that is.'

Rita had nothing else to say to that. She was still angry at being railroaded into the Halloween idea.

'So...' Marcus went on. 'Do you want to see it?'

Rita frowned. 'See what?'

'What it is that I'm doing upstairs.'

Rita was caught off guard, given the privacy Marcus had demanded over his activities up there.

'Is there something specific you want to show me?' she asked.

'Kind of. And I think it will be of interest.'

What could Rita realistically say to that? So, she simply nodded her head.

'Excellent!' Marcus exclaimed. 'We'll wait until Ray returns, since I want him to see it, too.'

15

'JESUS CHRIST,' Ray said when shown the room on the top floor. He didn't know what he was looking at, exactly, but it was equal parts impressive and... creepy as hell.

The large room he, Rita, Marcus, and Vincent had all gathered in was near the front of the building, clearly originally used as a bedroom. Now, it was a storage area for things Ray didn't really comprehend.

'Quite something, isn't it?' Marcus asked, the grin he wore wide and proud.

'It... really is.'

The space was jam-packed with bookshelves, display cases, and boxes that all contained—as far as Ray could see—things that were... *odd*.

Ray could see strange artefacts in some of the display cases: weird sigils, daggers, and unrolled parchments. There were even small, dead animals floating in jars full of yellow liquid, forever preserved.

'You two haven't been sacrificing goats up here, have you?' Ray asked, unable to help himself.

Thankfully, Marcus took the remark in good humour and bellowed out a laugh.

'No,' he said. 'No sacrifices, I can promise you that. However, it may or may not surprise you to know this: Perron Manor isn't a stranger to such things.'

Both Ray and Rita turned to look at him. 'Sacrifices?' Rita asked, shocked.

Marcus nodded. 'Yes. You see, when I divulged some of the history of this house to you, I may have left a little bit out. Partly due to time, and partly because I wanted to ease you into it.'

'You're going to have to explain that further,' Rita replied as she started to walk around the room. She squeezed herself between boxes and bookshelves, taking an interest on what was on show.

'Understood,' Marcus said. 'You see, while Perron Manor has a... shall we say... bloodier than average history, for its age—'

'Hold up,' Ray cut in. 'I thought you said *all* houses like this have dark elements to their history. Now you're saying it's bloodier than the average?'

'What I said was certainly true,' Marcus replied. 'But yes, this house has seen more than its fair share of darkness. I believe a lot of it is self-perpetuating, of course, given the early years. Word travelled about the murders that took place here when the building was used as a monastery. The house gained a reputation and attracted a certain type of person to it. People like Edward Grey, and especially Robert Perron. Those who had an interest in the darker things in life.'

'Would you add yourself to that list?' Rita asked, stopping at a waist-height display case, one with a glass top and a plush red lining inside. It contained a single book, bound in black, creased leather, and had gold symbols and wording on the cover. Ray walked over and looked down at it as well.

The title isn't written in English, he noted.

'Well, it is my stock and trade,' Marcus replied, casting his arms about the cluttered room. 'But, of course, there is a difference.'

'Which is?'

'In my view, people like Robert Perron absolutely believed in the things they were studying.'

'And you don't?'

'No, I don't,' Marcus confirmed, shaking his head. 'I find it fascinating, for sure, seeing how the uglier side of human nature can manifest. But do I believe human sacrifice has any material bearing on the world? No, of course not. Other than people ending up dead.'

'Wait,' Ray jumped in. '*Human* sacrifice? I thought we were talking about goats and stuff?'

'Well, I suppose there could have been some of that. But many of the tragedies that have befallen Perron Manor are borne from the wrong kind of people being attracted to the house. People known to go to the extreme.'

'And it just so happened to fall into your family's possession?' Rita asked. She continued to stare at the book. Ray even saw her run a finger over the glass case.

'It wasn't by chance,' Marcus said. 'My grandfather wanted this place precisely *because* of what it was. Given its past, it became well known among his colleagues. And since I've followed in his footsteps, why would I ever sell up? It was just a shame it stood empty to rot while my father was in possession. It wasn't really his kind of place. He was far too... short-sighted. Thankfully, he was wise enough to keep it in his possession, knowing its value would only increase. I suppose I'm grateful dear old Daddy had at least that much sense.'

'You don't sound very fond of your father,' Ray noted, and Marcus shook his head.

'No, I don't believe I am. Don't get me wrong, he wasn't a bad person by any stretch. In fact, his problem was the total opposite. He was quite vanilla and pedestrian and... well, *boring*. He didn't really make the most of life. And I don't have much time for people like that.'

'So why show us this room now?' Rita asked. 'I'm sure you didn't really bring us up here to talk over your daddy issues.'

Ray was a little shocked at how confrontational Rita was being. He'd noticed a small change in her demeanour recently, but put it down to exhaustion and stress. However, she'd always toed the line with Marcus. Until now.

Marcus narrowed his eyes. 'Indeed not,' he replied, flatly. 'I came to show you what this house is *really* all about. I believe one of the reasons you are struggling to attract guests is because of some preconceived notions people have about the house. And I think Ray hit on something when he said we'd be better served embracing its true nature.'

'Well,' Ray began, 'I don't think I put it *quite* like that.' He didn't want this to come back on him, given Rita was dead set against it.

'Regardless,' Marcus said, 'you were correct in your assertions. Let me tell you both something—I have dealt with a lot of people doing what I do. A lot of *wealthy* people. All are very intelligent, and all are very successful. But one thing many of them had in common was that any time discussions turned to the occult or the... dare I say, supernatural... their ears all pricked up. Interest heightened. I believe that is because to be successful you need something of an edge. And that is what we're currently lacking with the Blackwater Hotel. That edge, which would separate us from the norm.'

'So, people will come here to look at all of *this*?' Rita asked, gesturing to the macabre treasures within the room.

Marcus took a moment and rubbed his chin. 'Well... in all honesty, I hadn't considered that. I was just thinking of playing up to the house's reputation. But I suppose we could put some of these things on show. Another good idea. Of course, anything of true value will need to be safely locked away.'

'But don't you see,' Rita argued back. 'There isn't a large market for that kind of thing—otherwise, it would have been done before. Even if October is a success, it won't sustain the hotel long-term. We need a solid brand so the business can grow organically.'

'We've tried it your way,' Marcus said, with finality. 'And now we will try it mine. If it doesn't work, then we will see where we land. For now, I want you to focus your efforts on October, and making this happen.'

'And if I say no?'

Marcus smiled, but his eyes contained only anger. 'Then I'll thank you for your service thus far and we can part ways.'

An awkward silence descended over them all. Vincent looked to the floor, seeming like a lost puppy, and Rita had a face like thunder. Marcus continued to stare at her, neither giving any ground.

'So, in the meantime,' Ray cut in, hoping to play peace-maker. 'Can we try and build the business as Rita suggested? See how things grow? Then, come October, we have the event and see where we're at. We might surprise ourselves and find we're filling the hotel up every day of every week by then.'

Marcus eventually broke his strong eye contact with Rita and looked over to Ray. He rubbed at his chin again with his thumb for a moment, then nodded. 'Seems like a fair compromise.' He turned back to Rita. 'Agreed?'

Just agree, Ray pleaded internally. Thankfully, Rita nodded as well.

'Good,' Marcus said. 'Now, Ray, I need to speak to you about a few modifications I want to make up here. As you can see, space is a little tight, so I want to convert two rooms into one.'

'Okay,' Ray said. 'That should be no problem.'

'I'll leave you to it,' Rita cut in, her voice curt. 'I have things to be getting on with.' She then walked away, leaving Ray in limbo. He desperately wanted to stand up for his wife, but at the same time he didn't want to make them homeless.

'Don't worry about her,' Marcus said. 'She'll come around.'

Ray shook his head. *You obviously don't know my wife very well.*

16

ONCE RAY HAD LEFT THEM, Marcus walked over to the display case that contained *Ianua Diaboli*.

The Devil's Door.

Vincent approached and stood beside him, an ever-present shadow. One that had its uses, of course.

'I thought my sister was going to quit right there,' Vincent said, his voice soft, mumbling... pathetic.

'She won't quit,' Marcus replied, still eyeing the precious book. 'They have nowhere else to go.'

'I suppose. How are the translations coming?' Vincent asked.

Marcus lifted the lid and then picked up the thick, heavy book. 'Getting there. We should have plenty of time, though. I believe my grandfather had been largely accurate... for the most part. Such a shame he didn't have the courage to make use of the knowledge he had.'

Vincent just nodded uselessly. 'And... it's going to happen *then*? In October?'

'Yes,' Marcus confirmed. 'I think Ray stumbled upon a good idea with that. It should give us the bodies we need.'

'And my sister...'

'Is proving less than compliant,' Marcus finished. 'I'll need to change that.'

17

'IT'S A JOKE!' Rita spat, struggling to keep a handle on the rage that bubbled through her.

'I know,' Ray agreed, 'but what can we do?'

She wanted to scream. Ray was right, there was nothing they could do. They were trapped here, and she *hated* it.

The whole venture suddenly felt like it was spiralling and collapsing down around her. After being tasked with putting together a fucking haunted house tour, Rita might as well have been working at a carnival.

She and Ray were back in the office, tucked away from anyone else in the house. Rita checked the clock and saw that it was close to three in the afternoon, which meant one of them would soon need to go pick up Chloe from school.

'I guess we just have to bend over and take it,' Rita snapped. 'All because you couldn't keep your mouth shut.' She saw Ray's face fall. She knew her words hurt him, but it didn't stop her. 'Next time, leave the ideas to me, got it?'

Ray's shoulders slumped and his head dipped a little. In an instant, Rita felt terrible for taking her anger out on her husband like that. All he'd done was put forward an idea.

Granted, it was a stupid one, but it was Marcus that had picked up the idea and run with it. *He* was the one imposing his plan of action onto Rita, whether she agreed with it or not.

And *that* was the real root of her anger. Early on, Marcus had insisted that this was Rita's show. However, he'd been quick to enforce his will when it suited.

Her early enthusiasm had been stamped out. Rita now realised Marcus was no different from the other men who'd screwed her over—all that mattered to them was what *they* wanted and what *they* thought was best.

Everything else was just lip-service.

'I'm sorry,' Rita eventually said to her husband.

Ray shook his head. 'No, you're right. I *should* have just kept my mouth shut and let you do your thing. I'm an idiot.'

Rita walked over to him and placed a hand on his cheek. 'You're not an idiot, Ray. I'm just tired and angry, and I'm taking everything out on the wrong person.' She cupped a hand under his chin, raised his head up, and looked into his eyes. 'You are *not* an idiot,' she repeated.

Then, she kissed him. Hard. Before Rita knew it, she was clawing her nails through Ray's thick, black hair. A sudden surge of desire ran through her, and Rita wanted desperately to find some kind of release to her frustration. She started to undo the buttons on Ray's shirt.

She didn't want to use sex as a way to brush over the apology she'd just given, but right now the need to feel him inside her was just too strong.

Ray pulled away a little, visibly shocked. 'Do we have time?'

She just nodded and kissed him again. 'We'll make time.'

Ray was then pushed onto the desk, and Rita climbed atop him.

'Erm... hello?'

Both Rita and Ray stopped at the sound of a voice from the entrance lobby. Her teeth were still clamped over Ray's top lip. She released him and turned her head.

'Yes?' Rita shouted back, feeling a sting of frustration. She had recognised the voice, and it belonged to Mrs. Tenant, one of the few guests they currently had staying.

'I... I have something of a problem that I need you to have a look at.'

'Shit,' Rita whispered. Then, louder, she called over to the waiting guest. 'I'll be right out.'

'Guess we'll need to pick this up later,' Ray said.

'I guess so. Come on, let's go and see what the issue is.'

'You go first,' he replied. 'I'll follow up in a few minutes.'

Rita frowned in confusion. Ray then raised his eyebrows, and Rita felt his hardness against her.

'Ah,' she said, realising his issue. She laughed. 'Okay, you take a few minutes to calm down first, and then you can follow us up there. It's room ten.'

'No problem,' Ray replied, and Rita climbed down off him, making sure to give him a teasing squeeze with her hand as she did.

18

'Yes, I can certainly smell it,' Ray confirmed. 'But I'm sorry, I have no idea what it is.'

After calming down, Ray had made his way up to the room and arrived just in time to hear the end of the complaint from the guest.

Mr. and Mrs. Tenant were a couple in their mid-forties. He was a tall, broad-shouldered man who had a few inches even on Ray, and she was the polar opposite—petite and lithe, with long dark hair, heavy makeup, and a tight top that accentuated her breasts.

Their room was one to the rear of the house, with pale green wallpaper, white curtains and throw pillows, and a runner that was a slightly darker green than the walls. The room also had an adjoining en-suite, which all four of them were currently squeezed into.

The smell in question was potent and not an odour that was easy to distinguish. Close to rotten cabbage, but a little sweeter.

'We will of course move you to a new room straight away,' Rita said. 'And I apologise for the smell in here. It wasn't something we were aware of. If we had been, we would have never put you in here.'

'I'll take a look at it,' Ray confirmed, knowing it would have to be done after he picked up Chloe. If the guests were changing rooms, that would tie Rita up, meaning he would be on school-run duty.

'No problem,' the large man said, rolling a thick, golden ring around one of his pudgy fingers. The couple seemed amenable and perfectly pleasant, which was a relief to Ray. Often, when guests had a complaint, they *really* let you know about it.

'Something else you may want to look at,' the woman offered, 'is that there is sometimes a draft in here. I noticed it earlier when I first picked up on the smell. I felt what I thought was someone breathing on my neck. It was the weirdest thing. Obviously, I think you may just have a crack in the walls or something where the air was getting through. It really gave me the shivers, though.'

'Thanks for letting us know. I'll definitely make sure it gets taken care of. And, again, I'm sorry. We do inspect the rooms thoroughly before check-in, so we must have missed it.'

'Oh it's fine,' the lady said with a wave of her hand. 'Don't worry too much about it.'

'I'll still look into it,' Ray promised. The smell in the en-suite was undeniable—and unpleasant. So much so that he wanted to be out of the confined space and get a little fresh air.

'How about we move you into a similar room, just on the opposite side of the house, would that be okay? You'd still have a private bathroom.'

'That's fine,' the man said. 'Absolutely no trouble.'

'We'll move your bags over,' Rita added. 'And a few

drinks on the house are in order, I think. So, if you'll follow me...'

Rita led the couple out of the en-suite. Ray was pleased by the agreeable demeanour of the guests. They certainly could have made things more difficult.

Just as he was leaving the bedroom himself, however, Ray felt a sudden gust of air roll over his cheek. As it did, that vile smell suddenly intensified, and Ray's cheek tingled from the cold.

He looked around, puzzled, and felt the air with his hand. However, he could not detect any further breeze or airflow.

The guest was right. And it *had* felt like an exhalation of breath on his skin. But there was no one around, and the horrid smell soon dissipated as well.

At a loss, Ray closed the door behind him and left, knowing he could come back to this later. For now, Chloe was waiting.

19

MAY.

It was their fifth month of living at Perron Manor and Ray was getting more and more concerned about his wife.

There were times that she would drift off and just stare at nothing, in a zombie-like state, and wouldn't come out of it unless he shook her or repeatedly called her name. She was also starting to look gaunt, with sunken cheeks, and she had to wear heavier makeup to hide the bags under her eyes.

After Ray had finished converting the two rooms on the top floor for Marcus—which involved knocking out the separating wall and a bit of redecorating—he had been allowed to convert one of the bedrooms on the mid-floor into another living area, this one for him and his family to use in the evenings. The living room downstairs was now used by the guests exclusively... when they had any.

The mid-floor living room, situated on the opposite protruding rear wing to their bedrooms, contained only a black-and-white television and some sofas and side tables, and was basic but adequate.

The family was gathered in the newly converted mid-floor living room, with Chloe reading on her own sofa and Rita snuggled up with Ray. If any guests needed them, then there was a note at reception to either come up to this room or, if it was late and there was an emergency, dial a direct number to Ray and Rita's bedroom. Thankfully, it hadn't been needed as yet. Still, he found it difficult to truly switch off and relax.

Rita was looking over at the television, though she wasn't really watching it. It was close to nine in the evening, and normally Ray liked to have Chloe in bed by then. Given Rita was looking exhausted as well, he decided they should all turn in. Only two nights ago, he had woken to see that Rita wasn't in bed with him, and he found her sleepwalking down the corridor outside of their room. He hoped not to have a repeat performance of that tonight.

'Come on,' he said, kissing Rita on top of the head. He then stood up and stretched out, feeling his vertebra give a satisfying pop. 'I think we should all call it a night.'

'Awww,' Chloe complained, 'can't I stay up a little longer?'

Ray shook his head. 'Not a chance. You have school tomorrow. We've already let you stay up late enough as it is.'

'Fine,' she huffed playfully, slapping her book closed. Ray walked over to the television set and clicked it off. He turned back to Rita, who was still staring blankly at the screen.

He moved over to her and gave her a gentle shake on the shoulder. Rita blinked a few times, and then her brown eyes focused onto him. 'Everything okay?' she asked, her voice distant.

He laughed. 'Yeah, but we're going to bed. Come on.'

Holding her hands, he pulled his wife up to her feet,

then the family walked over to their rooms. Ray put Chloe to bed after reading her a few chapters from her story—one about a secret society of witches.

Once back in his own room, Ray saw that Rita was already under the covers, lightly snoring.

Good. I'm glad she's getting some rest.

He used the toilet then brushed his teeth, changed into pyjama bottoms and a t-shirt, and finally climbed into bed next to his wife. He lay in the dark, running over the family's situation in his head, wondering if there was a way to move away from the hotel and start again, should they need to. He didn't get very far, however, as sleep soon claimed him.

It felt like he'd only just drifted off when he was woken by an urgent ringing sound. Confused and disoriented, he lifted his head from the pillow. Fragmented remnants of a dream clung to him, though they were hard to piece back together. He could only remember the feeling of falling. Or, rather, being dragged down. Had he been underwater? No, everything around him had seemed too solid for that.

Other than the ringing, which he soon realised was coming from the phone in the room, everything else seemed quiet. He checked the clock, squinting through the dark.

A quarter past three.

If a guest was calling this late at night, that meant there was a problem. A *serious* problem.

He got up and walked over to the nightstand on Rita's side of the bed. Rita didn't seem to be stirring, which was a blessing. However, Ray knew that there was a good chance he was going to have to wake her anyway. The cold in the room bit at his arms, and there was the faintest of odours that seemed... off.

Ray lifted the receiver and brought it up to his ear. 'Hello?' he said into it, trying to hide the grogginess in his voice.

He then waited for a response. There was none initially, but he could hear heavy breathing down the line, so thick that it gave off a crackling effect with it. Ray waited a little longer before asking, 'Anyone there?'

'*Yesssssss*,' came the throaty reply. '*I'm... here.*' That was followed by a giggle. Ray felt a chill, and could only think that one of the guests was drunk and making a prank call.

'Is everything okay?' Ray asked, attempting to stay professional. Another long pause. Too long. 'Hello?' Ray went on.

'*I... want... you,*' the voice eventually replied in a hoarse whisper. The line was crackly and distorted. '*We... want... you... Ray.*'

Ray gritted his teeth and held his breath. He was certain it was a drunk caller now—some woman who was feeling randy with no inhibitions—though he wasn't sure which guest it was. Ray wasn't sure he wanted to find out, as he had an intensely uncomfortable feeling about the whole thing.

'*Do... you... want... me... Ray? Do... you... want... us?*'

He didn't know what the hell she was talking about. *Us?* Did this woman have multiple personalities? Or was she referring to another guest involved?

'I'm going to end the call now,' Ray said. 'This isn't appropriate. So, go back to bed and sleep it off.'

He then replaced the handset. The cold air around Ray felt heavy, unusually so, and his skin was lined with goose-bumps. He realised that the call had him a little freaked out, though he wasn't certain why. Sure, it had been unusual, but even so, it was just some idiot who'd had too much to drink. So why had it unnerved him so?

He looked down to Rita, who still lay asleep—which he was thankful for. In truth, he was surprised the ringing of the phone hadn't woken her. As Ray turned to walk around the bed again, keen to lie down and put the call out of his head, the phone rang again, loud and urgent.

Ray sighed, clenched his teeth, then picked up the receiver once more, desperate not to wake his wife. He knew who was on the other end of the line, of course, and didn't even bother to say anything as he placed the receiver against his ear.

When the voice spoke this time, it was male.

'*Helloooo, Ray.*'

A drunken husband, or boyfriend, perhaps?

'Who is this?!' Ray asked through gritted teeth.

'*We... are... friends,*' the man replied. Like his female counterpart, he spoke in a whisper. '*Come... with... us. Through... the... door.*'

'Look,' Ray snapped. 'I don't know what you're talking about but I'm warning both of you, you and your girlfriend, hang up the phone, go to bed, and don't call me back. Guest or not, I won't put up with shit like this. Understand?'

The only response was a mocking titter, one that rose in frequency until it became indistinguishable from the rising static that surrounded it. Soon, there was a clicking sound, followed by the long tone which signified the call had ended.

Perhaps Ray's threats had worked. He again replaced the handset but stood by the phone, watching it and waiting for it to ring again. After a few minutes of nothing but his wife's deep breathing, he was satisfied the couple had called it a night. He then turned to walk back around the bed. As he did, however, Ray stopped dead.

The door to the room was ajar.

Ray hadn't heard the handle move, or any squeak of the wooden door swinging on its hinges. There was no way a door as heavy as this one had simply drifted open of its own accord. Ray had made sure to click the thing shut after coming inside. Although, he wasn't certain if he'd actually pulled the security chain across.

But someone else had clearly opened it.

Ray's sense of unease only grew. He realised that someone could be standing just outside the room right now. The most obvious suspect was the woman he'd spoken to first, given the door had most likely been opened while he was talking with her partner.

If they were playing games like this they were either stupid or maybe a little unhinged. And that thought scared him. Had they brought Chloe into a potentially dangerous environment?

Ray strode out into the corridor, fists clenched, only to find it empty.

He quickly moved to his daughter's room but saw that the door was still closed. Ray didn't want to take any chances, so he quietly opened it—she wasn't allowed to use the security chain in case there was an emergency—and peeked inside. He saw Chloe fast asleep and under her covers.

That meant his late-night visitor had run off in the other direction.

Ray then quietly closed Chloe's door and walked back to his own room, stopping just outside of it. He could go back to bed and hope that whatever fun the couple was trying to have was now finished with. However, that did not sit right with him at all. He needed to make sure it was over, and the only way to do that was to confront the culprits and put a stop to this nonsense himself.

But first, he needed to figure out who the culprits actually were. Ray closed his eyes and tried to remember all of the people currently staying at the hotel.

He wasn't great with names but recalled there was a little old lady staying, though she was alone so Ray could rule her out. The other three rooms in use were taken up by couples, so they were the obvious candidates.

The first was occupied by two men, who said they were staying for business. However, Ray could tell it was anything but business. Instead, their rendezvous seemed like something they were hiding away from people, which Ray felt was a shame for them.

So, given the call had been from a woman *and* a man, those two gentlemen could also be checked off the list. The next couple were in their mid-to-late sixties, and prank calling didn't seem like something they would do.

Which left only one other pair, and the most likely culprits. Ray was far from Sherlock Holmes, but to him, his process of elimination had been solid. It was the only viable explanation.

Ray tried to remember the surname of the younger married couple. Was it Watson or Wilson... something like that. *Screw it*, he thought, *I'll just go with 'Sir' or 'Ma'am.'*

He'd guessed the couple to be in their thirties, and they were at the hotel for a romantic weekend away. Ray noticed earlier that they had been enjoying their evening drinks quite a bit, laughing and giggling together. If they had kept that pace going after Vincent had taken over the evening shift, they may have ended up quite soused.

He would still never have guessed they'd be the type to go on and act like naughty children in the middle of the night, but they were certainly the most likely candidates. They were staying on the same floor as Ray, but on the opposite side of the house.

He started towards their room, trying to keep as quiet as

possible, but still walked with purpose—and still simmered with annoyance and anger.

He decided to try and keep it polite... at first. If they didn't listen, well, then he intended to get a little more stern.

Don't do anything stupid, a voice inside warned. Wise words, but Ray didn't intend to go in swinging. He would just make sure their behaviour improved.

When he reached the door to their room, he saw it was closed. Everything was quiet. Ray moved his head closer and listened through the thick wood, trying to pick up anything: movement, whispering, giggling, any sign of life. He heard something, but not what he'd expected.

The man inside was clearly a snorer—a loud one—and the rumbling came in constant and steady waves. Ray seriously doubted that whoever had made the call would have had the chance to legitimately fall asleep in such a short time. Which meant either the guy was faking, or it hadn't been him in the first place.

If he knocked, and it turned out the couple had genuinely been asleep, then he would have to explain himself.

But, if Mr. and Mrs. Wilson, or Watson, or whatever the hell their names were, *had* been responsible, and he just left it alone, then they would have gotten away with it. That would give them confidence to start up their shit again.

As he was internally debating the issue, quick and sudden footsteps made Ray jump. He turned his head and heard the sound continue again, from around a corner up ahead. He realised someone was heading towards the stairs of the entrance lobby.

Ray quickly hurried in that direction as well, hearing whoever it was thunder down the stairs, not making any effort to be quiet in the dead of night. That only angered him further.

Ray then broke through to one of the high-level walk-ways in the lobby and looked over the rail, hoping to see the person he was chasing. But the rapid footsteps had already moved out of view, and he heard a door below him slam closed. Ray followed as fast as he could, but always seemed too slow. For someone he'd assumed to be drunk, this stranger could certainly move fast.

When Ray broke through into the great hall, he stopped and looked around. The area was dark, with the night outside visible through the rear glazed doors. All was quiet. No running footsteps, no doors opening or closing... nothing. Only the sound of his own breathing. That meant the person he'd been chasing was down there with him now.

Ray looked around the space for any kind of clue and noticed all doors except the one to the basement were closed.

If a guest had gone down there in the dark, then they had put themselves in danger running down a steep flight of steps.

Stone steps, no less.

Also, all the guests were made aware that the basement was strictly out of bounds.

Ray was through fucking around.

He marched over to the open door and stepped through, into the small room that housed the steps. It was a small area, with nothing else of note except the drop to the level below. He looked down into the dark, which seemed infinitely deeper than that of the ground floor. The shadows were thick and heavy, looking almost impenetrable. The light switch for that lower level was at the bottom of the steps and had not been flicked on yet.

Ray descended, taking slow and steady steps. There was no other route out of the basement, so he was now in no rush. They couldn't get away.

The air grew colder the lower Ray got, rolling over his exposed arms. An intense chill ran up through his bare soles as they pressed down on the hard stone steps.

When Ray reached the bottom, he held out a hand and felt along the wall until his fingers crept across the light switch. He flicked it, and the lights above slowly blinked to life.

Once his eyes adjusted to the light, he looked around the now-lit area, searching for the wayward guest.

He saw the furnace, piles of wood and coal, the small cells... but could see no one down there with him.

At first.

It was only when he turned away from the cells and back to the furnace that he caught a glimpse of a face peeking out from behind the giant metal structure. The sudden sight made Ray jolt in shock.

He didn't get much of a look before the head pulled away out of sight, but it seemed to Ray that something was wrong with the person's eyes. They just looked... blank. Devoid of pupils. But that could have just been because of the distance and the poor lighting. Regardless, Ray could not dwell on that point for long, as he intended to put a stop to the whole thing now. However, no sooner had he taken a step forward did the lights cut out and again plunge him into darkness.

Ray was unsure if the bulbs had blown or if the electricity had been tripped, but he could see nothing now. Not even his own hands that he raised up before his face.

All he could do was to listen. After a few moments, Ray heard something: breathing, which was slow and laboured, almost exaggerated. It was coming from directly ahead of him, though it was hard to pinpoint the exact distance. Maybe ten feet away, he guessed.

'Hello?' Ray called out, hearing his own voice echo. He received no response and heard only the continued breathing. Ray backed up and felt for the light switch again. Once he found it, he tried it a few more times, flicking the switch back and forth. Nothing happened.

Anxiety began to creep up, and his skin started to crawl. Some primal sense inside warned of imminent danger, and his heart began to beat faster and faster.

That horrible odour he'd experienced throughout the house recently again made itself known—a sickly sweet smell, foul and rotting. Ray moved his foot back again, and his heel made contact with the lowest step. He knew he could simply turn and scramble back upstairs.

But before he did, another sound made his heart seize.

From up ahead, Ray heard a throaty cackle, immediately followed by rapid footsteps that slapped against the stone floor. They moved towards him, quickly getting louder and louder, and they moved so fast Ray scarcely had time to turn around before the sounds were right on top of him. Ray felt a blast of cold air slam into him, followed by something much more... solid.

A body. After the impact, Ray was thrown backwards. He landed hard on the steps behind him and let out a grunt of pain as his shoulders collided with the edge of a step. He felt something move over him, and those quick footsteps started again, running up the steps to the level above.

Ray turned to his front and looked up the flight of steps, hoping there was enough light to make something out, but he could see nothing beyond faint movement in the darkness.

He suddenly had a desperate need to be out of the base-ment, but that meant following the stranger. That thought filled him with dread. Ray couldn't fully explain what was happening, and that allowed his fear to rise.

Who the hell was that person? A guest? Someone else?

He hadn't gotten a good enough look to know for certain.

Regardless, Ray pushed himself up and ascended the stairs as quickly as he could. He stumbled a couple of times on the way and banged the front of his toes on one of the steps edges, causing him to yelp in pain. He kept going, but was limping now, thinking he may have cracked a few toes. He soon reached the top and hobbled back into the great hall.

'What are you doing?' a weary voice asked, causing Ray to jump in shock. However, he soon saw his wife standing alone in the great hall, a light-blue dressing gown wrapped around her and a confused frown nestled on her sleepy face. 'Were you just down in the basement?' she asked.

'I... yes, I was,' Ray eventually replied, unsure of how to explain what had just happened. He was breathing heavily.

'Why?' Rita asked.

Ray took a breath, steadied himself, then recapped the night's events, starting with the phone calls.

When he was done, Rita raised a sceptical eyebrow.

'I didn't hear the phone ring,' she stated. 'Are you certain it did?'

'Of course!' Ray exclaimed. 'Twice. I had *two* conversa-tions... if you can call them that.'

'Okay, okay,' Rita replied defensively, 'it's just something that would have normally woken me.'

That was true, but Ray had assumed it was Rita finally catching up on some much-needed sleep.

'So... you didn't find whoever was down in the basement, then?' she asked.

Ray shook his head. 'No. Well, I saw *someone*, I think, but the lights went out, and they got past me and ran up here.'

'Well I didn't see anyone,' Rita stated. 'No one came running up before you did.'

Ray couldn't explain that, unless the mystery person had gotten out of the hall before Rita entered. Ray's head hurt trying to make sense of it all. He knew there had to be a logical explanation for it all, and still put it down to one of the guests causing mischief.

'Come on,' Rita said, 'let's go to bed.' She held out a hand, and Ray walked over to her and took it.

'So why are you down here, anyway?' he asked her.

'I woke up again—another bad dream—and saw you were gone. You weren't in the bathroom, so I came looking for you. I was a little worried. You normally sleep like the dead and never stir.'

'True enough,' Ray agreed, and they headed back upstairs. Ray kept himself alert, looking and listening out for anyone who may have been up and skulking around the hotel. But there was no one. Now that everything seemed to be calming down, Ray had a feeling that this was a mystery he would not solve.

20

JUNE.

The translations were now complete.

Marcus looked over the ledger with a sense of pride. Indeed, his grandfather had put in the bulk of the work transcribing the ancient book, but there were some areas that Marcus had improved upon, making things more accurate.

He'd also added his thoughts to the back of the ledger his grandfather had started all those years ago, and was now satisfied he could move ahead with the plan in a way that was safe.

At least, safe for him.

He closed the ledger and got to his feet. The room around him, formerly two rooms, now offered more space for his collection thanks to Ray's improvements. It was hard to imagine how he'd managed when it was just a single room. Though it was still cluttered, he at least had space to properly display his most prized possession.

The *Ianua Diaboli.*

Marcus moved over to the case it was stored in, lifted the

lid, and then took hold of the precious book—one that contained knowledge and power beyond what most people could comprehend.

The black leather of the cover was worn, but at each corner there were pristine, gold-embossed symbols, each different from the others. The top left marking was an eight-pointed star. The top right, a simple cross. The bottom left symbol was a triangle with another inverted triangle set within it. Finally, in the bottom right, was eight intersecting lines, arranged like the lines of a compass.

Marcus knew what these symbols were. Not just decorative markings; they had a purpose. They had *power*.

They protected the book from the influence of forces that lay beyond the natural world. Forces that may try to destroy the book, given what was inside. The protection offered by the symbols went beyond just warding off any supernatural entities, but also extended to any people that may be possessed.

Of course, as well as a dangerous and sacred knowledge, there were things written in the book that would be of great interest to those same forces. *If* they were to become aware of what the incantations could do.

After a moment's admiration, Marcus set the book back down and locked the display case again. He then made his way downstairs to the office, hoping to find Rita there. Preferably alone.

He walked down to the entrance lobby and over to the reception area, where he saw Rita checking out some guests: three women, all in their thirties. They may have been businesswomen, and were dressed in suit jackets, professional skirts and heels. Marcus stared lustfully at the women, who had their backs to him, appreciating their lines and curves.

Very nice.

Rita noticed him over their shoulders and offered a curt nod to acknowledge his presence. She still wasn't happy with him, but he didn't care. She would wear down soon enough.

She'd never really liked him, but he aimed to change that. And, luckily, Rita was very easy on the eye. She would do nicely for what he needed.

At least, he hoped she would. There were no guarantees with a plan like this.

Marcus listened in to the conversation that Rita was dealing with, and he heard one of the women talking animatedly. She was shorter than the others, and her skin the colour of burned butter.

'Well,' the woman said, 'we didn't really want to wake you and cause a fuss. But I've never smelled anything like it before in my life. It's like there was a dead animal in the room.'

'Again,' Rita said, 'I'm so sorry for that.'

'And it was *so* cold,' the tallest of the women went on. 'I mean, when we woke up it was like we were in a fridge. We could see our own breath.'

The last of the women finally noticed Marcus and turned around. She was dark-haired with Latin features and high cheekbones. Her hazel eyes fell on him, and Marcus held a confident smile.

'Hello?' she said with a frown.

'This is Mr. Blackwater,' Rita said as the others turned to see him as well. 'The owner of the hotel.'

The dark-haired woman's expression immediately softened. 'Oh, pleased to meet you. In that case,' she continued, 'I suppose you need to know that your hotel needs work.'

'How so?' he asked, feigning a genuine interest.

Another of the women spoke up, the tallest of the group.

'Last night, we were woken by someone running up and down outside our room, for one. And the radiators weren't working so the room was stupidly cold. And the smell...' She wrinkled her nose and stuck out her tongue. 'Urgh.'

Marcus forced his eyes wide, putting on an expression of shock. 'Oh dear,' he said. 'That is no good at all.'

They were so oblivious. What the group had experienced were actually *signs*, indications pointing to the presence of other entities. The women would have been safe enough, of course. While the spirits of the dead trapped in this house could influence the living, given enough time, Marcus had taken steps to ensure no person could be physically harmed in the bedrooms.

That had been done by having protective symbols drawn onto the floorboards beneath the beds, completely hidden from sight. Those markings were similar in nature to the ones on the cover of *Ianua Diaboli*.

In addition, Marcus had taken extra precautions in his own room, as well as Vincent's, by marking the Eye of Horus onto the floorboards there as well. That would ensure his and Vincent's minds remained uninfluenced.

The rest of the house, however...

Still, Marcus didn't feel like the building was quite 'alive' enough. Certainly not enough to cause anyone any true harm. Yet.

'Tell you what,' Marcus said. 'We'll knock fifty percent off your room hire. How does that sound?'

The women looked shocked but pleased, and after casting a look to each other to make sure they were on the same page, they all nodded.

'That seems fair,' the taller woman said.

It was more than *fair*, and Marcus knew it. But he didn't care. Rita seemed bothered, however, and shot him an angry frown. Obviously, her offer of compensation would have been much more restrained.

'Excellent,' Marcus went on. 'And we'll look into the smells and the cold, I can promise you that.'

'And you might want to keep your guests in check,' the woman with Latin features added. 'Get them to stop running round in the night.'

'Will do,' Marcus confirmed.

The guests soon finished their business with Rita, checked-out, then left. Ray went with them, helping with the bags, leaving Marcus and Rita alone together. He followed her back into the office after she tried to walk away without another word.

'Fifty percent was too much,' she said, circling her desk to get to her seat.

'Fair enough,' Marcus replied. 'I'll leave that to you in the future. Just trying to help.'

She shot him a look that told him his help was not wanted. Even angry, Rita had a certain allure. One he wanted to act on.

Needed to act on... in time.

'The thing about the guest running around outside of their room concerns me,' Rita said.

'How so?'

'A little while ago Ray said he heard the same thing. It would have been strange enough if it happened just *once*. But multiple times?'

'Strange,' Marcus said with a nonchalant shrug. 'Something to keep an eye on, I guess.'

'I guess,' Rita repeated, but she narrowed her eyes. 'I have to ask, it isn't you or Vincent, is it?'

'What do you mean?'

'I mean... is it the two of you that people are hearing in

the night?'

Marcus laughed. 'What, you think we get up and play 'tag' when everyone else is asleep?'

'I don't know *what* the hell you two do,' Rita shot back.

'Well, I can't speak for Vincent, but I can assure you that I'm asleep in my room during the night. Not running around the hallways like a child.'

Rita continued to cast him an accusing glare, but it soon softened. 'Fair enough,' she eventually said, and then began busying herself with a file on her desk. 'It's still strange.'

'I definitely agree. Now, I came down here to speak to you about the event we have coming up in October.' He saw her jaw tense up, and he held up his hands defensively. 'I know, I know, it isn't something you're too enamoured with. *But*, I did want to check up on how the preparations are shaping up.'

'They're ongoing,' Rita replied flatly.

Marcus paused, expecting her to go on. When she did not, he prodded a little further. 'Care to go into detail?'

She sighed. 'Well, I've blocked those dates out of the diary, so we don't make any cross bookings.'

'And that's it?'

'Look, Marcus, we have bags of time until the event. We can't start building hype too early or things will fizzle out. And other than getting the word out and taking bookings, there isn't much more we can do.'

'So you've done *nothing*?' He didn't hide his disappointment. At the same time, he didn't show his true anger, either. Not yet.

Rita took a deep breath, held it, then slowly exhaled. Marcus had to fight from snarling. He took exception to her acting like he was an annoyance. She was in his own house, no less—where *she* worked under *his* employment.

After standing up, Rita walked over to the filing cabinet and pulled out a thin blue file. She then walked back, sat down, and set the file on her desk, opening it up to a series of handwritten notes on the first page.

'I've made a list of all the local newspapers and magazines where we can advertise, or at least start some stories running to help get the word out. I also have details of the editors and journalists at those publications. I've looked into magazines that deal in the paranormal and things like that, and begun to make some inroads. I'm sounding out the reporters and trying to get on friendly terms. It's no good trying to hound them for page space if they don't know who you are. So, I'm busy putting myself on their radars. When the time comes, I can then leverage those relationships. And not just for October's event, but for the hotel in general, if needed.'

Rita flicked over to another page. 'I've also done some research into paranormal groups in the surrounding areas as well, which hasn't been easy. But, I've found a few. I have to be honest, I was surprised to see they're primarily made up of older people in the upper class, so you were right about that. I have the contact addresses of the people who run these groups, as well as telephone numbers. When the time comes, they will be perfect to target with a leaflet drop and follow-up phone call. I've also—'

But Marcus cut her off. 'Alright, alright, I get it,' he said, raising his hand. 'You've done a lot of work. I don't know why you didn't just tell me all of that when I asked.'

'Because I hate people looking over my shoulder when I work,' Rita told him. 'You hired me to do a job here, so just let me get on with what needs doing.'

Rita took another breath, then pinched the bridge of her nose with her fingers and squinted in pain.

'You okay?' Marcus asked.

'Headache,' she stated. 'Comes and goes. Probably because I'm feeling a little run down. It's nothing to worry about, though.'

'You're working too hard,' Marcus told her, and he walked over to her desk.

'If I don't work hard, then I can't get this place where I want it to be.'

He came and stood behind her, looking down at the nape of her neck, which was just visible behind her pony-tail. Rita rubbed a hand over the area where her left shoulder met the upper trapezius muscle, working out an obvious ache.

'Rita, I probably don't say this enough, but you really are doing a good job here.'

She let out a humourless chuckle. 'I wouldn't call it a 'good job.' The place has been more than half-empty since opening. I'd call that a piss-poor job.'

'It's a work in progress,' Marcus offered. 'Rome wasn't built in a day. You'll get us there. I have faith.'

'Faith enough to push the Halloween thing on us, even though I don't think it's a good idea?' She then turned to look at him, wincing as she did. Rita again began to rub her neck.

'Humour me with that one,' Marcus replied. 'Please. You might be surprised. If you don't mind me saying, you look tired. Not sleeping well?'

She shook her head and turned back to her paperwork. 'Not really. I wake up just about every night.'

Marcus smiled but didn't let her see it. 'Any particular reason?'

She shrugged. 'Bad dreams, I guess.'

'Sounds like stress.'

'Maybe. It always seems to be between three and four in the morning, as well. It's weird, and annoying as hell. I can't get more than a few hours of unbroken sleep.'

Excellent, Marcus thought to himself. *That will help make her much more compliant.*

'A stressed mind can do funny things,' he told her, then tentatively laid his hands on her shoulders. He felt her immediately tense up.

'What are you doing?' she asked.

'Nothing inappropriate. Just relax.' Marcus then began to firmly massage her neck and shoulders, pressing his thumbs deep into the muscle and tissue. Rita let it continue, if only for a moment. But it was a little longer than he had expected, which was a good sign.

'That's okay,' she eventually said, batting his hands away and slipping out from her seat. She turned to face him. 'Thank you, but I'm fine.'

He held up his hands in submission. 'As you wish. I was merely trying to help, but appreciate you may not be comfortable with it.'

There was an uncomfortable silence, which Rita eventually broke. 'Well, I have a lot to catch up on, so... if that is all?'

Marcus smiled and gave a polite nod. 'Indeed it is, at least for now. Have a good day, Rita.'

And with that, he left her alone, happy with how things were going.

21

JULY.

Ray stretched, feeling the heat from a sliver of sunlight that had penetrated through a crack in the curtains. He yawned and slowly opened his eyes, ready for another day —another day where his wife continued to deteriorate and drive herself mad with stress.

When his eyes adjusted, however, he was shocked to see Rita standing just next to the bed, looking down at him. Her eyes were half-closed, and she swayed ever so slightly, as if in a trance.

'Rita?' he asked, quickly sitting up. 'What's going on?'

She didn't answer and just continued to stand. He quickly realised she was still asleep, but had obviously been sleepwalking and decided to stop close to him. The image of his wife looking dazed and unresponsive like that was more than a little unnerving.

Ray put a hand on her arm. 'Rita,' he whispered. 'Wake up.'

He still got nothing in response. So, Ray pulled himself out of bed and tried guiding her back to her own side. She came willingly. As he led her, he glanced at the clock and saw that it was a little after six-thirty. Rita's skin felt cold to the touch and he wondered just how long she'd been standing there like that, watching him.

After helping her into bed and pulling up the covers, Ray watched Rita slowly close her eyes completely. It was only then that her body seemed to relax a little more. After a few moments, she started to breathe deeply, and he was satisfied she was completely asleep.

Ray didn't plan to wake her now. The hotel would run under his supervision today—all day, if it needed to. He would stumble his way through while his wife was resting. There was a knot of worry in his gut. Ray had already been concerned about Rita, given her exhaustion and obvious stress, but now it seemed she had taken to walking around in her sleep—hardly the sign of a contented and healthy mind.

Something had to change.

For now, though, Ray knew he needed to get ready. Chloe needed to be dressed and taken to school, and they had to be ready for today's guests as well. So, Ray took a quick shower, readied himself, and then went to check on his daughter, happy to let Rita continue to sleep.

Chloe was already sitting up in her bed, which Ray wasn't surprised to see. Nor was it a shock to find her reading. She looked up at him and smiled.

'How you doing, kiddo?' he asked. 'Been up long?'

'A little while.'

'Well, we need to get you ready for school. I'm letting your mum have a lie-in today, as she has been working really hard recently.'

'Okay,' Chloe replied and hopped out of bed. She then paused and crinkled her face. 'Is she okay?'

'She's fine,' Ray said. 'Just tired.'

That seemed acceptable enough to Chloe, and they both prepared for the day before getting breakfast. They then jumped into the family car and set off for school.

En route, Ray wanted to get more of a feel for how Chloe was coping with life at the minute.

'How's school?' he asked as a segue.

'Okay,' she replied.

'Really? Just I know you had a rough start, with kids telling you stories about the house and everything.'

Chloe just shrugged. 'They still do, and they ask about it all the time as well. But they're mostly my friends now, so it's fine.'

'Mostly?' Ray asked.

'Well, yeah. Some of them are just 'okay,' I guess. Not really friends.'

'But no one is bullying you or anything like that?'

She looked at him, frowned, then shook her head. 'No. Why?'

'Just checking up on you, kiddo, that's all.'

'Okay.'

'And what about living at the house?' he went on. 'Still think it's cool?'

The grin that broke out over Chloe's face told the whole story even before her words did. 'Oh yeah! I love it. It's like a castle!'

Ray chuckled. 'Well that's good,' he said.

In truth, though he—and more specifically Rita—had been feeling the effects of running a hotel full-time, Chloe had always seemed to enjoy it.

It was good this adventure of hers hadn't lost its shine just yet. Though Ray wasn't certain how much longer it could continue, as he wasn't prepared to let his wife continue to suffer. In truth, he'd been considering getting his family out of there anyway. *Especially* after the previous month's experience where a guest had been running around in the night. Ray hadn't felt comfortable in the building since then. But, after seeing his wife this morning, Ray knew he had to broach the subject of their long-term plans with Rita sooner rather than later.

They still had nowhere else to go, of course. Ray would just have to figure something out.

Marcus and Vincent might not be too happy, but if Ray was being honest, he didn't give a fuck what they thought.

22

RITA SCRUBBED her skin with the coarse washcloth as firmly and quickly as she could. The water she sat in was luke-warm at best, since she hadn't had the time to run the bath correctly.

How could I have slept in for so long? And why had Ray let me?

It was past midday when Rita had opened her eyes, still feeling tired, and with a thumping headache. But when she'd sat up and saw that she was alone in the bedroom, Rita instantly knew something was off.

She checked the clock... and panicked.

Once finished in the bath, she all but leapt out, then dried herself off as fast as possible. She hurriedly changed into her clothes and threw on some makeup before running down to the reception area. There, she found Ray behind the reception desk, dressed in his suit as normal. There was no one else around, which meant she could give it to him full-force for not waking her when he had gotten up.

She marched up to him, teeth clenched and jaw set. Ray

smiled when he saw her, but that smile faltered when he noticed her demeanour.

'What the hell are you doing?' Rita snapped as she walked around to the back of the desk, standing over him.

'What'd you mean?' he asked, sounding genuinely confused. *How could he be so dense?*

'It's half-past-*fucking*-twelve, Ray! Why the hell didn't you wake me up?'

He frowned and shook his head, somehow surprised at her attitude. 'Because you *needed* it,' he replied. 'Jesus Christ, Rita, I woke up this morning and found you standing above me. Do you even remember that?'

Rita stopped in her tracks, and the mountain of anger she was readying to unleash was momentarily held back. 'What the hell are you talking about?'

'This morning,' he repeated. 'I woke up, and you were standing next to my bed, looking down at me.'

'That didn't happen,' she snapped back with a frown. However, deep down, Rita knew there must be some truth to it. Ray wasn't the type to make up things like that.

'It did happen,' Ray stated calmly. 'I don't know if you were sleepwalking or what, but I put you back to bed and you dropped off almost instantly. So, like I say, you *needed* the sleep. God knows how long you'd been standing there like that.'

Rita was stunned. She had no idea. 'Jesus,' was all she could mutter.

'Tell me about it,' Ray said, then got up from his seat and guided Rita into it instead.

Her mind sprang into action. 'But what about the guests that were due to arrive?'

'Two lots are already checked in and up in their rooms,' Ray said. 'The rest haven't arrived yet.'

'And what about Chloe?'

'At school. She's fine.'

She let out a sigh of relief, but then had to wonder why Chloe was the *second* thing she had worried about, after work matters.

'Look, Rita,' Ray began, 'I think we need to have a long talk about what we're doing here.'

She looked up at him. 'What do you mean?'

'Well... is this place good for us?'

Rita wasn't quite sure what he was getting at. 'It's kind of essential, Ray,' she replied. 'We need it so we don't end up on the street. You know that.'

He nodded. 'Yes, I know, but is it *healthy* for us? For *you*?'

The point then registered, but Rita didn't like what he was implying at all. 'Are you saying I can't handle it?'

Ray quickly shook his head. 'No, that isn't what I'm saying at all.'

'Yes it is,' she shot back. 'That's *exactly* what you are saying, isn't it? Just admit it,' she challenged.

'Rita, when is the last time you had a proper night's sleep? You always look exhausted. We spend more time working and looking after strangers than we do our own daughter. And now you're getting up and wandering about in the middle of the night. How can I not ask the question? I'm worried about you. About all of us.'

Rita stood up, furious. A sharp and sudden anger cut through her, tearing its way to the surface. 'Bullshit, Ray!' she snapped. 'You're just like all the others, aren't you? You don't think I can do this at all. Do you think I'm incapable? Is it because I'm a woman, Ray? Is that why I can't do it?'

Ray looked genuinely stunned, but Rita didn't care. She knew what the truth was now.

'That isn't it at all,' Ray replied. 'You're the most capable person I know. It's just this house, the hotel... I think it's a lost cause, and I don't want you killing yourself trying to prove it's not.'

'I'm not going to kill myself, Ray,' Rita snarled. 'But I *am* going to prove you all wrong. We are *not* leaving this house.'

'Rita, listen to reason, for God's sake,' he went on, but they both had to stop when they heard the front door open.

'Just keep quiet,' Rita told him. 'More guests are here. I don't want to talk about this again, understand.'

She expected a subservient nod in response. Instead, he just stared back at her, incredulous.

Four new guests entered the reception area, and Rita greeted them with a beaming smile. 'Hello. Welcome to the Blackwater Hotel.'

23

Two Days Later.

Chloe was bored.

She lay on her bed and stared up at the plaster ceiling above her, admiring the intricate patterns to the edging.

Given Chloe had read all of her books countless times before, she was starting to grow a little tired of them; it was still a little while until her birthday, where she could ask for more. Television didn't intrigue her, and it was raining outside, heavily, which kept her from going out to play in the gardens again.

What Chloe really wanted to do to help pass the time, however, was to explore more of the house. It seemed like a cruel torture to live in a place like this but be confined to only a few rooms.

The house was a mansion—like something out of one of her stories—yet she hadn't seen half of it in any great detail. And there were many places she hadn't seen at all. Going down into the basement appealed to her in a spooky kind of way, and when she'd told her friends at school about it, their eyes had lit up.

'Is that where the ghosts live?' Trevor had asked. And she had to tell him yet again that the house wasn't haunted. Even so, the one time she had been down there with her dad, it was cold and uncomfortable, so it would have been an ideal spot for a ghost.

Chloe decided that she wasn't brave enough to venture down there on her own. And besides, her mum and dad would probably ground her if they found out she had gone against their strict instructions to stay away from the basement.

There was still the rest of the house, but her parents had given Chloe similar warnings about running around. It was fine before the hotel had opened up, but not any longer.

With a house like this and all the secrets it must have had hidden away, it was hard for her to accept.

She had snuck around the house once already, without being caught. So, if she was careful, she could probably have another little adventure and relieve the boredom.

She bristled with excitement. Regardless of the consequences, the appeal was just too much. Chloe reasoned that her mum and dad were either too busy with guests, or too busy ignoring each other at the moment to really worry about her. She knew that something had happened between them recently. They didn't fight often, but when they did the two tended to keep away from each other and not talk until one of them saw sense. Even Chloe knew that wasn't the best way to resolve a disagreement, but what could she do?

In truth, she was a little worried about them—particularly her mother, who always seemed tired and cranky recently.

Chloe jumped off her bed and grabbed Emma before running over to the bedroom door. She pushed it open and peeked out into the hallway. No one was around.

She set foot outside and felt her excitement rise, trying to decide where to go first. The ground-floor had the library and great hall, as well as the kitchen, but she had seen those rooms more than enough times already. She craved something new. The floor she was on contained mostly bedrooms, which were predominantly empty, so she could try and explore those to see if there was anything cool hidden inside.

That was as good a plan as any.

She set off, creeping through the halls and checking doors, but only after listening through them to make sure the rooms were empty. Much to her disappointment, however, all doors she tried were locked.

So that just left the top storey.

Chloe knew she shouldn't go up there, but then again she shouldn't have been wandering around at all, so if she was going to break the rules, why not go all-in?

She brought Emma up to her face and looked into the two button-eyes of her doll. 'Should we do it?' Chloe asked. The stitched, permanent smile from her friend was all the answer Chloe needed. 'I agree,' she said. 'Let's go.'

On tiptoes, Chloe snuck around towards the stairs that led up to the top floor, then placed her foot on the bottom step. She took a breath and started her climb, being as light on her feet as possible. As she continued up, she knew that if anyone turned the corner at the top there would be no hiding at all. Thankfully, she made it without detection and stepped up to the top storey for only the second time since moving in.

Chloe worked her way around to her right after exiting the stairs, and at the end of the corridor saw something that hadn't been there before: a new wall that blocked off the way. It ran the width of the hallway and had a door set in it.

The wall was not like the old ones and consisted of basic plasterboard, but without wallpaper, and it had no detailed coving at the head. The door did not look as ornate or heavy-duty as the rest, either, and Chloe could only assume her dad had installed both but had not quite finished.

She knew the way ahead led to the room she'd heard Vincent and Mr. Blackwater in the last time she was up here. Listening now, she could hear something through the door —a muffled, but steady and rhythmic scratching. No, that wasn't quite right. It was more like a *scrubbing* sound.

She took hold of the handle on the door and slowly turned it, certain it would have been locked.

Instead, the door swung open smoothly and soundlessly, revealing more of the hallway beyond. With the door now ajar, the scrubbing sound became louder. Intrigued, Chloe crept onward. She saw the room Vincent and Marcus had been in last time, but that door was now shut, and the sounds she heard were coming from farther away—from another room up ahead and just around a corner. Chloe snuck around and saw that another wall and door had been put in as well, which boxed off a front corner of the house completely.

The scrubbing noise drew her attention further, and the door to the room it was coming from hung open. Chloe crept over to it and peeked inside.

She saw Vincent on his hands and knees on the floor, a rag in hand and bucket of soapy water next to him.

The bed had been pushed aside, and the carpet was pulled back across most of the room, revealing the floorboards beneath that Vincent was rubbing with a wet rag. His shirt was damp and clung to his skin, and he appeared to be scrubbing away what looked like an old, painted pattern on the floorboards.

That looks like a symbol.

A crudely drawn eye looked up to a top eyelid, though there wasn't much else left to see.

Chloe could make out the very edge of another symbol farther along, but the carpet had not been pulled back far enough to completely reveal that particular one.

The ends of Vincent's fingers looked raw and scabby. Chloe's first thought was that he was scrubbing too hard and had cut his fingers up, but the scrapes around his nails looked old.

Looking around the room, Chloe quickly figured out that it didn't belong to Vincent, since none of the clothing looked like what he wore. The outfits were mostly dark and a mix of suits, blazers, crisp shirts, and pressed trousers—a far cry from the type of clothing Vincent always wore, such as the frayed chequered shirt and chord trousers he had on now.

Chloe realised it was Marcus' room. And it seemed Vincent was doing some kind of cleaning.

He suddenly paused his movements and looked up. Chloe was too slow in ducking back behind the door jamb and was seen.

Annoyed with herself, and now panicked, she looked back down the corridor and considered running away. She could just deny everything to her parents when Vincent inevitably told on her.

'Chloe?' she heard her uncle say softly from inside the room.

She held her breath, considering her options while dreading the telling-off that was no doubt coming. But, running away was pointless. Chloe knew it would solve nothing. Her father had always told her that running away didn't make anything better; it just put off what was coming anyway. So, she might as well face up to what was in store.

'Yeah,' she replied and stepped back from around the door frame, head hung low.

'What... what are you doing up here?' he asked, still gripping the wet and stained cloth.

Chloe shrugged. 'I was just bored,' she admitted. 'So I came up here to explore. I know I shouldn't have.'

He squinted his eyes, then nodded. 'Okay. I bet it's a little bit boring for you here sometimes, huh?'

'Sometimes,' Chloe admitted. 'It's an amazing house. But I always have to stay stuck in the same old rooms all the time.'

Vincent leaned back on his heels. 'I get that.'

'Isn't it boring for you, living here?' she asked. 'You always seem stuck up on this floor all the time.'

Vincent chuckled, then shook his head. 'Boring? No. One thing about this house, if you know what to look for, is that it's never boring.'

'Really? But you've lived here for a long time, haven't you? Doesn't that mean you've seen everything?'

'I haven't seen everything yet. I can promise you that.'

She smiled, but it quickly faded. 'Are you going to tell my mum and dad I was up here?'

Vincent cocked his head to the side. 'Don't you want me to?'

'Well, I'll get in trouble because I'm not supposed to wander around like this. But it's my own fault, I guess.'

'Hmmm, that's true,' Vincent said. He then smiled, but it wasn't a happy smile. To Chloe, it was more mischievous. It looked like the tiger in one of her books, one who came and ate all the food a family had in their cupboards. 'You know,' Vincent went on, 'I could just keep it all a secret.'

'Really?' Chloe asked, surprised.

'Really. As it happens, I'm not really supposed to be in here either.'

'In Mr. Blackwater's room?'

Vincent nodded. 'That's right. He doesn't like it when people come in here without him knowing.'

'So... why *are* you in here?'

'Cleaning. You see, Mr. Blackwater isn't the neatest person in the world. He has gunk like this on the floorboards,' Vincent gestured to the markings on the floor, which to Chloe looked like more than just 'gunk.' 'I'll bet it's been here for years and has never been cleaned up. So... I'm just helping him out. Of course, he probably wouldn't appreciate it. Which is why I've come in here while he's out. Understand?'

Chloe nodded. Though, if she were honest, it didn't make a whole lot of sense. What did it matter if there was something on the floorboards, especially since the carpet covered it anyway? But Chloe wasn't about to look a gift-horse in the mouth, and had a feeling a compromise was about to be offered.

'I guess so,' she said.

'Good. So, how about this: you don't tell anyone you saw me up here—and I mean *anyone*, not your parents, and certainly not Mr. Blackwater—and I won't tell anyone that I saw you, either. It can be our little secret.'

Chloe nodded enthusiastically. 'Yeah, I can do that.'

'You have to promise me now,' Vincent added sternly. 'If we promise each other, then you can't go back on it. Do we have a deal?'

'We do!' Chloe said.

Vincent held a hand out towards her, and Chloe frowned in confusion.

'Shake on it,' he said.

'Huh?'

'You know, 'shake on it?' If you make a deal with some-one, then you have to shake hands to seal the deal. It makes it unbreakable.'

'Oh,' Chloe replied, unaware of the tradition. She put her own hand into his—it felt warm and sweaty—and he shook.

'There we go,' he added, smiling. 'Now it's a *real* promise. So, you have to keep it. Forever.'

'That's a long time,' Chloe said with a laugh.

He just shrugged. 'Depends on your perspective.'

Chloe frowned, not really understanding his comment in the slightest. She then just giggled. 'You're funny.'

'Well, I do try,' he replied, and let go of her hand. 'Now you run along and I'll get finished up in here before Mr. Blackwater gets back.'

'Okay,' she said, then turned away to leave.

'And Chloe,' Vincent added, causing her to turn back. She saw him make a motion over his mouth like he was pulling a zipper closed. He then mimicked turning a key at the corner of his lips.

'Don't worry,' she said, realising what he meant. 'I won't say anything.'

'Excellent,' he replied. 'That's a good girl.'

Chloe skipped away, heading straight back to her room. She was confused at the interaction with her weird uncle, but definitely glad she had avoided getting into trouble.

24

Rita's head hurt. A lot.

It was another dead weekend—not a single guest. The hotel was dying, and it made Rita feel like she was trying to push a river of water uphill. Nothing she did worked and nothing was good enough.

Ray had suggested, given the weather was nice, that they spend the day outside in the garden. They worked on tidying up the space a little, which was a welcome reprieve from being stuck inside the house all the time.

She had agreed and was now kneeling on a foam pad, trowel in hand while she churned over a soil bed that surrounded one of the lawns. She picked out any weeds that she could find as she went. Given the heat, Rita was dressed in only a light summer dress—which was strapped at the shoulders—and sun hat. Though it wasn't a lot of clothing, it still felt like too much, and her brow was sweating.

Ray was manning the riding lawn tractor up and down one of the long stretches of grass, and the machine gave off a constant and annoying hum as it rolled along. Chloe was playing outside as well, free to roam around the gardens as she pleased.

Vincent and Marcus, as ever, were tucked away up on the top floor.

After scooping up another pile of dirt, movement in the soil drew Rita's attention. In the dirt, she saw the frantic wiggles of a long and thin worm as it desperately tried to burrow its way back into the muck. Creepy-crawlies had never bothered her, but looking down at the pathetic, writhing thing, she had a sudden urge to bring up her trowel and split the fucker in half. In fact, her trowel was already rising up when Rita caught herself.

She instead reached down and pinched the small worm between her gloved fingers, then dropped it farther along the soil bed, in an area she had already finished. That would allow the little guy to burrow back to safety.

She and Ray still weren't on the best of terms. It had been close to two months since the fight, where Ray had brought up the idea of leaving the Blackwater Hotel. He wanted to cut and run like a coward.

He'd tried to push the idea a few more times as well, coming at her with what he called 'logic and reason.' Each time it had happened, she'd cut him off, telling him in no uncertain terms that they *weren't* leaving. If he wanted to, he could go alone.

Rationally, Rita knew she should try and find a way to patch things up with her husband. However, she couldn't bring herself to do it. She felt like he'd betrayed her by not believing in her abilities. It was only a few days ago that he'd insisted she 'wasn't herself at all, acting like a completely different person.'

Well, maybe she was a different person. Maybe she had become a person who was tired of being walked on.

No more.

Rita would make the Blackwater Hotel a success if it took her the next ten years. Hell, they had a fantastic home here that they didn't even have to pay for. *She* had provided that for them. Granted, it was because of her brother, but what had Ray done to help their situation in the last few years? Nothing. He was an archaic creature, lost in the new world, and fumbling around like a big, useless mammoth—aimless and ready for extinction.

Rita caught herself again, realising just how harsh she was being on Ray. *Do I really think so little of him?*

She thrust the trowel into the dirt again, angrily, though she wasn't quite sure who the target of her bubbling rage was: Ray, the world, or herself?

Rita carried on churning the muck and picking out the unwanted weeds, building more and more of a sweat as the hot sun burned in the clear blue sky. After another half hour of solid work, Rita leaned back and stretched out her spine, feeling a dull ache from being hunched over for too long. It was then, when she looked up to the back of the hotel, that Rita saw a figure looking out from one of the top-storey windows. The sight of the person shocked her for a moment before she realised it was Marcus. He raised a hand and waved.

Rita returned the gesture.

Marcus had been acting differently lately—less aloof, more engaging. It was a side to him she liked. Marcus then stepped out of view slowly but watched her the whole time; Rita realised she was smiling. She shook her head and got back to the job at hand. The sound of the lawnmower cut off, and she looked up to see Ray jump from the vehicle and start to walk over to her. She tensed up as he approached.

'Want some juice?' he asked. 'I'm pretty parched, so I'll go get some.'

'Sure,' Rita replied but offered nothing else.

After a few moments of expecting a little more in the way of a reply, Ray eventually nodded. 'Right, then, I'll be right back, I guess.'

He then trudged off. She knew she was being short with him, and also that she should feel bad for it. But she just... didn't.

He soon returned with a jug of orange juice and some glasses. The jug glistened, and droplets of condensation ran down the glass, reflecting in the sun.

He had three glasses pinched between the thick fingers of his other hand, which she hoped to God he'd washed. She had a feeling that wasn't the case.

Rita took the glass he offered, seeing the smudge of a fingerprint on the side, then let him fill it up. She took a long gulp of the tangy, refreshing juice, and it practically exploded with flavour on her dry tongue.

'Good?' Ray asked, eyebrows raised. She knew he was waiting for some kind of thanks, so she decided to throw the dog a bone.

'Very nice,' Rita said, nodding and smacking her lips together. 'Thank you, Marcus.'

She finished the rest of the drink and handed him back the empty glass. Ray didn't take it. Rita paused when she noticed his frown.

'What's the matter with your face?' she asked.

'Don't you realise what you've just done?'

She had no clue as to what he was talking about. 'I didn't *do* anything,' she replied.

Ray's frown deepened. 'You just called me Marcus.'

'What? No I didn't,' she argued.

'You did.' His voice was flat but certain and his stare unblinking.

Rita tried to remember the words she'd used, but couldn't be sure one way or the other. If she had said it, then it had certainly not been intentional.

'Well... I didn't mean it,' she eventually shot back defiantly. She then thrust the empty glass back into his hand. 'Go and give Chloe her drink, will you? It's hot out, and I don't want her to get dehydrated.'

And with that, she turned around, knelt down, and got back to work, not giving her husband the chance of a rebuttal.

Her head still pounded in pain, like something within her skull was trying to break its way out.

25

RAY WAS SEETHING.

Having stormed off, leaving the lawn unfinished, he headed back inside to the kitchen. He needed time to try and process what had just happened.

Ray couldn't remember ever being disrespected by Rita like that before. *Not ever.*

But ever since the day he'd expressed his concern over her wellbeing, she'd treated him as little more than the shit on her shoe.

This latest incident, however, when she'd actually referred to him as *Marcus*, was a new low.

He grabbed a whiskey glass and started digging through the cupboards. He needed something to scratch the itch. Towards the back of one of the cupboards, he found a twenty-five-year-old scotch that was unopened. Possibly one Marcus was saving for a special occasion.

Fuck it.

Ray twisted the cap free and took a sniff. He got hints of oak mixed in with the strong-smelling alcohol. He poured himself a hearty measure and drained the glass in one go, wincing as the whiskey burned on the way down. In that moment, he sincerely hoped Marcus *had* been saving the bottle. He poured another drink.

It was hardly a mature or productive way to deal with what had happened, but Ray felt like he had hit a brick wall every time he tried to speak to his wife about anything important recently. His opinions and concerns were simply dismissed out of hand. Worse, he was then accused of lacking belief and trust in his wife, which was the farthest thing from the truth. As far as he had seen, *no one* could turn this place around. Maybe it truly was cursed.

And now he had a fresh concern. Maybe his wife's slip of the tongue *had* been a simple mistake, with no further implications behind it. Or maybe... there was an underlying reason. Had she been thinking of him?

Or was he just being stupidly paranoid?

Regardless, Ray knew they couldn't go on like this. It felt like a pivotal point in their marriage, and there was too much at stake—Chloe, their mental wellbeing, and their very relationship—to let petty pride cause things to spiral further.

He was now certain they needed to leave this place in order to make things work. The house was toxic, and its poison was seeping into their pores.

Ray downed another whiskey—wincing again as he did —then replaced the bottle. He decided to try and speak to Rita again, though this time he would not let her divert the conversation. But, he would wait until that night to do it.

He was alerted to the sound of someone approaching, and Marcus entered the room.

The last person Ray wanted to speak to right now.

'Oh, it's you,' Marcus said, looking visibly disappointed.

'When I heard someone come in, I thought it may have been Rita.'

'Something you need to speak to her about?' Ray asked, trying his best to keep his voice neutral.

'Just... business stuff,' was the reply.

Just business stuff—as clear a lie as Ray had ever heard.

'Such as?' Ray asked. 'Maybe I can help.'

Marcus paused for a moment, then shook his head, almost as if the question had taken a few seconds to register. He seemed a little spaced-out. 'No, that's okay. Thank you.'

There was something different about Marcus recently, something Ray had been noticing more and more over the past month. For one, his impeccable appearance was starting to slip ever-so-slightly: his normally brushed-back hair was now a little frazzled, and his clothes hadn't been quite as pressed or pristine as usual. Plus, he looked tired as well—a lot like Rita—with dark bags beneath his eyes.

Ray wondered if the lack of success the hotel was having was beginning to take its toll on the owner as well. Marcus had always come off like money was never an issue, but maybe the hens were coming home to roost.

'Where is she?' Marcus went on to ask, referring to Rita.

Ray shrugged. 'Not sure,' he lied. 'But if I see her, I'll say you were asking after her.'

Another slight pause, then a nod of confirmation. 'Good. Thank you.'

Marcus then turned and walked away, leaving Ray more certain than ever that he needed to get his family out of the house.

26

AFTER FINISHING up in the bathroom, Rita walked back into her bedroom, only to see Ray sitting up in bed with his nightlight still on. She couldn't help but feel a pang of disappointment; she had deliberately taken her time, all in the hopes he would have fallen asleep. Then they wouldn't have to indulge in any small talk.

What the hell is wrong with you? This is your husband.

The dissenting voice was brief, and quickly pushed back down by the irritation she felt towards Ray.

He was a weight around her neck. Hell, if he could have even just looked a little more professional, then the guests may have accepted this hotel as a classy place. But no, all they saw was a gorilla dragging his knuckles.

How she wished that Marcus could make himself more available, if only to lend a little sophistication to proceedings.

Rita!

And there was that voice again, the one that was always getting in the way. Always holding her back.

'Hun,' Ray began. 'I think we need to talk.'

'Can we not?' Rita replied, padding over to the bed and slipping in next to him. She kept a healthy distance, however. Rita then reached over to her nightstand and grabbed a tube of hand cream. She applied some to her palms, and then started to rub it into the skin on the back of her hands. It smelled of butter. 'I'm tired,' she went on. 'And I have a pounding headache, so I just want to try and get some sleep.'

She hoped his silence was an indication of agreement. *Maybe he'll turn off the light and go to sleep.*

'I'm sorry,' he eventually said, shaking his head, 'but that isn't good enough.'

She turned to him with a scowl. When she spoke, her voice was laced with sarcasm. 'Oh, I'm sorry, is my exhaustion and suffering *inconvenient* for you, somehow?'

'No,' he replied. 'And that's exactly what I want to talk about.'

She shook her head. 'Not this again.'

'*Yes*, this again,' he said, but his tone was steady and soft, not confrontational. 'Honey, things aren't right here. They haven't been for a while now.'

'Things are fine,' she shot back. 'Maybe a little hard, but that's just life. If things get tough, you don't just quit and run. What kind of lesson would that be to Chloe?'

'I dunno,' he said with a shrug. 'Maybe one that shows there are more important things than work and money. Like your own health. That's a good lesson, I think.'

Rita couldn't help but grit her teeth. 'Spoken like a person who has never had to worry about either work or money, isn't that right, Ray?'

'What do you mean by that?'

'Since when have you provided either to this family? You've had a few odd jobs every now and again... when was the last time you brought us a steady, reasonable paycheque? Let's be honest; you're *hardly* the great provider.'

A dark expression clouded his face, and Rita knew her barbs had landed as intended. However, the brief flashes of anger she'd seen quickly dissipated.

'I don't want to fight, hun,' he said, turning away from her. 'I just want to make sure you're okay.'

'I *am*,' she stressed. 'So I wish you would stop going on about it.'

He again looked to her, then set a large, warm hand on her shoulder. Rita moved to shrug it off, but Ray's grip strengthened. Not to the point that he hurt her, but enough that she couldn't easily brush him away. Ray then sat forward, closer to her.

'Do you hate me?' he asked.

'What kind of question is that?'

'An honest one,' he replied. 'For the past two months, things between us have been terrible. I've tried to build bridges, but you just keep pushing me away. And I can't believe this all stemmed from me checking if you were okay.'

'No,' Rita snapped. 'That's not what you did. You wanted us to pick up sticks and move, just because *you* were having a tough time adjusting.'

'I'd stay here forever for you, Rita, if I thought it was good for us. I'd do it whether I liked it or not. And you *know* that. I don't know where this guard of yours is coming from, but can you let it down long enough for us to get this sorted out?'

'I'm done,' Rita said and tried to turn away again. His

grip, however, remained firm. Using both hands, he twisted her round enough to fully face him.

'What the hell is going on, Rita?!' he pressed, raising his voice. She shook her head petulantly, desperate to be away from him. She didn't want to give him an answer. What was the point? He wouldn't understand, anyway.

But then that voice inside popped up again. *Understand what, exactly? What are you expecting of him?*

'Look, Rita,' he went on, 'if you don't love me anymore, and you don't want to be with me, then that's okay, it's your choice.' Ray's voice cracked. She turned back and saw that tears were building in his eyes. 'Even though it would kill me, I'd accept it. But you need to think about yourself. *And* your daughter. When was the last time you played with her or gave her any attention that wasn't squeezed in-between work hours?'

'I've been busy, Ray,' she shot back, but the sight of his tears starting to fall broke something inside of her.

'If you can't find time for Chloe, then you're *too* busy. It isn't working. She needs you, Rita. We both do. But you just seem to be getting lost inside the house, sinking farther away from us.' He was sobbing now. 'You're driven and determined, Rita, but while you're here, you're also angry. You've never been that way. So I *know* you aren't happy here.'

'I... I *am* happy,' she whispered, but even as she spoke, a feeling of guilt rose up, washing away whatever misplaced anger she had been feeling. 'I am.'

Ray shook his head. 'You don't smile anymore, either. Not really. And it's definitely not the smile I know.'

That was true. She didn't.

Rita *was* miserable here. Completely and utterly broken. The walls she'd built fell away, and Rita started to cry as well. In an instant, Rita's recent attitude made no sense to her: the way she'd spoken to Ray, the neglect of her daughter, and not realising she'd been falling into a pit of self-loathing and depression.

'What the hell is wrong with me?' she asked quietly in between tears.

Ray took her in his arms, hugging her tightly. 'Nothing is wrong with you, Rita,' he said. 'You've just taken on more than anyone should, and it's been overwhelming.'

That might have made sense, logically, but Rita couldn't believe it. She'd been in prolonged and stressful situations before with other jobs, but she'd never become so isolated and angry during those times. This seemed different, somehow, like she'd been on autopilot and someone else had been at the controls. Someone she didn't like.

Rita pulled back a little and looked deep into Ray's brown eyes. She saw a lingering hurt there, a pain that *she* had caused.

'You're right about this place,' she told him. 'It's a cancer. The hotel isn't going to work, and I'm tired of being... tired.'

Ray smiled. He looked visibly relieved.

Rita felt a release as well. The weight that lifted from her shoulders made her feel physically lighter.

She went on. 'You're right, we should leave. Start over somewhere.'

He nodded enthusiastically. 'Where?'

'We'll figure something out,' she replied. 'As soon as we find somewhere, and have a plan in place, we're gone.'

Ray pulled her in again and hugged her tightly. She could feel the relief in him through his powerful hold. 'Chloe isn't going to be happy,' he said. 'She loves it here.'

'She'll understand. She's a smart kid.'

He nodded. 'She is,' Ray agreed, pulling away. He brought a hand up to her cheek. 'I'm glad to have you back.'

Rita kissed him. There was still so much for her to process after her realisation, and she needed to figure out how she'd allowed things to spiral so much, but right now she was just happy to have seen the light. And she hoped that might even lead to a good night's sleep.

27

Down.

Farther down.

Rita fought and fought, but those hands—grasping hands she couldn't see—continued to pull her through the earth.

She wanted to scream, but something covered her mouth. The rocky ground Rita continued to fall into changed its consistency. Soon, it was not earth that engulfed her but glistening skin. In it, mouths moaned and eyes rolled. However, even the skin that surrounded her soon changed, turning into exposed meat and flesh. The temperature continued to rise, as did the incessant stench.

And then Rita woke up to find she was standing in the dark. She wasn't in her room anymore, and she was completely naked.

It took Rita a moment to figure out just where she was, since she couldn't see anything. However, her first clue was the cold, hard ground underneath her bare feet. She felt rough and uneven stone beneath her soles. Rita could also feel a light circulation of cold air around her, and it bit at her exposed skin.

It had to be the basement.

Rita turned her head, looking around, but saw nothing beyond blackness. She was encompassed by it. *Smothered* by it.

How the hell did I get down here?

Rita had been asleep only moments ago, so there could be only one explanation. But as she was now alone in the dark, panic surged through her, further fuelled by the confusion she felt.

'Ray, are you here?' she called out desperately, hearing a meek echo accompany her words. The lack of response indicated she was alone. Rita held her arms out before her, feeling the air, but couldn't even see her own hands. She had no memory of coming down here. And to wake actually standing up... she must have been sleepwalking.

Rita was shivering, the cold around her having seeped into her bones. *How long have I been down here?*

She tried to keep her ever-rising panic under control and think logically so she could get herself back upstairs. The problem was, she had no way to navigate back to the steps.

She debated screaming, hoping her cries would draw the attention of someone above. However, if it was still the middle of the night, then her voice would have to travel up through at least two solid floors, and then wake a sleeping person.

Think.

She had to move, as staying put simply wasn't an option. If she couldn't see, Rita knew she could at least feel. Therefore, it seemed like the only option was to try to find a wall, and then work her way around until she found the steps.

So, Rita started to move forward, taking small shuffles, sliding her soles across the ground so as not to trip. Her hands were still held out before her, fingers moving and feeling, ready for contact of any kind.

It was so fucking *cold*.

After a few moments of incredibly slow progress, Rita felt her fingertips finally brush against something hard. After an initial shock, she then let her hands run over the object, soon realising it was made of wrought metal. She squatted, feeling her way down, finding that the metallic object ran all the way to the ground. It didn't take Rita long to figure out it was the furnace.

If the furnace was in front of her, that meant the stairs should be behind, just off to the side a little.

That was good.

At least now Rita was oriented. She turned around and began to sidestep to her right, eventually finding the side wall. From there, she started to follow that wall, moving forward, knowing she would soon find the steps. However, no sooner had she taken a few steps did Rita hear something from behind—a dull thud from *within* the furnace.

Her body seized, and her hands instinctively balled into fists.

'Hello?' she called out.

There was no reply. *Get a grip*, she told herself. The noise from the furnace could have been anything—the metal contracting in the cold, or even a rat that had gotten inside. *Don't let yourself lose control.*

That was easier said than done when stripped of her sight. Fear was the easy and obvious option.

Rita began to move forward again. She knew that she just had to keep calm long enough to reach the steps, and she refused to let herself think of anything else.

As she moved, the temperature around Rita dropped, seemingly with every steady step forward. To compensate, Rita tried to concentrate on how warm and comfortable it would feel when back in her bed, wrapped up in the thick duvet.

Then, sounds of whispering in the darkness made Rita stop in her tracks.

The whispering had come from her side, a few feet away from her, and she let out a gasp.

And it wasn't just one voice she heard... but multiple.

Fear gripped her, tightening her chest and making breathing difficult.

'Hello?' Rita called out again. This time, however, she heard something in response—more whispering, though the actual words were too quiet to make out.

Oh Christ, oh Christ, oh Christ.

Who the hell could be down here with her? Perhaps Vincent, Marcus... Ray?

But that didn't make any sense. If it had been any of those, they surely would have responded. Hell, none of them would have been hiding down here in the first place.

'Who's there!' Rita managed to muster. She waited. Then there was a quiet, child-like giggling.

'*We're... here,*' a young, male voice whispered back. Rita screamed.

Rita ran, no longer concerned with moving carefully, driven now by fear and adrenaline. As she sprinted, her shoulder bounced off the wall next to her and she felt a sting, but she kept going, knowing she would be soon at the steps... though she'd likely slam her feet and shins into them. Rita didn't care. She needed to keep moving. Especially when she heard more giggling from the unseen children. This time, the sounds had a distorted, almost demonic quality to them. Definitely inhuman.

Shit, shit, shit!

This couldn't be real. Couldn't be happening. There was no way...

She suddenly cried out as the toes on her left foot collided with the solid bottom step, and an intense pain exploded up through her foot.

Rita then fell face-first into the stairs, the impact driving the wind from her. She quickly became disoriented, feeling like the dark world around her was spinning. Her foot continued to ache, and Rita thought she might have broken a toe. In addition, her shins were scraped to hell, and her face throbbed where it had bounced off the corner of a step. However, she was so close to getting out, so she pushed the pain away and started to scramble quickly upwards... until something grabbed her ankle.

She screamed.

The tight grip was unrelenting, and Rita could feel only three appendages on the hand, each with sharp ends. The grip brought with it a fierce cold, and it made the skin of Rita's ankle feel like it was burning. She tried to kick against the thing that gripped her, but couldn't even move her leg. Whatever had hold of her was infinitely stronger.

'No!' she cried out, terror and panic now completely gripping her. 'Help me!'

Rita felt a nauseating breath roll over her back, one that was accompanied by a sour-smelling odour. Something was leaning over her. The whispering from the unseen children continued in the background, but now it sounded fearful. She heard the quick pitter-patter of small footsteps moving quickly—running-farther away from her.

'Please,' Rita begged, but she was then pulled savagely backwards, away from the steps and deeper into the darkness.

28

'RITA?' Ray called out from his position in bed.

At first, he thought she was maybe in the en-suite, but he could hear no movement from within the adjoining bathroom. He got up and checked inside, but it was empty.

Strange.

The clock showed the time to be a little after eight in the morning, so Ray dressed himself for the day, keen to find his wife after last night's breakthrough. It felt like the real Rita had returned, and he was glad to have her back.

They'd talked late into the night, not settling down to sleep until it was close to two in the morning. He felt much better for it, especially after listening to his wife talk about her confusion over how she had been acting.

Once they were away from this house, then they could start again.

Of course, they had to find somewhere to go first, and that would not be an easy task. He and Rita had discussed using the savings they'd built up while working at the hotel, which would hopefully cover them for a few months. Rita said she would reach out to her old contacts to try and find something—*anything*—for now.

He would do the same, but also resolved to apply himself better. Whether Rita was acting like herself or not, she had made a good point about him not providing. He'd tried, of course—God knows he tried—but the skillsets of a handyman seemed to be in less and less demand these days.

That meant he would need to adapt, for the good of his family.

Once dressed, he used the toilet and brushed his teeth, and then went looking for his wife. There were no guests due that day—the same as the previous day—so the hotel was empty except for his family, Marcus, and Vincent.

Ray walked over to Chloe's room and lightly knocked.

'Come in,' his daughter called, and he pushed the door open. She was inside, reading again, but was alone.

'Have you seen your mother this morning?' he asked.

She shook her head. 'Nope, not yet.'

'Huh. Okay, you read a bit longer. I'm going to find her, and then we'll all get breakfast.'

'No problem,' Chloe said, then went back to her book.

Ray considered broaching the subject of them leaving with Chloe, but decided against it. Both he and Rita needed to be present for that, and there was no need to ruin his daughter's day so early on.

He tried to think of where Rita could be. It was doubtful she would have started work so early, given the conversation last night plus them not having any guests, so the office seemed unlikely. The kitchen was a possibility. If she hadn't slept well, then maybe she was down getting a coffee— something he suddenly craved. If she hadn't already eaten, Ray could fix them all breakfast as well.

Ray made his way along to the entrance lobby and

descended the stairs. As he did, he heard voices, male and female, both of which he recognised.

They were both coming from the office area.

Ray quickly made his way down, not quite believing his ears—the unseen pair actually seemed to be discussing the upcoming Halloween event, and they were speaking with clear enthusiasm.

It can't be. Not after last night.

But his suspicions were confirmed as he walked into the office. His heart dropped.

Rita was seated at a desk, and Marcus was planted on the table next to her leaning over her as they both looked through some paperwork she had laid out on the desk.

'What's going on?' Ray asked, his tone reflecting his confusion.

But the pair kept talking between themselves, and Ray felt like he was invisible.

'I think we can count on this guy to put a story out,' Rita said, tapping a handwritten name on one of the loose sheets of paper. 'He seemed quite amenable. And if I press, I think I can get some good press in his newspaper.'

Rita was back in her business clothes—black jacket over a navy blouse, and her hair was immaculate. She looked tired, which seemed to be a normal thing these days. But today seemed particularly bad. Her skin was practically ashen, and her cheeks had sunken farther seemingly overnight.

Marcus, too, had dark circles under his eyes, though he was dressed stylishly in a black suit with a silk, navy-blue shirt beneath.

'Excellent,' he said. 'I think we move on this straight away.' He then patted Rita on the shoulder, like a pleased owner. Ray noticed that his hand lingered on after the pat.

'But I'll have the story worded as though space here is running out. Scarcity breeds interest,' Rita added.

Marcus nodded. 'Good idea.'

Ray coughed loudly, and eventually drew the attention of the pair.

Rita gave a half-smile. 'Morning. Sleep well?'

'I guess,' he said. 'What are you both up to?'

'Planning the October event,' Rita answered with an enthusiastic smile.

'We've agreed that we need to get moving on it,' Marcus said. 'I think we've all let things slip recently, so it's time to ramp up our efforts in order to make the weekend a success.'

Ray was reeling. Surely Rita wasn't *actually* going along with this so willingly, not after their talk the previous night. He wondered if she was perhaps just humouring Marcus, to throw him off the scent of their new plan to leave. It was a possibility, but he needed to get her alone to find out for sure.

'Can... can I talk to you for a moment, Rita?' he asked. 'In private.'

A frown crossed her face. 'Well, I'm a little busy with Marcus at the minute, dear. Can you give me a little time and I'll come find you later?'

Ray didn't know what to say. He wasn't sure if Rita was playing a game here with Marcus to keep up appearances, or if something had drastically changed since the previous night.

He was unsure as to whether he should comply. His first instinct was to decline and insist on a moment with his wife. He chewed at his lip.

'Sure,' he eventually said, deciding to trust her for now. 'Come find me when you're done, okay?'

Rita nodded but was already looking at the paperwork again with Marcus. 'We need to start with the leaflet drops as soon as possible as well,' she said.

'I know someone who can get them produced quickly for us,' Marcus told her. Ray walked out of the room.

What the hell is going on?

He left it a couple of hours, but Rita did not come and find him as promised. Ray had even seen Marcus head back to the top floor alone, but his wife was nowhere to be seen. After another fifteen minutes of waiting, he reached the end of his tether and walked back down to the office.

There she was, still seated at her desk, with the phone receiver tucked between her jaw and shoulder as she spoke and scribbled down notes at the same time.

'Thank you,' she said to whoever was on the other end of the line. 'I really appreciate it. We'll look out for the story. And yes, Mr. Blackwater will be able to sponsor your event in return, no problem.'

She then hung up the phone and continued with her notes.

'Rita?' Ray said, stepping inside.

She briefly looked up to him before she quickly turned back to her writing. 'Hi,' was all she said.

Is she trying to piss me off?

'I thought you were gonna come find me when you finished with Marcus. You know... so we could talk.'

'Oh, sorry,' she said, still not looking up. 'It completely slipped my mind.'

She carried on working as if nothing at all were wrong with that statement. Ray took a moment, hoping she would just look up and say, '*Just joking! Now, how do we get out of this place?*'

But she continued scribbling her notes, almost feverishly.

'Are you fucking serious?' Ray snapped, unable to hold it in.

Rita lifted her head, and actually had the nerve to look shocked. 'What did you just say to me?'

'I asked if you were serious,' he repeated angrily.

'About what?' Rita's own tone was defensive.

How could she be so dense?

'About what you're doing,' Ray replied, exasperated. 'You're ploughing ahead with that stupid thing on Halloween!'

'It isn't going to plan itself, Ray.'

'Fuck it!' he said. 'Why are you planning it at all? Do you even remember our conversation last night?'

A look of realisation then washed over her face, and she eventually nodded. 'Ah, now I see,' she answered, and gave a tight-lipped smile—one that was almost condescending.

'About that... I've been thinking,' she started, but Ray couldn't believe what he was hearing.

'Don't you dare,' he cut her off.

'Look, I wasn't thinking straight last night. If anything, I think you blindsided and manipulated me when I was feeling down.'

'What?! You can't be serious.'

'I am.' Her tone was forceful and certain. 'And I'm *not* leaving this place, not when there is so much to be done.'

Ray walked over to her, standing on the opposite side of the desk, and set his palms down on the surface. He then leant over his wife. As he did, Ray detected a strange but faint smell, one which he thought was coming from Rita. Not body odour, exactly, something more... musty.

'Tell me this is just some sort of joke,' Ray said. 'I can't believe you could flip so much in the span of one night.'

'I'm not joking,' Rita said and stood up to meet him, staring him down.

'It's Marcus, isn't it?' he asked. 'He's said something to you that's scared you, made you change your tune.'

Rita shook her head. 'Marcus has been nothing but supportive,' she said. 'Actually, you could do with taking a leaf out of his book. If you can't do that, then just stay out of my way.'

Rita then walked around the desk and past him.

'Where are you going?' he asked, struggling to keep his voice even remotely calm.

'To run an idea past Marcus, I'll see you later.'

Rita walked out of the room and closed the door behind her, leaving Ray alone, raging, and in utter disbelief.

29

VINCENT WATCHED on in silence as his sister spoke with Marcus. They were on the top floor, tucked away amongst Marcus' artefacts.

Vincent's fingers felt sore, and there was a raw pain from where some of his flesh had been scraped away. He kept his hands hidden in his pockets.

Rita had just informed them both of what had happened downstairs with Ray, and how he wanted to leave. Marcus was then a shoulder to cry on and was currently comforting her with an arm wrapped around her waist.

'Then he's an idiot,' Marcus said.

'He is,' Rita agreed, nodding. 'He doesn't understand me or what I want to achieve here.'

'Some people have no vision,' Marcus soothed, and laid a hand on her upper arm, gently squeezing it. Rita did not pull away. In fact, she smiled.

It was all happening before Vincent's eyes: everything Marcus thought he wanted.

Destroying the seal in Marcus' room had clearly worked. His thoughts were not quite his own anymore.

'I'll give you two a moment alone,' Vincent said and left the room. The pair didn't even notice; they were too busy staring into each other's eyes. With the door shut behind him, Vincent took in a deep breath, feeling both fear and electricity buzz through him.

It was small relief to Vincent knowing he wasn't ignorant to what was happening around them. Not like Marcus, who thought he was still in control of his own actions.

From his left, Vincent heard the sound of rasping breathing coming from down the hallway. He turned his head and only just kept from yelling out in fright.

There stood a woman at the very end of the well-lit corridor. She wasn't trying to hide her presence, grotesque as she was. Vincent knew she *wanted* him to see her.

The strange woman's hair was long, patchy, and scraggly, and what strands she did have were greasy and shiny. Her skin was mostly pale but smattered with dark-purple blotches. She wore a short, filthy, and torn nighty that covered little of her rake-thin frame. One shoulder-strap was undone, and a drooping and twisted breast popped free. Her legs were bent inwards at the knees, and her feet were black, with toes missing from each.

Through strands of long hair, Vincent could see her blank and milky eyes looking at him, staring with a wide gaze. Her nose was bent to one side and she had a cleft lip, which showed some yellowed teeth behind. Her breathing sounded like that of a person close to expelling their death-rattle.

What he was looking at was her soul. Or rather, a twisted version of it. And it terrified him.

Vincent looked up to the ceiling above and addressed the house, rather than the horrifying vision at the end of the hall. 'I did what you asked,' he whispered, voice shaking.

The woman then took an unsteady step forward.

'Please,' Vincent begged, close to wetting himself. He then repeated himself. 'Please... I did as you asked.'

The woman drew closer, but Vincent knew he could not flee. It would do no good. In fact, it would make things worse. The twisted hag shuffled her way to his side. Her stench—one of rotted and fetid meat—overcame him. She brought her mouth to his ear, and he felt an icy chill radiate over him.

The woman began to whisper to him... and Vincent nodded his understanding.

30

MARCUS' hand was cupped behind Rita's head, and his fingers gripped a handful of hair. He tilted her chin up towards him, pulling her mouth closer. Her eyes were smouldering. She wanted him.

And he wanted her.

It was quite the turnaround, considering how things had started between them. Marcus was a man who was used to getting what he wanted, though usually without as much resistance. However, this woman had rebuffed him, even challenged him, and had been a tough nut to crack.

However, he wasn't naïve enough to think he'd actually cracked it himself. Marcus could see it in her attitude now. Hell, he could even smell it on her. Rita wasn't herself anymore. But that suited him perfectly, as Marcus needed a much more subservient Rita than the one who had first set foot in Perron Manor.

'Are you sure you want this?' he asked, and brought his other hand up to her mouth before running his thumb over her bottom lip, then gently down her chin.

She nodded. 'I do.'

'What about your husband?' Marcus' voice was a teasing whisper.

'He...' Rita took a moment, struggling with the answer. 'He isn't important,' she eventually replied, though the pause annoyed Marcus. He'd seen a look of doubt and resilience flash across her eyes. It quickly vanished, however, and her carnal lust returned. The real Rita was once again quashed, replaced by a puppet.

A puppet for the house. One where he controlled the strings.

'Tell me how much you want me,' Marcus pushed, enjoying the control.

'I ache for you,' she whispered.

'And you'll stay here with me? And do as I ask?'

Rita gave a slow, deliberate nod.

'Excellent,' Marcus said, sliding his thumb back up to her lips. She took the digit into her mouth and lightly sucked on it, maintaining strong eye contact the whole time.

Her compliance was an important step. Marcus needed to ensure her servitude was upheld until the time was right.

In the meantime, however, he'd earned himself a little fun. Marcus knew he could have *lots* of fun with her until his plan finally came to pass.

He grabbed her hair, hard, and kissed her. Rita's tongue darted into his mouth, and he yanked at her jacket, pulling it down so he could slide it from her arms. Marcus then got to work on her blouse, lost in his desires.

They were soon on the floor, both completely naked, and Marcus mounted her.

As they fucked, neither saw the dark figure with burning yellow eyes watch them from the corner of the room.

31

Early October.

The eggs Chloe was eating were slightly overdone, and the accompanying bacon was soggy and stringy. That definitely wasn't the norm from her mother.

At least, it didn't *used* to be the norm. Over the last couple of months Chloe had noticed that her mum hadn't been putting in the same effort, care, or even love that normally came with her cooking.

It was the weekend, which meant no school, and Chloe's father had promised to take her out into town and then to a park, saying the fresh air would do them both good.

Her mother was too busy to go, apparently.

All three were currently in the kitchen, eating breakfast in silence. Another recent normality that Chloe didn't like.

Her parents weren't the same anymore, and she was scared for them.

'When you're ready, we'll get going. Make a full day of it,' her father said after draining the last of his coffee.

'We do have guests this weekend,' Chloe's mother said.

'Marcus and I could do with your help carrying their bags up to the rooms.'

'You and Marcus can cope on your own,' her dad said. His voice was stern, and Chloe couldn't help but note he never used to speak to her mother that way.

'Fine,' her mother shot back, before shovelling more food into her own mouth and swallowing without chewing. 'You two enjoy your day. I'll just keep the hotel going on my own.'

'You do that.'

No eye contact was made. Chloe's mother then got up and left the room without another word. She looked sickly, Chloe thought. Thinner than normal, and paler, too. Chloe wasn't sure if her mother was brushing her teeth correctly, either, given her breath always had a weird, metallic smell to it.

'Is Mum okay, Dad?' Chloe asked, a little afraid of what the answer might be.

Her father didn't respond straight away, but he looked at her with sad eyes. He took a breath. 'I honestly don't know, kiddo. We're just under a lot of stress at the minute, that's all.'

It perhaps wasn't the answer Chloe was looking for, but at least it was truthful. She could always count on that from her father.

'Are you two going to split up?' Chloe asked.

She couldn't help herself. The thought had been playing on her mind recently, so she had to ask.

He gave her a smile. A false one. 'We'll work it out, don't worry.'

The answer terrified Chloe. Because, for the first time that she could remember, she could tell that her father had just lied to her.

'Come on,' he then said, getting up. 'Let's go try and have some fun.'

~

The autumn breeze in the park had a chill to it, but Ray had made sure both he and his daughter had wrapped up warm. She was wearing her thick, red cotton coat, a grey skirt with white tights beneath, and a black beret hat. Ray was in his standard jeans, boots, and navy jacket.

While not bustling, the park was far from quiet, with couples walking, children playing, and dogs running free through the fallen, golden leaves. Up ahead, Ray saw a play area for kids, with a climbing frame, swing set, see-saw, and some balance beams.

'You can go play in there if you want,' he offered, hoping to break the silence between them. As they had been walking, he'd noticed Chloe carrying an expression of concern, one that had been more and more frequent recently—like the weight of the world was on her small shoulders. It reminded him of Rita.

The old Rita.

'It's okay,' Chloe said, kicking at a pile of leaves. The whole situation was breaking his heart, and it was clearly taking a toll on their daughter. Ray didn't know how to fix it.

'Nope,' he said, putting on a big smile. 'Afraid I can't accept that. I'm making it an order.'

Chloe gave a half-smile in return, but her eyes said she wasn't up for it. He knew she was about to politely decline again, but he instead scooped her up.

'Let's go!' he ordered and carried her over to the play areas.

'I don't think I want to,' she said, looking over at the swings. 'I think I just want to walk for a bit instead.'

But she didn't take her eyes off the play equipment, and Ray saw through the false reservation.

'We can walk soon enough; I think your legs need a rest!' He tried his best to sound enthusiastic and then set off running as he carried her. Chloe jiggled up and down in his arms, giggling as he pretended to trip and jostled her more vigorously. 'Oops, best make sure I don't do that again,' he joked before giving another exaggerated stumbling step. Chloe laughed again.

Ray quickly reached the swings, and out of the three that were there, only one other was in use. He carefully let Chloe drop into the free one nearest the frame. Her legs dangled through the gaps in the plastic seat, and he trotted around behind her.

'Now,' he said, 'you best hold on tight, 'cos I've got a lot of energy to burn, so I'm gonna make sure you go *really* high. Are you ready for lift-off?'

Another giggle, and the sound started to warm his soul. It may have been temporary, but for now it was a welcome reprieve.

'Ready!' Chloe exclaimed, letting the brief happiness and excitement overcome her as well.

Ray grabbed hold of the seat that supported her and pulled it back. The chains squeaked as Ray lifted her higher, all the way up to his chest. He then held Chloe stationary for a moment. 'Three,' he bellowed playfully, beginning the countdown. 'Two...'

Chloe started to laugh, but Ray didn't wait for the 'one' and pushed her down early to surprise her. It worked, and his daughter cackled and shrieked with joy as she went sailing forward in the swing-seat, hitting the apex of her climb and getting as high as Ray's own head. Before her descent back the other way, he saw Chloe kick out her feet with a laugh, and then she came swinging back. He pushed her again, keeping the momentum going.

'Higher,' she ordered, still laughing. He did as instructed, pushing harder. Her beret flew backwards off her head after one particularly strong push, and she squealed, slapping her hand to her head but missing the hat. Ray was quick, however, and caught it with his free hand.

'Got it!' he announced, stuffing it into his pocket while using his other hand to keep her momentum going. Chloe's brown hair flowed behind her as she moved through the air, and Ray couldn't help but feel that he was having an important and much-needed moment with his daughter.

Rita should be here for this.

He tried not to ruin the time they were having. *Concentrate on the here and now.*

It was strange to think that blocking his wife out of his thoughts was a way to actually make him happy. But that had become more common since the day she'd reneged on her promise to him. Since then, it was like she'd plunged even further into the abyss after she'd come up for a moment's clarity.

'Keep going!' Chloe shouted. Ray realised he'd missed his cue, and she had started to slow.

'Aye, aye, captain,' he said, and pushed her again when she swung back to meet him.

While Ray would be crushed if he and Rita split up, he knew the one who would be hit hardest was the one they both cared about most. If Chloe wasn't worth fighting for, then nothing in this world was.

Surely Rita would come back to them for her?

Ray and Rita had been together for what felt like forever, so what was a few months on the rocks compared to all those years of happiness?

But there was only one thing that scared Ray. One thing he wasn't certain they could come back from. Rita had been spending a lot of time with the owner of the hotel recently... and that worried him. In the early days, Marcus had almost been a phantom presence in their lives. Now, however, it seemed like Rita spent more time with him than she did her own family. And if the two of them were...

Ray didn't even want to think about it. He'd always trusted his wife completely. Surely she wouldn't be so selfish as to do something like that, regardless of any trouble they were having?

After ten more minutes on the swing, Chloe decided her time was up. 'I'm starting to feel a little sick,' she said.

Ray wasn't surprised; she'd been going non-stop for quite a while, so he caught the swing and slowly lowered her down to a stop before lifting her out. She was a little unsteady, legs wobbling a little, but soon found her footing.

'You okay?' he asked, squatting down to her level. After she took a few deep breaths, the colour started to return to her pale cheeks.

'I'm fine,' she said with a toothy smile.

'Glad to hear it. How about we go into town and get a cup of hot chocolate?'

Her enthusiastic nod was answer enough, and Chloe skipped ahead as they walked back to the car.

∽

The day out with her father had been a great one, and Chloe didn't really want to come home. As much as she loved the house, things were always frosty and cold there now.

No one seemed to smile or laugh anymore. Even her father, who had been chatty and happy all day, had quieted down again as they drew closer to the house.

The car rolled down the long driveway, and Chloe could hear the gravel crunch and shift beneath the tires. The sight of the building was still something Chloe savoured, especially from this distance. Its three peaks stood tall and proud against the backdrop of the security wall and the hills and trees beyond.

With all that was going on between her parents, she felt like their time at the house was drawing to a close. Chloe dearly hoped her parents would fix things so they could go back to how things were when they first moved in. But, she knew that wasn't likely.

When they drew closer to the house, Chloe noticed something in a window on the top floor. It was a figure, looking out—possibly Marcus, her Uncle Vincent, or even her mother. Whoever it was, they were too shrouded in shadow to make out clearly. It did confuse Chloe why the person just stood motionless like that and didn't wave. Chloe considered waving first, or even pointing the person out to her dad, but after staring for a few more moments, the strange figure simply wasn't there anymore. They hadn't stepped from view, just blended into the darkness, which made Chloe unsure if she had even seen anyone there in the first place.

Obviously not.

Her father pulled the car to a stop in the carport and switched off the engine.

'Ready to go back in?' he asked her, forcing a smile.

'Yeah,' she lied. Chloe wanted nothing more than to go back to the park with her dad.

32

LATER THAT MONTH.

Marcus was busy with Vincent's sister again. Vincent heard them fucking in Marcus' room when they no doubt thought everyone else was asleep.

But Vincent didn't sleep too much anymore.

Which, he knew, was true of Rita and Marcus as well. Vincent knew *exactly* why that was, though the other two were ignorant to the truth.

While Marcus was... occupied, Vincent took the opportunity to sneak into the room upstairs, using the keys he had stolen from Marcus' room earlier. He moved to the door of the locked-off area, noticing the walls Ray had recently put up were still undecorated.

The Halloween event was quickly approaching, and while the hotel wasn't full, the majority of rooms had been booked out. Hopefully, the number of souls staying that weekend would be enough for what was needed.

Vincent unlocked the door and opened it, moving to the area where Marcus stored his collected treasures. Vincent flicked on the light.

The true value of the many artefacts inside was probably far in excess of even what Marcus had estimated, especially when considering the true power contained within the room. Vincent had been made aware of the power mainly by the house itself. It spoke to him nightly through its avatars, their words like worms burrowing into his brain and infesting his thoughts.

There was one thing in particular that the house was interested in. One which spoke to its true nature.

Ianua Diaboli.

He walked to the display case that contained the book, lifted the lid, and took it out. Not for the first time. There was something about the tome, something that drew him back again and again; a compulsion just to hold it and touch it that Vincent couldn't explain. The author of this ancient book was, as far as Vincent knew, unknown. As was the book's place of origin. That it was written in Latin was probably some clue, of course, but neither he nor Marcus had been able to find out much in the way of its history, beyond what Marcus' grandfather had uncovered.

Vincent leafed carefully through the pages, knowing which in particular he was headed to, without actually being able to understand what was written.

Marcus had never let him near *Ianua Diaboli* before, so he always had to sneak in here in the dead of night just to be near it and fulfil the compulsion. He was allowed to inspect and study all other artefacts in the room, but not the book. Vincent had respected that at first, even gone along with it, as he was just so happy to be learning more under Marcus' tutelage.

He was thrilled to be in a house like Perron Manor—one that was alive with spirits from beyond. It was both terrifying and liberating. Knowing there was more to life than just death gave Vincent purpose. Over time, he'd actually begun to have experiences with entities and had seen spirits roaming the halls. But he soon also felt their insidious nature, as well as their cold presence. Vincent had even laid eyes on the more powerful and evil things that existed in the house as well. Not just the souls of the dead, but demonic beings that had never truly lived. Not in this world, anyway, even though they desperately wanted to.

Through snippets of what Marcus divulged, Vincent had slowly learned more of the nature of the house and how it tied directly to *Ianua Diaboli*.

Vincent had needed more. He grew resentful of the fact that the most powerful artefact in Perron Manor was being kept from him. It wasn't *fair*.

It was an incident in the basement, midway through the previous year, that changed things for him. Vincent had been down in the depths of the house alone, hoping to catch a glimpse of the burned man who lived in the furnace; he was the one who screamed in agony every time the equipment was fired-up as it boiled his blood. Instead, he saw something else. A yellow-eyed demon, only partially visible from the shadows. It spoke to Vincent without moving its mouth, but said its name was Pazuzu.

It was a demon Vincent had heard about.

He had been terrified in that moment, but the entity put forward a proposition that offered knowledge, as well as eternal life. Vincent just had to destroy the protective seals in his room.

Vincent had struggled with the offer for days after, knowing there were inherent dangers, but he was equally frustrated at being held at arm's length by Marcus. Blackwater had cast doubt over his ability and aptitude regarding the dark arts.

Eventually, even though it filled him with terror, he had eventually complied. From that point on, his room was no longer protected from Perron Manor. The effect of the house, subdued so far thanks to the Eye of Horus keeping it at bay, was unleashed, like water finally surging past a broken dam. Perron Manor had already tasted both him and Marcus, so with the last obstacle removed, its subsequent hold on them was quick to tighten.

Vincent was well aware he was possessed. Evidently, the house did not care that he knew. Was Vincent so subservient and easily controlled he wasn't considered a threat? Marcus, in contrast, seemed ignorant to his situation.

Soon after Vincent's compliance, he started to see more and more of the spirits in the house, and the demons as well. Though the entities terrified him, they never tried to hurt him.

Slowly, the spirits began to speak to Vincent. His dreams changed. He realised what he had to do.

It was at that point Vincent had gained the courage to go against Marcus' wishes and look at the book.

Vincent recalled the very first time he held *Ianua Diaboli*. He was instantly beguiled, though he understood nothing of the foreign language written within its pages. After leafing through the book, he'd stopped at a section titled *Impius Sanguis*, immediately realising there was something special about it. He'd then moved on to the back of the book, and when he got to the last passages titled, *Claude Ianua*, a sudden revulsion overcame him.

Just looking at the words, as well as at the drawings that littered the pages—mirrors and pools of water all with horrible things in their reflections—was enough to make him nauseous. He was forced to close the book as a sudden and unexplainable *hate* rose up within him, aimed at those particular pages and the simple ritual narrated on them.

However, that made no sense, given he couldn't even understand the words.

Vincent knew it wasn't really *his* hate that was being channelled, but that of the house. He was compelled to rip out the offending pages and destroy them, but was physically unable to. Something stopped him. A protection on the book, of some kind, tied to the symbols on the cover.

Over the months that followed, he'd tried many times to tear out those pages, or alter the markings on the cover, but could not. The symbols on the cover stopped any who were possessed from destroying or altering the book.

Out of curiosity, Vincent flicked to the back of the book again to try once more, though the result was as expected. He took one of the pages and tried to pull... but his body did not respond.

So instead, Vincent just continued to enjoy being in the presence of the book. It lent him a sense of peace he couldn't seem to find anywhere else in the house.

He knew he could not indulge in that peace for long. Marcus and Rita would be finished soon, and preparations for the ritual of *Impius Sanguis* needed to be carried out. Vincent had no doubt that Marcus would seek *him* out to complete the more menial tasks involved.

Vincent set the book back in its case and laid a loving hand on top. He noticed that his fingers were beginning to look worse. One nail on his left hand had come away completely, and angry red flesh showed through where strips of skin had been rubbed away. Vincent knew he should stop the scratching, but just couldn't. It was too much of a release.

He left the room and walked back to his small, sparse

bedroom. Only twenty minutes later, there was a knock on his door.

'Come in,' he called, already knowing who it was. The door opened, and Marcus stepped inside, wearing a dark blue t-shirt and black jogging bottoms. His feet were bare, and his normally pale cheeks were still slightly flushed. Marcus moved into the room and closed the door behind him before walking over to Vincent and sitting down next to him. Vincent couldn't help but notice that his 'friend' smelled of sweat and sex.

'How are you doing, Vincent?' Marcus asked.

'Okay,' Vincent replied.

'Glad to hear it. I wanted to come by on the off-chance you were still awake.'

'I don't sleep much,' Vincent said in response.

Marcus nodded. 'Me either, at the moment. I've tried to figure out why, and I think it is because of what is coming. I suppose I'm nervous. And excited.'

You're a blind idiot, Vincent thought, and wanted to say it aloud. While they were both puppets now, at least Vincent could see his strings.

The actual response he gave was much more sympathetic. 'I guess that makes sense. You know... you never did tell me the full extent of what is going to happen here.'

'I know,' Marcus said, looking ahead, his eyes lost in thought. 'But the time has come to indulge you, I think. I need your help to see it through.' He then turned to Vincent. 'Will you help me?'

'Of course,' Vincent said.

'I'm glad to hear that. I think you know that the book I treasure so much—*Ianua Diaboli*—has a connection to this house. Or, rather, for places like this house. The book was written to utilise a power that exists at certain points in our world. Points that have a connection with—'

'Hell,' Vincent finished.

Marcus looked surprised. 'That's right. How did you know that?'

Vincent smiled, then lied: 'The translation of the title. Or, at least, one of the possible translations. A Devil's Door. I've heard of such things.'

The house. The house has shown *me.*

'Impressive,' Marcus said, eyebrows still raised. 'Maybe I underestimated you and your knowledge. But yes, that's right. The house is built on one of those gateways. That is why it's special.' Marcus then looked at the walls of the room, admiring the structure around him. 'My grandfather only learned what this place truly was after finding *Ianua Diaboli*, and that is why he moved ahead with buying the house. But... he was too afraid to use the power himself. I will make no such mistake. That is the reason we turned the house into a hotel.'

'To get bodies in here,' Vincent said in confirmation. 'Souls the house can feed off of.'

'Correct. Even if it is just tiny bites, for now, the constant stream of fresh souls are enough to keep things building and growing. And that is needed for a ritual in the book. *The* ritual, as far as I'm concerned. Vincent... I need you to know something. I won't be here after the ritual is done.'

'You won't be at the house anymore?'

'That's... complicated. However, as a thank you, I've added you into my will. You are to be the sole heir of the house, which you will inherit after I'm gone.'

Vincent made a show of looking surprised. 'Wait... are you saying you intend to die? Is that part of the ritual?'

'It is. And it is unavoidable,' Marcus said. 'I have to go

through with it. Though, I can promise you it won't be the end for me. Even so, I need someone here in the house to keep it safe. A gatekeeper, if you will, until the time is right. That gatekeeper is you.'

'Thank you,' Vincent said. 'You have no idea how much that means to me. But, Marcus... does it have to be that way? I mean, dying is a big price to pay.'

It was all lip-service. They were both just acting out a charade, even dancing to the same tune, but Marcus wasn't actually aware of it. Vincent could only assume the house controlled people in different ways, and the strong-willed were easier to fool if they believed they were still in control. Not so with himself, he knew, as he had submitted out of fear.

'Believe me when I tell you,' Marcus went on, 'the price is *nothing* compared to the reward.'

'So, what can I do to help?' Vincent asked, though he already knew the answer.

'We need to get the boundaries for the ritual set up. To do that, we need to mark the house with certain symbols.' He reached into his pocket, pulled out a crumpled piece of paper, and unfurled it. It showed a hand-drawn circle, which had a large dot in its centre.

'A circumpunct,' Vincent said.

'Correct.'

'I thought that was a sign of God. Order withholding chaos.'

'It is. And that is why it needs to be drawn on the *outside* of the house. The dot represents the chaos of the house, and the outer ring would represent the outer world.'

'So we contain the chaos within.'

'You're quick on the uptake,' Marcus said. 'I need you to draw this at specific points. But, there is one more thing...

each marking will need blood added to it. Just a drop, from a pinprick in your finger or something.'

'That is no problem,' Vincent said, taking the paper.

'Also, the protective markers in most rooms—besides mine, yours, and the study upstairs—will need to be removed.'

'I can do that.'

'Excellent. Now, I have to ask something else. Are you feeling okay?'

Vincent lifted a confused eyebrow. 'What do you mean?'

'Well, we need to be sure we are... pure, for the ritual to work as expected. My blood will be spilt, and your blood is being used as well.'

'What do you mean by pure?'

Vincent knew *exactly* what Marcus meant, but played dumb in order to keep this dance going and make sure Marcus still felt in control.

'I've ensured our rooms are protected in this house, as you know, so that our minds are not poisoned by the house. My plans could get a little... derailed... if it turns out either of us are not fully in control of ourselves. Do you understand??'

Vincent gave him a look of realisation, then nodded. 'I understand,' he said. 'But I'm fine. I still feel myself. Do you?'

Marcus nodded with misplaced confidence. He even gave a condescending chuckle. 'I'm fine, dear boy,' he said, patting Vincent on the back. 'I know what I'm doing. Believe me, I'd know if something was wrong.'

It took everything Vincent had to keep from laughing at the poor, misguided fool.

'Then I'll get to work,' Vincent said, standing up and waving the scrap of paper.

'Now?!' Marcus asked.

'Perfect time. No one is awake to see me doing it. Best not to raise any suspicions with Rita or Ray.'

'Good thinking,' Marcus said and stood up as well. He held out his hand. 'Thank you for everything, my friend.'

They shook. 'No problem,' Vincent replied, almost taken aback by the man's ignorance. 'It has been my pleasure.'

33

October 29th.

The weekend was upon them.

Rita and Marcus had worked so hard to reach this point and now it was time.

Ray had intentionally kept out of it recently; his focus instead had been on reaching his wife again. Mostly. However, he'd failed to reconnect with her and had been routinely ignored. Every now and then he'd seen flashes of regret and sorrow in her eyes, but they had been brief.

She had given him a promise, however, though he didn't put much stock in that.

'Just let me get Halloween out of the way,' she'd said. 'Let me make a success of at least *one* thing in this hotel, and then I'll be happy. After that, we can hand our notices in to Marcus and leave here. I promise.'

She hadn't been as emotional and readable as that night the previous month, where she'd broken down crying; instead, she appeared guarded and robotic, but at least it was something. It was a promise Ray could cling and hold her to. So, he'd reluctantly agreed to that.

It was early, and they had all gathered in the office—
even Vincent and Chloe, who had tagged along out of interest. Marcus stood before the group with his hands behind
his back and serious expression on his face, like a general
about to give orders to his men.

'This is it,' he said, wearing a prideful smile. 'All we've
worked so hard for. We may not be fully booked, but thanks
to Rita's ingenuity, guile, and persistence, we have more
guests staying this weekend than ever before. So,' he looked
directly at Rita, who was beaming, 'I want to say a big and
personal thank you to you, Rita. This is all because *you*
made it happen.'

Marcus then started clapping enthusiastically, clearly
wanting everyone to join in, but it just came off as awkward.
Still, Ray didn't want to simply stand with his arms folded
while another man showed appreciation to his wife, so he
joined in as well. Chloe followed, as did Vincent, though he
seemed less than enthused. Since Ray's arrival ten months
ago, he hadn't really seen too much of Vincent, probably
even less than Marcus. Even though Vincent was Rita's
brother, he'd been little more than a ghost to them, popping
up every now and again but always staying in the background. A non-entity of a person, in Ray's eyes.

Still, Ray preferred him to Marcus when all was said and
done.

'Now,' Marcus went on, raising a hand to bring the
applause to an end, 'we need to stay focused. All the hard
work needs to continue for just a few more days. Later this
afternoon our guests will start to arrive, and things are going
to get busy. There will be a lot of requests and demands for
you all to deal with. I myself will take the lead on the events
we have planned.'

Ray raised an eyebrow. 'What kind of events?'

'It was Marcus' idea,' Rita replied with a smile. 'Give the people what they want. This is a paranormal weekend, after all, and since Marcus and Vincent have a huge amount of knowledge in that field, Marcus will be running workshops and tours.'

'Workshops?' Ray asked, still not quite understanding.

'You know,' Marcus cut in, 'Ouija board sessions, vigils, and I'll even go over the history of the house and its supposed paranormal influences.'

'But you said you didn't believe in any of that rubbish,' Ray retorted.

'I don't,' Marcus snapped, and Ray saw him bristle. 'But like Rita said, we must give the guests what they have paid for. Understand?'

Ray shrugged. 'I suppose so.'

Marcus glared at Ray for a moment, then turned to the others and forced a smile. 'So, I want everyone looking their best and ready to roll no later than two o'clock this afternoon. You need to be energised and battle-ready.'

'We will be,' Rita replied, looking at the hotel owner like he was some kind of fucking idol. It sickened Ray seeing his wife act like a cheerleader, and he wasn't naïve enough to fully trust she would go through with her promise.

But he had to give her the benefit of the doubt... for now. If it turned out to be a lie, then he knew their marriage was truly in the gutter. There would be no way back, despite how much he didn't want that to be true.

Ray had also needed to stifle a laugh when Marcus had instructed everyone to look their best.

The nerve of it.

While their boss had access to some truly nice clothes, they didn't hide that the man still looked ill; he was gaunt, pale, and absolutely exhausted. But, the same could also be said for Ray's wife.

'Rita, you will welcome the guests and man the reception desk,' Marcus ordered and she quickly nodded in assent. 'Ray, you will take the guests' bags up to the rooms on arrival. Vincent will help you. I'll need you both working as quickly as possible, because I think people will start to arrive thick and fast.'

'No problem,' Ray answered, though his tone was nonchalant. He then looked to Vincent. 'Right, partner?'

Vincent gave a blank expression like he wasn't even listening. 'Yeah, I guess so,' he said, which hardly filled Ray with confidence. Still, he only had to last one more weekend, so he didn't mind picking up any of Vincent's slack if he needed to.

Ray had made a decision: no matter what Rita said come Monday morning, whether she was coming with him or staying, Ray was going to leave this place forever.

And he was going to take Chloe with him.

34

CHLOE HAD BEEN GIVEN strict instructions for the weekend, and her mother had been firm and uncompromising when dishing out the orders.

Her father, however, had been a little gentler in his explanation: that the weekend was going to be extremely busy in the hotel, with lots of people wandering around. Lots of strangers. He'd told her it was very important that Chloe kept to her designated rooms.

She'd agreed to do as she was told. And she had fully intended to stick to that promise, too. However, the guests had been arriving in a constant stream for the past hour, and Chloe realised she was going to find it difficult to stick to her word.

The whole thing was just too exciting!

There was a buzz throughout the building, one that made it feel somehow *alive*. Chloe was used to experiencing the hotel as a big, empty, and even cold place. It always had the feeling of being an echo of the past. Large and grand, but somehow... lonely. Now, however, with the chatter and noise of people filling almost every room, the atmosphere was different.

Chloe couldn't help but constantly peek out of her room when she heard people walking close to it and passing down a nearby corridor. Adults dressed in the finest clothing—pressed suits and beautiful dresses—who all seemed thrilled to be here marched past her room in a never-ending line, all being shown to their rooms by her father. They chatted enthusiastically about what the weekend ahead would hold.

More voices approached, and again Chloe cracked open the door to her room and looked out. Through the gap, she could see her father pass by her line of sight, struggling with three large bags while sweating and red-faced. Then, she spotted an elderly couple follow behind. Chloe heard a brief snippet of their conversation.

'I don't think we'll see anything,' the man said. 'But it should be fun all the same.'

'Oh tosh,' the lady replied. 'I've heard a great deal about this house. So I'm hoping for the best.'

Chloe knew what they were referring to. Her father had prepared her for what was happening that weekend and the reason everyone was coming. Because, he'd said, it turns out that even some grown-ups like a good fairytale.

When Chloe had asked what that meant, he'd gone on to explain that the people who were coming all had one thing in common: they believed in things that simply didn't exist.

Ghosts.

Chloe knew what ghosts were, but her dad had gone to great lengths to make sure she understood they weren't real.

'Then how come some grown-ups believe in them?'

He'd paused. 'It makes handling certain truths easier.'

She'd asked what that meant, but he said he'd explain it another day, when she was older. What was important now, he'd said, was that there was nothing to be scared of in the house.

But Chloe wasn't scared at all. She'd fallen in love with the house since the first day they'd moved in.

Still, she wished she could be a part of what was happening right now. Fairytales or not, everyone seemed excited, and the house was full of happy sounds—it seemed like one big party. She wanted to be a part of it, not hidden away in her room while everyone else had fun.

So... would it really be so bad if she snuck out again to see what was going on? She'd become quite adept at that in her time living here, and it had worked well for her so far. Sure, with more people around there was much more chance of her getting spotted. But, considering most people wouldn't even know who she was... was that really a problem?

Chloe just had to make sure her mum, dad, Uncle Vincent, or Mr. Blackwater didn't see her.

After a few moments of deliberation, she made up her mind. She *would* be part of what was happening this weekend. And, if she got caught, then so be it, she'd accept the punishment. With a tingle of excitement, and after waiting to make sure her father was far enough away to not be a concern, Chloe left her room and pulled the door closed behind her.

35

To SAY that Patricia Cunningham was looking forward to the weekend ahead was an understatement.

Everyone had gathered downstairs in the great hall, and what a hall it was—an impressive space with a high, ornate ceiling, stone flooring, and aged but elegant wallpaper. Patricia could practically *feel* the history seep out of the surroundings. Tables had been set with plates and cutlery ready for the evening meals, but one table in particular looked different from the others, which were draped in tablecloths. This one looked very old, made from fine oak, and was much bigger than the others. If possible, she aimed to be sitting there when the food was served.

Patricia had been enamoured with the building from the moment she and her best friend Betsy had been chauffeured down the driveway and had seen the three peaks of the proud, old house come into view. Such a magnificent and stately home would not have been out of place in her native Scotland.

She and Betsy had travelled down to the hotel from their home on the borders. It had been a relatively short trip, made easier thanks to their chauffeur Norm, who was staying a few towns over and would be back on Monday morning to take them home.

Patricia had first heard of the event through a paranormal society she was a part of. What lay beyond death was a subject that had always interested her, but it had become something of an obsession since the passing of her dear husband fifteen years ago. Betsy, too, was in a similar position, having lost her partner six years prior. Patricia was not a naïve person and knew one of the main draws the subject held for her was one of comfort; she wanted to know that maybe her Andrew still existed out there somewhere, instead of just having been snuffed out of existence completely.

Both Patricia and Betsy had worn their finery tonight—it seemed like the occasion for it—with Patricia in a royal-blue, strapless gown, one that suited her busty frame and hung down to her feet. It was embossed about the chest with a delicate floral pattern over see-through netting that showed a little skin beneath. Despite being in her mid-sixties, Patricia thought she was ageing well and was pleased with how the new dress looked on her, especially when complemented by her makeup and greying-blonde hair styled in an elegant and sweeping bun. She was relatively short, standing at around five-foot-six in the heels she was wearing, but she always ensured her posture was confident. Her mother had always taught her that a straight back and high chin would make her appear taller in other peoples' eyes.

Betsy, who was taller and thinner, was dressed a little more conservatively, with a silk blouse and a long, ankle-length black skirt. The outfit matched well with her dyed, curly dark hair.

People were chatting and mingling and enjoying a few glasses of complimentary champagne. It was nice to be surrounded by people who shared her interests and beliefs. But as good as this socialising was, Patricia was eager to kick the weekend off proper; they were all waiting for the owner of the hotel—Mr. Marcus Blackwater—to make an appearance and officially welcome them. They had been told he was going to give a speech to go over what they could expect in the coming days.

She and her friend were currently talking to a nice couple who had travelled up from Newcastle in the northeast of England. Their thick Geordie accent was sometimes difficult to understand—with lots of abbreviations that confused her—so she found herself smiling and nodding a lot.

Finally, Patricia detected a sudden change in the atmosphere and the talking around her dulled. Heads started to turn, and Patricia looked in the direction everyone else was. She saw a well-dressed man making his way through the crowd. He had dark, brushed-back hair, a smart black suit, and piercing blue eyes. He was certainly attractive, though he had a quality about him that seemed a little... tired. He was gaunt, with an ashen pallor. The man carried a glass of champagne, gripped at the stem.

She knew it was Mr. Blackwater.

He was followed by the young lady that had checked Patricia and Betsy into the hotel earlier that day. The woman carried a footstool lined across the top with plush red velvet. She was a very pretty girl, though she seemed afflicted by the same weariness as her boss.

Perhaps they were all working too hard here.

Mr. Blackwater moved close to the rear door that looked out over a courtyard, and the lady put down the footstool.

Mr. Blackwater then stood atop it, elevating himself above everyone else. He was handed a butter knife and, though it wasn't needed, he tapped his glass with it, signifying he was about to speak. The last of the small murmurs in the room faded to silence, and an easy and charming smile crossed Mr. Blackwater's lips.

'Ladies and gentlemen,' he began, 'welcome... to the Blackwater Hotel!' A polite round of applause rippled around the room. The owner waited for it to peter out before carrying on. 'I'm so glad you could all join us this weekend, and I trust your surroundings are to your liking. But as fine a building as this is, I think we all know the reason you are here... and what you hope to see.'

A few people cheered, and there was another smattering of clapping. Patricia could sense the energy in the room. That everyone here could all get so excited over their shared passion was nice, and it gave a sense of camaraderie that, in truth, Patricia hadn't experienced a whole lot of in her life. It made her feel like she belonged.

'Now,' Mr. Blackwater continued, 'some of you may know a little about the building already, and some of you may not. But the history of the stately home is a long and extremely interesting one. It was built all the way back in the twelve-hundreds but has seen much in its lifetime, including more than its fair share of death. It is supposedly cursed, and well known in certain circles for being one of the most haunted houses in the country. Well, after living here for a while now, I can confirm that to be true. I have personally experienced things here that I still can't quite believe. I am not just talking about creaking doors or unexplainable noises, either. I have actually *seen* the spirits of the dead walking the halls.'

There were a few gasps, and Patricia felt her buzz of

excitement grow. *This could be it.* She had been hoping this house could provide what so many other locations had failed to deliver.

Hoping... but not really believing it would be so.

However, if their host was to be believed, then maybe, just maybe, the weekend ahead would give Patricia the answers she so desperately sought.

'We have a whole host of activities for you to indulge in during your stay here,' Marcus went on. 'Those, however, will begin tomorrow. Tonight is about fun and getting to know each other. Food will be served shortly. So please, eat and drink your fill. But!' and he held up a finger of warning, 'make sure you are all fit and ready for what tomorrow brings.' He smiled. 'So no hangovers.'

The gathered crowd chuckled.

'Can't promise that!' someone called out, drawing more laughter.

'Well, don't say you weren't warned. Now, I've spoken enough. Speeches are boring, and there is fun to be had. I will be here for a little while longer for those that wish to speak to me, but I do plan on getting an early night. I ask that we meet here after breakfast is served in the morning, and from there I will lead a tour around the building and give you a little more of the history.' He then raised his glass. 'To a fantastic weekend.'

Everyone's glass raised in unison. 'Here here!' Patricia said, and took a sip of the delicious champagne, feeling almost giddy.

36

RAY HAD to force a polite smile as the guests all toasted along with Marcus like he was some kind of celebrity. He also had to watch as his wife looked up at the man in admiration as well.

It turned his stomach. As did all the rubbish that Marcus had spouted about the house being haunted. Ray had lived here for two months short of a year, and despite a few odd things that could surely be put down to the building being old, he had seen nothing that would back up Marcus' claims.

It was all bullshit, said only to play to an eager crowd.

Ray stood out of the way at the back of the room. His body ached, especially his arms and legs after a hectic day of checking in guests and humping their bags up to their rooms. He'd then had to set up the great hall for the evening before serving drinks.

Vincent was locked away in the kitchen, doing some last-minute preparations to the banquet of food for that evening, so he had been no help. And Rita had been following

Marcus around like a little lost sheep. Ray felt like he'd had to handle the bulk of the manual work himself.

Only a few days to go.

He had arranged accommodation a few towns over and booked enough space for all of them: himself, Chloe... and Rita. Whether his wife would actually join him come Monday would depend on if she kept her word.

After a little while, people started to take their seats, and Marcus looked over to Ray, giving him a deliberate nod.

This was what Ray had to show for his thirty-seven years on this Earth—relegated to being a bloody waiter for a bunch of toffs, all at the behest of an egomaniac who had designs on his wife. Hell, maybe that man was fucking her already.

Ray swallowed his anger and went to fetch the first plates of food.

Only a few days to go.

37

'GOOD NIGHT, DEAR,' Betsy said to Patricia before giving her friend a peck on the cheek.

They were in the corridor outside of their respective rooms, and the hour was just past midnight. It had been a most enjoyable evening, but Betsy could feel the effects of the alcohol she'd indulged in—perhaps *over*indulged.

Both women were staying on the ground floor, to the back of the house in one of the rear wings. Theirs were the only two rooms in the corridor that looked out into the courtyard. It was pitch black outside and a little unnerving, especially when juxtaposed with the great hall behind them that continued to give off the hum of life, with the last guests still chatting and laughing. The sound was dulled by the separating doors and walls, making Betty feel somehow like she was just on the edge of safety.

'I'll give you a knock just after eight,' Patricia said. 'Then we can go for breakfast.'

'Sounds good,' Betsy replied. 'Sleep tight.'

'And let's hope nothing goes bump in the niiiight,' her friend replied in a sing-song voice. They both laughed, the terrible joke made funnier by their inebriated state, and Betsy walked to her room at the farthest-most point of the wing.

Once inside, and with the door closed behind her, Betsy turned on the light. The room was certainly to her tastes, fitting of a grand stately home. The four-poster bed was a very nice touch and lent the décor a regal feel. She noticed that the room was cold, however, which it hadn't been earlier that day. She then walked over to the black cast-iron radiator that was positioned between two bay windows and put her hand cautiously onto the metal. Though not exactly hot to the touch, it was certainly warm and should have been enough to heat the room at least a little.

Still, the bedsheets looked thick and comfortable.

Betsy paid a visit to the en-suite and then readied herself for bed, switching off the main light to the room and leaving on only the bedside lamp while she tucked herself in. No sooner had she gotten into bed did something draw her attention. She turned her attention to the far wall to her left, where two windows looked out over the rear grounds. The heavy curtains that hung either side of the bay windows remained open and tied back, and Betsy scolded herself for not shutting them before getting into bed. Maybe she was a little tipsier than she thought.

And it was from one of those windows that she saw movement from outside, drifting past the aperture. From her position in bed, Betsy stared out into the night, but the blackness beyond the glass looked like a heavy, impenetrable blanket, and nothing moved within it. Still, she was curious, if a little spooked, so got up to investigate—and to close the curtains.

With the light from the room, she could see at least a few feet out into the courtyard, but there was nothing obvious there that would have drawn her attention, and certainly no movement. Betsy could only think it had been a bat flying past the window.

She grabbed one of the curtains to pull it closed, but paused when she heard something behind her from the connecting en-suite: a banging noise, which she quickly realised was the sound of the toilet seat dropping and hitting the porcelain rim.

But... she had left the seat down.

With her heart in her mouth, Betsy slowly made her way towards the bathroom door. Could it be? Was the very reason she had come to this house for the weekend about to present itself to her?

It was indeed what she had wanted, but now that she was on the cusp of possibly seeing something, Betsy was terrified. She instantly regretted not sharing a room with Patricia.

Finding enough strength to push on, she opened the door and flicked on the light.

'Hello?' she called out to the empty room. There was a slight buzz from the light above, but she couldn't hear any sounds other than that. And there was certainly no one visible inside. Her breathing quickened, and Betsy considered running next door to Patricia's room, silly as it may be.

Instead, after a while, she switched off the light again and pulled the door shut. Leaving it open wasn't an option, as she would have been constantly looking over to it from her bed and expecting to see something peeking back at her from the other side. While she dearly wanted to believe there was something after death, the idea of actually *seeing* it was now a scary one. Especially since she was alone.

She again walked over to the bay windows and reached

for the curtains. Her hand found the fabric, but when she was about to draw the curtains closed, her body froze up.

A breath, from behind, loud and cold. It rolled over her bare shoulders. The smell that flowed with it was foul.

Betsy wanted to scream. She knew instantly that someone—or some*thing*—was standing directly behind her. She could feel a spiking cold and could hear steady and rasping breaths. She managed only a pathetic squeak.

A feeling of immense dread came over her, and Betsy realised at that moment that coming to the Blackwater Hotel had been a huge mistake. That was made blindingly obvious by the sinister chuckle she heard. The unseen thing in the room with her now was *not* benign. Betsy looked into the window before her, terrified of what she may see in the reflection.

It was difficult to make out the shape clearly, as it was a dark mass instead of a human figure. But something was definitely there, without doubt. Goosebumps lined Betsy's skin. She needed to get out of that room.

And quickly.

Her body started to shake, and tears welled up in her eyes. Deep within her gut Betsy thought she was going to die.

There was only one way out of the room, and that would require getting past whatever the black entity was that blocked the way. She reached down within herself and used every ounce of strength and bravery that she could find and turned around. But when she did, she saw the way ahead was clear. There was only an empty room, and nothing blocking her escape to the door.

Betsy didn't want to stop and doubt herself, to question if she had even seen anything behind her in the first place or if it was all imagined. She only wanted to get out and to run to her friend. While she still might not be safe in Patricia's room, at least she wouldn't be alone. She made to run, and had just taken her first step when there was a knocking on the window behind her. A deliberate *clink, clink, clink* on the glass.

Don't look. Don't look. Don't look.

But she did. How could she not? As she gazed upon the horror that stood outside, Betsy was finally able to push out the scream that had been trapped inside of her.

There was a man standing directly outside of the window, so tall that his head was close to the edge of the frame. He was completely naked, skin blotchy and pale, and his penis hung limply, dangling just above the line of the window sill. His abdomen was sunken so much that Betsy was surprised she couldn't make out the spine through the skin. Cracked ribs poked free from the dried flesh, and his arms and shoulders were so thin Betsy could read the outline of every bone. The man's eyes were a dirty, milky white, with no pupils, and they stared wildly at her, almost popping from the sockets. A thin mop of black, greasy hair sat atop his head, but the most striking feature of all was his mouth, where the man's jaw looked to have long since been ripped off, along with his top lip. Betsy could see the line of his teeth, and the jagged flesh where they should have met the jaw was dark and purple. The man's tongue flopped freely down to his throat.

He had one hand pressed against the glass, and he brought his head forward to rest on the window. She heard him moan, even above her own screaming. His other hand slowly moved to his penis, which he began to rhythmically stroke. The demonic person then slowly ran his tongue up the glass.

Betsy clutched her chest. Her heart felt like it was going to burst and hammered wildly.

She ran.

Though her legs threatened to buckle beneath her, Betsy was able to make it out of her room and across the hall, and she started to pound on Patricia's door, desperate for her friend to let her in. Even out in the hallway, well away from the window in her own room, Betsy felt exposed and vulnerable. Panic had overcome her, and she pounded and screamed.

'Let me in!'

It felt like she was standing alone in that corridor for an eternity. However, she eventually heard the click of the lock from the other side, and the door opened to reveal her friend looking both tired and confused.

'Betsy, what on Earth—'

Betsy didn't allow Patricia to finish. She fell into the room, and into the arms of her dear friend, sobbing and wailing and shaking uncontrollably.

38

'ARE you sure I can't persuade you to stay?' Patricia asked her friend as Betsy finished checking out.

Betsy firmly shook her head. 'Not a chance.' Her expression was as serious as Patricia had ever seen it. Betsy then went on to ask, 'But Patricia, are you sure I can't convince *you* to leave?'

Since Betsy had burst into Patricia's room the previous night in a state of panic and fear, she had been trying to get Patricia to leave with her, insisting the house simply wasn't safe.

Patricia had listened in awe—and a little bit of jealousy —at the story of what Betsy had seen outside of her window. Patricia could understand the fear her friend had experienced, certainly, but there was no way Patricia could leave now. What Betsy had experienced was the *precise* reason they had attended this event, and no amount of fear would sway her.

Patricia was staying.

Betsy had spent the night in Patricia's room, sharing a bed. Patricia knew the woman hadn't slept much, though nothing else had happened. As soon as Betsy had gotten up, she'd arranged her own transportation home.

The young lady—Rita—handled the formalities of the check-out and apologised for any distress the hotel may have caused.

A few other early risers had gathered around, listening in with great interest.

'I just don't want you to regret not staying,' Patricia said as the hotel manager finished the check-out. 'Scary or not, you've seen something we *all* want to see. Just think what else might be in store for us.'

But Betsy was unmoved. One of the hotel workers—a large man in a suit, whose nametag read *Ray*—gathered up her bags. Betsy shook her head. 'Patricia, I'm scared of *precisely* what might be in store, don't you see? And I think you should be, too.'

'Oh tosh,' Patricia replied. 'Nothing here can hurt us. We're perfectly safe.'

Betsy just gave her friend a sad look, then hugged her. 'I hope you're right,' she said. Betsy then nodded at the gentleman carrying her bags and walked outside with him. Patricia felt sad her friend was leaving, and even a little guilty that she wasn't going to follow to lend support.

But finding out what had happened only strengthened Patricia's resolve to stay and see how everything unfolded. It gave her hope that, after years of searching, she would see with her own eyes that there truly was something on the other side.

39

AFTER PUTTING her luggage into the boot, Ray helped the lady into the taxi she had called.

She looked shaken. He was worried for her, though he didn't believe the story she had told. Maybe that was harsh —perhaps she *thought* she was telling the truth, but he figured she was likely confused or misguided somehow. Perhaps it was a nightmare that just seemed real?

The guest dropped into the back seat of the car and swung her legs inside. Ray saw tears build in her eyes, and her hands were trembling in her lap. He leaned in a little closer.

'Are you okay?' he asked.

The woman didn't look at him. He knew it wasn't because of any snobbery, but because she was just struggling to hold it all together.

'I'm... not sure,' she eventually said. 'What I saw in there will stay with me forever.'

Ray considered his next words carefully. 'Well, you are leaving now, so you're safe.'

He didn't actually believe she was in any danger, otherwise he wouldn't have allowed his daughter to remain inside. But at the same time, Ray didn't want to see the woman even more upset and scared.

It was only after he'd finished speaking that she finally turned to look at him, eyes wet and sad. 'Look after my friend in there, will you, sir? I'm just worried about what will happen.'

'She'll be fine,' Ray replied with a friendly smile. 'I'll make sure of it.'

The lady managed a half-smile and nodded her thanks. Ray then closed the door and banged on the roof of the car, signalling to the driver that he could set off. As the vehicle made its way down the driveway, Ray took a breath. He was enjoying being outside, if only for a moment. The weekend had been hectic so far, and only one night had passed.

Still, he was edging ever closer to freedom.

40

CHLOE KNEW she had a few hours until her father came to check up on her. So she decided it was again time to sneak out of her room—which was feeling more and more like a prison—just as she had the previous day. Moving around the house when so much was going on was a huge amount of fun for her, and Chloe hoped today would bring the same amount of excitement.

She had taken no more than a few steps down the hallway when she heard many footsteps marching towards her. She heard a male voice, speaking like a teacher addressing a classroom. Chloe quickly ducked into her parents' room, but kept the door open enough to peek out. Mr. Blackwater passed by her view first, followed by what seemed like every guest staying in the hotel. It was a tour, Chloe quickly realised, and Mr. Blackwater was divulging some of the history of the house.

'...and it was in the eighteen-hundreds that Perron Manor became an orphanage,' he said as they all walked by. 'As is symptomatic of the house, there were a great many deaths here during that time, explained away as a cholera outbreak. However, there is a great deal of doubt about that, and much of the evidence I have found shows cholera was used merely as an excuse to disguise the truth.'

'And what was the truth?' one guest asked.

'That nobody could accurately explain the deaths. There were stories, spread by the children who lived here, about a strange, pale man who came in the night—one who brought with him a horrible stink...'

Eventually his voice faded out, and the words became unclear as the group moved farther away. Chloe took the opportunity to leave the room and slowly move in the opposite direction of the crowd. She was interested in the story Mr. Blackwater was telling, but she didn't want to get too close for fear of being caught. So instead, Chloe snuck downstairs... or tried to. However, she had to stop when she heard her mother and father talking in the reception area, hidden away from her view.

'Just don't forget what you promised,' she heard her dad say. 'Once this weekend is done...'

'I remember,' her mother said, but she didn't sound happy. In truth, she hadn't sounded happy for a *long* time. Chloe felt her heart drop a little. While it didn't seem like her parents were having a full-blown argument, they still weren't being friendly. They were speaking to each other like they were enemies, rather than being in love.

She didn't want her mother and father to be like that. It hurt her knowing their formerly happy life was now on a knife-edge.

'Good,' her dad said. 'I'm going up to check on Chloe to make sure she's okay. Feel free to go see her too, if you can carve out the time.'

'I can't, I'm too busy,' was the response.

Chloe clenched her teeth together. She knew her mum was working hard, and Chloe tried to be understanding, but to hear herself spoken about so dismissively caused her to feel sad. She started to silently cry, then quickly turned and ran back to her room.

41

With some time to spare as the lambs wandered the halls of his home, Vincent hid himself away. He heard them pass by outside. They were awed by the house and the stories Marcus was spinning.

Their awe would soon be replaced, however, with a terrible and horrific wonderment. It would be brought on by the very things they wanted to see, but things their minds would not be able to comprehend.

He had locked his door, and now sat on the floor of his small room, just in front of his wardrobe, the doors of which were pulled open. He didn't have many clothes inside—Vincent didn't have too much of anything anymore—but the clothes were not his focus. Instead, he leaned forward and brought his hands up to the back wall of the wardrobe, feeling the scratch marks on the wood. Things were building up inside him again. His head felt like it would explode.

While Vincent knew he couldn't stop what was going to happen, or even act on his own impulses anymore if the house did not wish it, there was still a rising feeling of guilt.

After all, he'd condemned his own sister, bringing her here even though he'd known what lay in store.

And not only that, he'd brought his niece into this hell as well.

The poor, innocent child.

He pushed the tips of his fingers into the wood, applying as much pressure as he could withstand, and slowly dragged them down the back of the wardrobe. The imperfections and undulations poked at his flesh, causing ripples of pain to shoot up into his hands. That was just the beginning. He repeated the motion, this time applying even more pressure and speed. The previously scratched surface of the wood cut in deeper, and he felt his nails catch and pull on splinters. More pain seared through his fingers and it made him feel sick. But it also brought with it a twisted kind of relief. The stinging fire made him feel human and fought back against the numbness that normally absorbed him.

Vincent's scratching increased in intensity, and he felt the raw nerve endings become exposed as skin was ripped away. The nail of his middle finger tore back savagely, causing him to emit a small yowl. The pain was so severe that he couldn't carry on with that hand anymore. He looked at the ruined nail, which was bent back at ninety degrees across its middle, exposing some of the bed underneath. Blood started to pool up from the torn skin.

Still, his other hand could take more, so Vincent continued to scratch at the wood, the pain reminding him that somewhere beneath it all, he was still human.

42

It had been a marvellous day, but Patricia was a little disappointed to have not witnessed anything personally.

There had been stories from several of the others, where some guests claimed to have felt a presence down in the creepy basement; others told of seeing a little girl sneaking around behind them during the tour that morning, but Patricia had no experiences of her own to treasure. The second-hand accounts were interesting, even thrilling, but they were not what she had come here for.

Night had rolled in, and the guests gathered down in the great hall again for their evening meal. Without Betsy, Patricia had to join with another party made up of three couples. They all knew each other, so Patricia felt like something of an outsider, which she supposed she was. It would have been so much easier, and far more fun, had Betsy just stayed.

Service for the food was a little slow, with only two gentlemen on duty: the one who had helped Betsy with her bags that morning, and a rather scruffy-looking man. Both brought out the food and drinks, though they struggled to keep up with the demand.

While the hotel itself was something to behold, it seemed the owner had scrimped on the service staff. Before long, Mr. Blackwater himself strode into the room. He was accompanied by the lady who had checked Patricia in, and both looked more than a little flushed. The woman had a certain glow about her as well—one that Patricia was all too familiar with, even if she had not felt its satisfaction for a number of years.

She knew *exactly* what the two of them had been up to.

The woman walked straight through to the kitchen, presumably to help with the food service, while Marcus Blackwater started doing the rounds and speaking to guests at each table. It didn't take long for him to reach hers.

'I trust everyone is having a fun evening,' Mr. Blackwater said to them all.

There were nods of confirmation, as well as an, 'Oh yes, we are indeed,' by one enthusiastic lady. Patricia's response was a little more antagonistic, however. 'To be honest, I was hoping to see a little more.'

Marcus raised his eyebrows. 'Really? From what I understand, there has been a lot happening already.'

'I've heard the same thing,' Patricia replied. 'My friend even saw something last night which scared her off completely. However, as yet, my experiences have been left wanting.'

'Your friend was the lady who left?'

Patricia nodded. 'That's right.'

'I hope she is okay.'

'I'm sure she will be,' Patricia confirmed. 'Just a little spooked.'

'Glad to hear it,' Marcus said. 'I'm sure your fortunes here will change.'

'I do hope so,' Patricia said. 'I have been looking forward to this for a long time, yet it seems everyone else here is having all the fun.'

Marcus laughed, then asked, 'Have you partaken in any of the events so far?'

Patricia nodded. 'I went on the tour, which was very interesting, and sat in on a séance.'

'Well, we have a lot more planned for tomorrow. A full day of it! So make sure you get involved.'

'I plan to,' Patricia said. 'Care to give me an idea of what to expect?'

'We will be running some Ouija board workshops, vigils, and we even have a few guests who believe they have psychic ability, so I'll be conducting more séances with them. I'm hoping those prove interesting. And, after midnight, we have a special surprise, one that I will not ruin just yet. Make sure you are well-rested and get plenty of beauty sleep tonight... not that someone as beautiful as yourself needs it, of course.'

Patricia smiled at the compliment. It was nice, though it hardly sounded genuine. Patricia got the distinct impression that what they were seeing from Mr. Blackwater was something of a practised facade.

Not that she cared, of course. She hadn't come here looking for new friends.

'You have me intrigued,' she said as their food finally arrived: roast potatoes, mixed vegetables, and thick cuts of beef drizzled in gravy. Not exactly high-class food.

'I'll leave you to your meal,' the host said. 'Enjoy the rest of your evening, and I'll look forward to seeing you again tomorrow.'

With that, he moved on to schmooze with the people on the next table over.

'Wonder what the surprise is?' one of the gentlemen in Patricia's new group mused.

She had no idea, but she was certainly looking forward to it. Tomorrow was their last full day, and it felt like time was running out for her.

43

WITH THE EVENING FINALLY OVER, and the time pushing two in the morning, Ray was looking forward to whatever sleep he would be able to get before rising early again to help prepare breakfast for the guests.

He felt physically wiped out and was close to running on empty. *Just one more day.*

He sat up in bed, nightlight still on, his tired body screaming for sleep. But Rita was still in the bathroom, readying herself for bed, and he wanted to speak to her for at least a little while before closing his eyes. Her waiting for him to drift off before coming to bed had been something of a habit recently, and he didn't want it to happen again tonight.

Though his brain told him she was not going to keep her promise, his heart held out hope that she might come through for him.

Eventually his wife appeared, and she walked to the bed without even looking at him. 'Sorry I took so long,' she said. 'Thought you'd be asleep.'

You mean you wanted *me to be asleep*, Ray thought. But he simply asked, 'How was your day?'

'Fine,' she replied. 'Busy.'

'You disappeared for a good portion of it,' Ray went on. 'Right around the same time Marcus did. Where did the two of you get to?'

Rita got into bed and began her nightly ritual of applying hand cream. 'Dealing with guests,' she said as if it were the most obvious thing in the world.

Ray didn't believe it, but he had no way of proving what he suspected. He also knew confronting his wife about it directly would only lead to another blazing row. One he didn't have the strength to have right now.

Too tired to fight for your marriage? Pathetic.

He couldn't help but wonder if there was anything left worth fighting for. At the moment he just felt crushed and defeated, unsure of anything. All he knew for sure was that he was leaving on Monday. That much was a certainty.

'Fair enough. Big day tomorrow, then,' he went on, trying to draw a little more conversation from her. 'Grande finalé of the weekend.'

'Uh-huh,' Rita agreed but offered no more.

'So... what have you got planned for everyone?'

She shrugged. 'Same as today, really. Rinse and repeat.' She lay down and turned her back on him.

'Has the event all been a success?' he asked, pressing further. 'Has it given you the closure you needed?'

'I suppose so,' was all Rita said, and then she reached out a hand and flicked off her nightlight. 'Goodnight.'

Ray couldn't believe it. The total dismissal of him left him furious. He actually shook with anger. Was she *trying* to enrage him? Was this just a tactic to push him further away?

Any fragile hope that their marriage was salvageable evaporated in that instant. Ray knew that they were done.

He could do nothing else other than switch off his own light and lie down as well, even though what he *wanted* to do was to yell and scream, to unload all of his frustrations and let her know what she was doing was unacceptable.

But he didn't.

He sat on his anger—stewed on it. If Rita wanted to stay here permanently with Marcus, then she could.

Fuck her.

44

IT WAS another early start for Chloe, and she couldn't help but yawn as her father got her dressed and brushed her hair.

'Only one more early morning,' he said from behind her as he wrapped an elastic hair-bobble around the ponytail he'd formed. 'Then, things will change. I promise.'

'I don't mind being up early,' Chloe said, but she had to stifle another yawn—which would have given away the small fib she'd just told. 'But I don't like being stuck in my room all day.'

'I know,' her dad replied. 'That isn't fair on you. In fact, there's a lot that isn't fair about living here, don't you think?'

Chloe cocked her head to the side. 'What do you mean?'

She felt his hands fall on her shoulders and slowly turn her around. He was kneeling down, so his eyes were level with her, and he looked sad. 'I don't think we've been very good parents since we moved into this house, kiddo.'

'Yes, you have,' she replied, even though what he'd said rang somewhat true, at least in part. But Chloe knew her parents had been really busy, and were working hard to keep them here.

Her father just shook his head. 'We haven't. Not really. And I want you to know that things are going to change.'

Chloe paused, then asked, 'How?'

He smiled. 'I'll explain later. Now come on, I'll get you some breakfast before the guests start to wake up.'

She followed her father down to the kitchen, more than a little confused at what he'd said. She wondered what exactly was going to change for them.

45

'But I want you *now*,' Rita said to Marcus, pulling him towards her, her mouth finding his. They were in his study on the top floor, hidden away from everyone else.

'I know,' he said, though he held her firmly at bay. 'But we must wait. The time isn't right.'

'The time's always right,' she told him, and he could only smile. *Poor little puppet.* Marcus wondered what it was like for her to be so controlled. Was there a part of her that existed somewhere inside, screaming to be let out while she was forced to act without her own agency? Or was she completely oblivious to it all, believing her actions were her own?

He gripped her shoulders tightly and looked into her eyes. 'Now, Rita, I need something from you.'

'Anything,' she said.

'After midnight tonight, forget whatever it is you're doing and come up here, to this room. I'll be waiting for you. Then... you can get what you want.'

'Okay,' she agreed readily. After a moment, she added, 'You know, I think my husband suspects something.'

Marcus chuckled. 'He'd be a fool not to. But it doesn't matter. Because, after tonight...'

'I can be with you forever?'

'Yes,' Marcus lied. 'Now, I need you to go and keep things moving downstairs. I will be along shortly, but I need to speak to Vincent up here first. Can you find him and send him up for me?'

'Okay,' she said, then brought one of his hands up to her mouth and slipped his index finger inside. He felt her hot, wet tongue massage the digit as she slowly sucked on it while holding firm eye contact.

Once finished, she flashed him a naughty smile. 'Until tonight, then,' she said and sauntered from the room.

Marcus shook his head and started to pace while awaiting Vincent's arrival. He had decided that it was this room, this study, where the ritual would take place. It wasn't the most comfortable space in the building, granted, but then again, Marcus had no real concern for comfort.

The book was already here, along with the translations. And it had enough space for what he needed.

However, things also needed to be put into place. A pentagram needed to be drawn—a task he would delegate to Vincent. That would be the last seal required, since the rest were already in place around the building. The host, too, was ready. It was obvious she was under the influence of the house now, of the power that flowed through the Devil's Door. Which was a relief, as she had initially proven quite resistant.

Everyone fell eventually, if you didn't have the intelligence and guile to keep those forces at bay.

Like Marcus did.

With the possession in place, Marcus had moved quickly to complete the trickiest step in the preparation phase. A step not guaranteed to work. Thankfully, however, he knew that it had.

He could smell it on her. The stink of life grew in her womb.

∽

'You wanted to see me?' Vincent asked as he entered the study. Marcus stood in the centre of the room, hands behind his back, standing tall and proud. But his physical appearance was at odds with the confident and powerful posture, and he seemed to look more and more exhausted and haggard with each passing day. Vincent wondered if Marcus was even aware of the changes.

'Yes, I need a little more from you, old friend,' Marcus said.

Vincent just nodded. 'Of course.'

'The ritual will take place here, in this room,' Marcus said, holding his arms out to either side. 'The room needs to be appropriately set. I have instructions here'—he pulled a sheet of folded paper from his breast pocket—'that need to be followed. A number of seals need to be placed to protect the room, just in case. If you would be so kind as to prepare everything?'

'Of course,' Vincent agreed, and walked over to the other man to take the paper from him. After unfolding it, Vincent read through what was written.

'This all needs to be ready before midnight,' Marcus said. 'Then things can begin. After tonight, you will be in charge of the house. But, you will not be alone here. I need you to watch *her*, Vincent. That is your role now.'

Marcus went on to divulge further instructions to

Vincent, and also outline *exactly* what would be needed of him.

'You can rely on me,' Vincent said.

Marcus smiled gratefully. 'I'm very glad to hear that. And I appreciate it, old boy. Now, I have lots to attend to, but feel free to make a start in here.'

Marcus then left Vincent alone in the room, and Vincent finally started to feel the gravity of what lay ahead. His fingers began to itch.

The day was finally upon them. Everything was set.

Now Vincent just had to navigate what remained of the pantomime downstairs. But only until midnight. However, that meant the rest of his day would no doubt consist of running after the snobbish guests, who were all keen to indulge in a world they knew nothing about. They were lambs to the slaughter, destined to fill the belly of the beast. To feed it.

To make it strong enough for what lay ahead.

Vincent had felt the energy in the house change recently. It was almost electrified, yet heavy and oppressive at the same time. He had also seen more and more of the spirits inside, all watching as the weekend's events unfolded.

They were waiting—held at bay for the time being while things continued to build.

Vincent still had more to do. He had his orders.

Ironically, Marcus' instructions were the least important ones on his list.

46

THE GREAT HALL was full and bustled with life as all the guests sat down for their final meal.

The food was much improved, which pleased Patricia. While the meal was not huge, she was of the opinion that less was more. The dish was smoked chicken and blue cheese salad, which in and of itself could have been seen as quite basic. However, it was served with a beetroot sorbet, and that was something Patricia had never tried before. By rights, the combination shouldn't have worked. As it was, every element sang in harmony, and the meal was absolutely delicious.

Patricia had gotten word that Marcus himself had prepared tonight's dinner, which she thought was a nice touch.

The mouth-watering food was welcome, considering it had been another disappointing day. There had been a flurry of stories regarding experiences and sightings from some of the other guests, but Patricia always seemed to be in the wrong place at the wrong time.

She just hoped the weekend wouldn't pass without giving her a story of her own to take away.

Even though Betsy had been terrified to the point of fleeing the hotel, at least she had answers; she had something she could cling to for whatever remained of her life. She'd found proof that there was more after death.

Patricia didn't have that. Not really. Because secondhand accounts just weren't enough.

What was more, she now felt like something of a third wheel among her fellow attendees. She'd tried to mingle and join other groups, but never felt quite welcome, and the earlier camaraderie she'd experienced at the event had eroded away. Sure, people were polite and welcoming, but it was always at arm's length.

With an empty plate before her, and guests on either side who talked to each other rather than her, Patricia concentrated on what remained of her glass of red wine. She started to people-watch, noticing a certain buzz in the room. A lot of the chatter centred on the upcoming secret surprise Marcus had promised.

Patricia brought the glass up to her lips and inhaled, taking in the aroma of the wine, one that was infused with fruits and slight hints of pepper. She swirled the liquid, ready to take another sip, but paused when her vision switched from the deep red liquid to the face of the glass itself. Or, more specifically, the reflection in it.

Someone was standing behind her—a woman, pale and naked, with saggy and deflated breasts on show.

Patricia spun her head around with a gasp. Those nearby looked over to her, confused at the minor outburst. The only thing Patricia saw behind her, however, was the other patrons, all talking, laughing, eating, and drinking. There was no naked woman. Patricia quickly looked back to her glass—back to the reflection—but the pale woman was no longer there. Patricia cast her eyes about the room, feeling an unnerving sensation creep up on her.

What had she just seen?

The reflection in her glass had been quite clear, even down to the wide, milky eyes staring at Patricia. Despite her unease, excitement ran through Patricia's veins. Was that her first genuine experience?

'Are you okay?' a lady seated next to her asked.

'I'm fine,' Patricia responded. 'I just... think I saw something.'

'What?' the woman asked, her eyes widening in obvious interest.

Patricia held up her glass. 'I swear I saw the reflection of a ghostly woman in this.'

'Fascinating,' the woman said and elbowed the gentleman who sat on the far side of her. 'Peter, this lady here has just had an experience.'

Patricia then regaled her new captive audience with what she had just seen, brief though it had been. *Perhaps this is the start of something*, she thought to herself, feeling her excitement grow.

The night wore on, the drinks flowed, and—spurred on by what she had seen—Patricia started to have fun, mingling with others more easily. Before she knew it, the hour was close to midnight.

People began to ask where Mr. Blackwater was, and when they could expect this special surprise to take place. Patricia was deep in conversation when a commotion over near the rear door drew her attention. Cries of fright rose up from the people gathered there, and all in the great hall turned to look.

Intrigued, Patricia cut her conversation short and made

her way over to the door. Two women—both in their later years—looked shaken, and one was close to tears. They were being comforted by those around them.

'What happened?' Patricia asked to anyone that cared to answer. A man next to her leaned in, and Patricia realised it was one of the hotel workers, the one she had seen running around tirelessly.

'They saw something outside the doors,' he said. 'A monk, apparently. He was just standing there, peering in from under his hood.'

Patricia could scarcely believe what she was hearing. 'Did anyone else see it?'

The man shrugged. 'I don't think so.'

It may just have been due to the excitement in the room, but Patricia felt a change in the energy around her—like something was building.

Soon after, people's attention turned again, this time to the other side of the room as Marcus Blackwater entered.

'Ladies and gentlemen,' he announced grandly. 'The time is almost here. I am going to ask you to remain patient for a little while longer. Feel free to look around the house again at your leisure. You may well see that, soon, things will become a lot different. And you will *all* find what you are looking for. I guarantee it.'

He then cast a look through the crowd, focusing on one person in particular—the hotel manager. Marcus gave her an almost imperceptible nod, which Patricia found intriguing.

Without fielding any further questions, the host turned and walked from the room, leaving everyone utterly confused. Excited chatter started to build, and the hotel manager also began to weave her way through the crowd to the exit. She was stopped by Ray, who took hold of her arm.

'Where are you going?' he asked her.

'I have things to attend to,' was the curt answer.

'Can you check on Chloe? Things seem... weird tonight.' There was an element of concern in his voice. The way the man spoke made it sound like Chloe was his child. Patricia then realised that these two were a couple, though clearly not on the best of terms.

She instantly felt pity for the man, knowing what she had seen between the woman and Marcus Blackwater.

'I don't have time,' she said, then pulled away from his grip and walked off.

He sighed.

'Are you okay, hun?' Patricia asked, laying a comforting hand onto one of his broad shoulders. The smile he gave was a weary one.

'I'll be fine,' he said. 'But if you'll excuse me for a moment, I need to go check on my daughter.'

He then walked from the room as well, leaving Patricia confused as to how any parent could let a little girl stay in a place as haunted as this one.

She checked her watch just in time to see the hand strike midnight.

47

Chloe was finding it difficult to sleep. She kept alternating between being too hot and having to kick off her covers, to being too cold and then having to duck back under them again.

She certainly felt tired enough to sleep, but lying with her eyes closed just made her feel restless, and the darkness in her bedroom seemed thick and heavy. That confused her, as Chloe knew darkness had no weight.

On top of that, even though she'd lived in the house for many months and had never once been scared by it, she was now on edge. She felt the need to constantly open her eyes to check the room around her.

Which was stupid, as there was nothing to be scared of.

However, no sooner had Chloe admonished herself for being silly did she hear the sound of the door handle to the room start to turn. She lifted her head off the pillow, breath held, and saw the door slowly start to push open. It swung into the room, and the light from the corridor streamed in, highlighting the silhouette of a person standing within the frame.

Fear surged through her and Chloe began to shake. However, she was soon made to feel even more stupid. Her eyes adjusted and she saw just *who* was standing there.

'Dad?' she asked, squinting.

'Sorry,' her father replied in a whisper. 'I didn't mean to wake you up. I just wanted to come and check on you.' He then moved into the room and closed the door behind him. 'Are you okay?' he asked.

Chloe quickly nodded, even though she didn't really feel okay. Not tonight... though she couldn't explain why. 'I'm fine.'

'Why are you awake so late?' he asked, sitting down on the side of the bed.

'I don't know. I just can't sleep.'

He smiled and tightened the sheets around her, which made her feel safer. 'Have you tried counting sheep?'

She just laughed. 'That doesn't work, Dad.'

'I know,' he replied. 'But people seem to suggest it a whole lot, so I figured they might be on to something.' He looked tired. Not in the same way Chloe's mother did—especially recently—but exhausted nonetheless.

'Where's Mum?' she asked, curious.

Her father's smile faltered. 'She's... a little busy at the moment, sweetie. So she asked me to check on you. You sure you're okay?'

Chloe gave him her bravest smile. 'I'm fine, Daddy. You don't need to worry about me.'

He tussled her hair. 'Kid, I'm *always* going to worry about you.' He then gave Chloe a hug and got back to his feet.

'It's gonna be a late night for me, I think,' he said. 'But you try and get some sleep.'

'Okay,' Chloe said, then added, 'night night.'

'Night night, kiddo. Sleep tight.'

He then left her alone, closing the door as he left. Chloe felt much more relaxed after his visit and was thankful for him dropping in. Her unease had disappeared completely, and it didn't take her long to finally drop off to sleep.

~

'What's that?' Rita asked, pointing to what had been drawn in chalk on the floor of the room.

'A pentagram,' Marcus replied as they both looked down at the symbol. Lighted candles were set at each point of the star; their gentle and flickering glow was the only light afforded to the room.

'Okay,' Rita went on. 'But why is it here?'

'Because we need it,' was his answer. Rita then felt his hands take hold of her shoulders, and the black suit-jacket she wore was pulled free. 'And it is where I'm going to fuck you. Isn't that what you want?'

Rita didn't much care for the symbol, but she certainly did want him inside of her. And she would do anything to make that happen again. Her husband and daughter were like distant memories. More accurately, they were inconveniences she wished were gone

Stop! What are you saying?

And there was that annoying and dissenting voice again from deep inside. One that just wouldn't go away. However, Rita had at least learned to ignore it.

She unbuttoned her trousers and wiggled out of them, then did the same with her blouse and stood before Marcus in just her underwear. He guided her into the centre of the pentagram.

Being surrounded by all of those old artefacts and books

and then being laid down on the bare floorboards was hardly romantic, but Rita didn't much care. If Marcus wanted to get a little kinky, then she was game. Though, her abandon was momentarily brought into question when he pulled free a small switchblade from his pocket. Marcus unfolded the knife, and the flickering light from the candles made the metallic blade glint.

'Don't worry,' he said, standing above her. 'I need you to trust me.'

Marcus then undressed as well, completely. She smiled at him and raised a leg, nudging his dick with her toe. 'Come to me,' she said.

His smile bordered on a sneer, and he lowered himself towards her. Rita held her breath as he brought the knife to her shoulder and hooked it beneath the material of her bra-strap. He cut the material free and then repeated the process with the other side. The feeling of the sharp, cold metal on Rita's skin brought with it a flash of pain, but also excitement.

He then moved it down to her underwear and slid the blade in between the skin of her hips and the black fabric. This time, as he cut her lingerie away, Rita felt a fiery sting slide across her hip. She looked down and saw that he had drawn blood, which rolled down her leg to the floor below.

'Marcus!' she snapped, and put a hand to the wound, but he moved it away.

'Don't!' he shot back. 'Let it flow.'

Her initial reaction was to push back and tell him no, but something settled over her. It quelled her anger and fight, smothering it out like a thick blanket over a flame. Marcus squeezed her flesh around her cut, making more blood flow. The look in his eyes was animalistic, like a lion waiting to feed.

Marcus then brought the knife up to his own hand and placed the metal edge against his palm. Rita winced as he harshly slit his own skin, then wriggled his fingers to encourage the flow. The blood that poured free was much more generous than from her own cut, and Marcus made sure the small patch of red liquid that Rita had given up was completely covered by his own.

'That's it,' he said with an enthused grin. 'Perfect.' He then threw the knife away.

'Now what?' Rita asked, confused, but still willing.

He smiled, then tilted up his head before speaking loudly... though not to her. It was like he was issuing a command to the room itself. Or, rather, the house. The words Marcus spoke were lost on Rita. They were a language she wasn't familiar with.

'What was that?' she asked when he was done.

'An incantation,' was his reply.

Rita wasn't sure what to do with the information, but he then crawled on top of her. She felt his hardness press against her.

'Now,' he said, 'we fuck.'

Marcus was all over her, kissing and grabbing at Rita, devouring her. She arched her back and pushed up her hips, wanting him.

Rita let out a gasp of slight pain as he entered her; then she gave herself over to the ecstasy that was building.

48

PATRICIA WAS mid-conversation with one of the ladies who had seen the 'monk' outside when she heard it—an incredible, all-encompassing noise that shook the very walls around them.

Shrieks of surprise rose up around her, even from Patricia herself. There were lingering vibrations from the sudden and terrible sound, but they slowly faded away.

The great hall was not as full as it had been, with many of the guests having taken Mr. Blackwater's advice to again explore the house. However, those that were still present began to panic.

'What the hell was that?' one man asked.

Patricia had no idea. Given the magnitude of the sound, she could only assume that it was perhaps a brief tremor in the earth, not that she'd ever experienced anything like that before, of course. She had to wonder if everyone else in the house had heard it as well. *Surely they must have.*

Another equally loud boom thundered around them all. Patricia felt her heartrate spike. It wasn't an earthquake, and it sounded more like something was striking against their very reality, the horrible booms like the impact of an immense, invisible object.

After fading out to silence again, the noise came back with a third crashing impact. The screams of the terrified guests echoed again, and Patricia was able to hear them from other areas of the house as well.

She expected another boom to hit and was braced for it... but it never came. There was only the whimpering and fearful sobs from the guests, with many asking, 'What *was* that?'

The relative quiet continued, and it was only after a few minutes without any further incident that Patricia felt confident the sounds—whatever they had been—were over.

'Was that something to do with Marcus?' one guest asked. 'Was *that* part of his bloody surprise?' Patricia noticed the man who had asked the question was talking to Ray, who was back in the room. She could tell from the man's shocked expression that he was just as in the dark as the rest of them.

It was then that a feeling of intense cold rolled through the room. Patricia was wearing a long, black evening gown, which was strapless, and her hair was pinned up so that her shoulders were exposed. Her skin tingled as the breeze flowed past her. She then began to notice plumes of misty clouds—people's breath as they exhaled. Her own breath hung before her, giving an indication of the sudden drop in temperature. She hugged herself, trying to keep in some of her own body's warmth.

'Something's wrong here,' she said, stating the obvious. Everyone else was deathly quiet, just waiting for something to happen. Patricia's eyes wandered around the room and she held her breath. Her focus then stopped on a large mirror mounted on one of the walls, and in it she could see the reflection of the guests, all with terrified expressions etched on their faces.

However, there were others in the reflection as well. People who stood between the guests—ones Patricia had not seen with her own eyes when scanning the great hall.

These strangers were all deathly pale and stood stock-still. And they seemingly went unnoticed by everyone else. In the time it took Patricia to scream, she had already taken in numerous horrible details about the things she instantly knew to be spirits.

The dead in the reflection were a mix of men, women, and children. Their clothing was mostly from a past era, and were all dirty and tatty. Some were either completely naked or near-naked. All of their forms, however, were either mutilated or twisted in some way: withered arms, missing limbs, torn flesh, chests pulled open from neck to navel, and distorted and demonic faces that were frozen with blank, stony expressions.

When Patricia's scream actually tore free, those blank expressions suddenly changed to something much more insidious. It was at this point the other guests in the room turned in fright to see what had caused Patricia to cry out. It didn't take long for their focus to fall on the mirror as well.

Everyone in the room began to shriek in fright. Patricia turned away from the reflection, to see if those horrible things were actually standing between them all outside of the mirror as well.

But she couldn't see them. Only the other frightened guests.

However, when Patricia locked eyes with one particular gentleman, her heart froze. She suddenly wanted to shout a warning about the horrible thing that stood behind him: a rake-thin woman dressed in what looked to be old-style maid clothing. The left side of her head was completely crushed in, now little more than a concave mass of pulped black and purple flesh.

Her hand rose up and grabbed the man's neck from behind. He gasped in shock, and his eyes went wide. Patricia then noticed there were others around the group as well, just as she had seen in the mirror.

Patricia then looked back to the man, just in time to see his throat get ripped out completely.

49

CHLOE DIDN'T KNOW what to do. She was standing in her room, hands at her chest, tucked just beneath her chin.

Something was happening outside—through the whole house, in fact—but she had no idea what. A loud noise that she didn't understand had woken her. It was an almighty crash that seemed to come from all around her. Then, there was another, and another, and now people were screaming.

She heard running footsteps beyond the door to her room, and shouting, and there were other noises she couldn't place.

It sounded like chaos.

But Chloe wasn't sure if she should stay put in her room, or go outside and see what was happening. Staying inside felt like the safer, more sensible option, but what if there was a fire and she needed to get out? Chloe knew her mum or dad would likely come for her, but there was also a chance something had happened to them. Perhaps they were trapped or hurt... or worse.

She bit her lip and eventually decided to at least open

her door and look out into the hall. At least then she might have a better idea of what was going on.

So, fighting through considerable apprehensions, she moved forward and slowly opened the door. While the short corridor outside was empty, Chloe could see people running back and forth through the adjoining hallway, all of them yelling in confusion.

She could tell people were scared, and the thought of staying in her room when something potentially dangerous was happening seemed stupid. So, she stepped out and began to walk down to the adjoining corridor. People sprinted past her view every few seconds. The sounds around her were constant and sometimes... bizarre. The screams, shouting, and crying, though worrying, were relatively normal in comparison. It was the other noises that she had picked up on: moaning, crashing, and... growling, that confused and terrified Chloe.

Just as she reached the intersection point, she noticed that no one was running past anymore. Though she could still hear pounding footsteps and shrieking, the way ahead now seemed clear, at least for the moment. Did that mean everyone had already fled the area?

Sensing she should get out of there as well, Chloe broke into a jog, suddenly desperate to find her parents.

Just as she turned the corner ahead, Chloe looked up, and her eyes went wide. She braced for the unavoidable collision as a large man in a suit barrelled towards her, running desperately and looking back over his shoulder. Even if he had seen Chloe, there was simply no time to stop.

She quickly closed her eyes, an instinctive reaction, and started to bring her hand up. But it was all in vain.

The impact from the much larger person took Chloe's breath away, and she felt herself thrown back with savage force. A searing pain exploded in the back of her head. Chloe had just enough awareness to realise she had struck a corner point of the wall behind her.

She then felt herself drop heavily to the floor like a rag doll, and was unable to move her arms or legs during the quick drop. The dizziness and pain she felt was overwhelming, and Chloe quickly fell into unconsciousness.

50

Marcus was lost in his desires. He thrust hard against Rita, who lay submissively below him with her legs splayed.

But, he had to keep his composure, at least to some extent. The indulgence needed to keep going. It was, after all, the anchor that would allow *Impius Sanguis* to continue.

Sex was a sacred thing, despite what some people believed. It was the very act that created life. Indeed, with Rita, it already had.

This time, however, the sex was a subversion of that. It was an affront to God, and a staining of what grew within the host. Their blood had combined with the unholy seal below them, and now that he was inside of her, the ritual was in full flow. Above Rita's moans of pleasure, Marcus could hear cries of pain and agony echo from the lower floors of the house.

It was working.

Everything had built to this. The steady stream of bodies to the house had slowly built its power, while the protective symbols he'd placed had held it back. Now... everything was unleashed. Tonight, it was time for the house to break free from its shackles and gorge itself.

That was why he needed to hold out.

Marcus' own release would signal the beginning of the end, and he wanted the house to draw as much as it could before that happened.

51

IT WAS CHAOS.

Ray was rooted in place, unable to comprehend or believe what was happening all around him in the great hall.

This isn't possible.

How could he accept what his eyes were showing him? There were strange people who had seemingly appeared from nowhere in the room with them. He knew those deformed and twisted 'others' were not human.

Ray had never believed in the things Marcus and Vincent had talked about—things that supposedly dwelled within the dark corners of the house. It was just a fantasy, believed by people who hadn't accepted what death really was.

But, as it turned out, it was Ray who had been naïve. The evidence was there for him to see, killing the guests and ripping them apart.

One poor attendee had his head torn clean off while he screamed, the wails getting higher before being cut short as his spinal cord became visible. The bone glistened with blood as it slipped out from the meat of his torn neck.

Another lady was gutted by two pale children, one of whom only had black pits for eyes, the skin around the sockets torn and ruined.

Ray also saw a man fighting against a horde of undead spirits. The swarm around him pushed the man closer to one of the stone walls, where Ray noticed the consistency of the wall begin to change—the wallpaper warped and morphed, turning into something else entirely.

Becoming more like... skin.

Then, something emerged from the fleshy substance, ripping itself free like a demonic child fighting from a womb.

The creature from the wall was different from the other ghosts in the room, however. Its skin was obsidian, and its wild eyes were a fiery yellow with vertical black slits for pupils. Long arms grabbed the man, and he was pulled back inside the fleshy expanse of the wall. The demon—if that's what it was—completely disappeared along with him, fully claiming its prey. However, some of the unfortunate soul's facial features remained on the stone surface: wide eyes and gaping mouth merging with the skin of the wall. A night-marish prison, and one that Ray assumed would be for eternity.

That last horrible vision was enough to snap Ray back to life. As terrifying as all this was, Ray knew he had to act quickly.

Chloe.

The thought of anything like that happening to her filled him with dread the likes of which he'd never known before. He couldn't let his little girl succumb to this madness.

Ray didn't have time to try and make sense of what was going on. He just had to deal with what was before him and get to his daughter. His thoughts also ran to his wife as well, but Ray had no idea where she even was.

He felt an approaching cold behind him, one that grew stronger and more biting with each passing moment. He turned to see a tall man with no jaw shambling towards him, then reach out with pale arms and black fingernails.

Ray quickly broke into a sprint, fleeing from the approaching ghoul and weaving through the carnage in the great hall. His heart pounded in his chest, but the spike of adrenaline resulted in a kind of hyper-focus; every detail seemed to register, and Ray was able to duck and weave past clawing and reaching hands. Some were from the demonic entities, but others belonged to pleading guests who were being slaughtered.

Just as he was about to make it to the door, someone—or something—did manage to grab him, taking fistfuls of his jacket in a desperate grip. Ray quickly turned, but was thankful to see it was one of the guests—a lady dressed in a black, strapless gown. She appeared to be in her sixties, and her eyes were wide with panic as she clung to him.

'Help me!' she pleaded.

While Ray was desperate to get to Chloe, he wasn't about to shrug off someone who so dearly needed his help. So, he put an arm around her and ushered the woman along with him. They broke through from the great hall and into the adjoining corridor, where they saw bodies lying on the floor. But at least there didn't appear to be any spirits barring the way, though Ray could still hear the hellish noises from the hall behind them.

'We need to get out of here,' the lady said as they set off running again. Ray slipped on something squishy underfoot. He managed to keep his footing, but he looked down to see something red and mushy on the ground. Ray pushed on, not wanting to know what he had been standing on.

'When we get to the entrance lobby,' he said, 'I want you to keep going out through the main door. Don't stop running.'

'And what about you?' she asked.

Ray kept his eyes dead ahead, teeth gritted together in determination. 'I need to get my daughter.'

52

PATRICIA STRUGGLED FOR BREATH, running as fast as she had in a long time, which was made doubly hard since she was in heels. The exertion sapped her strength, but so too did the fear that overwhelmed her and pressed on her chest like a physical weight. That, combined with the running, made breathing difficult.

She had to keep going. Otherwise, she would wind up like those other poor guests back in the great hall. One *worse* than death.

But even as the intense panic threatened Patricia's sanity, the irony of finally seeing what she'd always wanted to was not lost on her.

Betsy had been right.

She should have left with her friend when given the chance.

The man that was guiding Patricia through the corridors ushered them both out into the entrance lobby. Body parts were scattered across the floor in rapidly expanding pools of blood. Thankfully, whatever massacre had taken place here now seemed to be over.

Patricia was turned and faced her guide, who stopped short.

'The door is there,' he said, pointing over to the exit. 'You just need to run through. Keep going to the road at the end of the driveway and don't look back.'

Patricia nodded, trying desperately to hold herself together for a little while longer.

Just long enough to escape.

'Good luck finding your little girl,' she told him, sucking in deep breaths. 'Go save her, and then get her the hell out of here.'

He gave half a smile, then turned and ran, making his way up the stairs. Patricia looked over to the door, towards her salvation, and drew every ounce of strength she had.

Just a little bit farther.

She ran. It was only a short distance to the exit, and she made it without incident. Judging by the wails and screams that sounded from other areas of the house, the entities seemed to be busy elsewhere. Patricia then pulled open the front door... and stopped dead.

On the porch outside a man was pulling himself across the stone ground. His bottom half was gone, and below his waist were only long, glistening red tendrils—intestines and guts that slithered behind.

One of his arms was twisted and deformed, a withered imitation of a limb. His head was a mess of cuts and lacerations, and there were bulging growths on one side. The skin of one of them was pulled down over one eye and connected to his cheek.

The withered hand reached out to Patricia, who shrieked in absolute terror. She took a step back, but there was something else blocking the way.

Arms suddenly wrapped around her. The skin was black

and scaly, and the fingers of both were long and had talon-like ends. A sudden and overpowering sulphuric smell assaulted Patricia. She started to scream. The touch of the thing that held her burned.

Patricia was hoisted up into the air like a doll, then dragged backwards. She kicked her feet frantically in the air, causing her shoes to fall free, but it was futile. Whatever had her in its grasp was simply too strong. She turned her head and managed to see a little of the nightmare pulling her backwards.

It was a frightful creature, with a face that was a mix of human and inhuman features, all melded together like they had been made from wax that had started to melt. A mass of yellow eyes, all different sizes, lined the face and head. Behind the monster, Patricia saw the wall she was being moved towards had changed—it was now an expanse of pulsating skin, and her mind ran back to the man in the great hall who had been pulled into a similar flesh wall.

Patricia wailed, and she kicked against the shins of the entity, but succeeded only in cutting the thick flesh of her heel on the hard, jagged skin. Something cold and wet found her ear. A long, thin tongue that pushed inwards, secreting a viscous liquid deep into her inner ear.

With tears in her eyes, Patricia felt herself dragged inside the enveloping flesh of the wall. It was thick and warm and moulded around her form. The demon that held her suddenly released its grip, though she had no idea where it disappeared to. However, she was not able to turn her head to see, or even move her body at all. The only thing she could do was to roll her eyes and silently scream.

53

VINCENT SAT on his bed with his hands over his head, pulling at his hair. He was desperate to block out the screaming outside.

He was also terrified of what could come into his room, either through the door... or by other means.

While the house had a purpose for him, Vincent knew it was difficult to control the poisoned and feral souls trapped within, even for something as powerful as Perron Manor. When not watched and controlled, those wild entities would always try to indulge in depraved acts against the living. Vincent could only hope the house could keep hold long enough for it to finish feeding.

A sudden rattling on his door caused him to jump.

'Help! Help me!'

'Go away!' Vincent shouted back. Tears were already streaming down his face, and his nose ran freely, with long strands of mucus dripping into his lap.

'Please! It's coming!' the person outside yelled.

The pounding on the door suddenly changed, becoming louder yet slower in frequency. He knew that whoever was outside was now kicking at the door, desperate to get in. Vincent was terrified that the person would also draw unwanted attention if they kept going like that. He needed to put a stop to it.

He got up, fists clenched, and strode to the door. 'I said fuck off!' Vincent then swung the door open, ready to confront the guest, but was met only by a look of surprise from a tall, rotund man in a suit. A rotted hand rested on top of the guest's bald head, and a young woman with long, stringy hair stepped from behind him. She wore a smile that, thanks to serrations at either side of her mouth, ran all the way up to her ears. She was naked, and her stomach had been cut open, with black, rope-like intestines bubbling free from the wound.

'Help,' the terrified man whispered. The entity behind him then thrust him forward, forcing him into the room. The screaming man crashed into Vincent and knocked him aside before falling to the floor. The manic spirit, screaming like a banshee, was quickly atop him. Vincent shrieked in terror as the ghoul's hand drew back its jagged and sharp nails. The hand then thrusted down. There was a crack, and the hand forced its way *through* skin and skull, destroying the back of the man's head.

Vincent then acted on impulse as his fight or flight instinct kicked in, very clearly favouring running for his life. He pushed himself to his feet once again and sprinted from the room, barging past anyone who got in his way.

The exit... I need to get to the exit.

But as he ran, Vincent was forced to stop when he spotted something up ahead: a small figure that lay in a crumpled heap on the floor.

Chloe.

The same demon that had first coerced Vincent into following its orders stood above her, looking down.

Pazuzu.

'Chloe!'

Vincent looked farther ahead to see who had called out, and saw Ray sprinting down the corridor towards them.

54

RAY COULD SCARCELY BELIEVE what he was seeing. The madness from the great hall was terrifying enough, but he now experienced a whole new level of fear upon seeing that... *monster*... standing over his daughter.

He had no idea if Chloe was even alive. She was just a small, crumpled form on the floor, her hair covering her face.

The demon that stood close to her had black skin, and its knees were bent inward like the legs of a beast. Its stomach was sunken, pulled in tightly beneath a serrated, overhanging ribcage. The arms were disproportionately long, and its mouth was a mass of jagged, spindly teeth with no lips to cover them, resembling the mouth of a piranha pulled into a wide and hideous grin. And the creature's eyes were fleshy orbs of fiery yellow protruding out from the sockets. The skin of its face was like dark, melted wax.

The terrifying monster was not looking down at Chloe, however, but at Ray.

'Leave her alone!' he screamed.

There was another figure beyond the grinning night-mare as well. It was also stationary, but very much human.

Vincent.

The demon started to lean down and reach its taloned hands out towards Chloe's fragile form. Ray didn't even think, but simply ran forward towards it, desperate to protect his child. Just as he got close, the obsidian demon swung a hand faster than Ray thought possible. The impact across his face was so sudden and powerful that his head snapped back and he was physically thrown through the air, crashing down to the floor several feet from where he'd stood.

Ray's face burned and the back of his neck throbbed with pain. His vision spun. It was a struggle for him to lift his head and look back at the creature.

It now stood in front of Chloe, putting itself between Ray and his daughter as if in challenge.

Ray had to stop that thing from harming his daugh-ter, even if it meant his own death. He got slowly back to his feet. He was unsteady and had to use the wall beside him for support. While sacrificing his own life to help Chloe was a given, what terrified him was the knowledge that it might not be enough. If he was dead, then the demon would just move on to her anyway. Unless...

'Vincent!' he shouted. 'Help! Please!'

However, his brother-in-law just looked scared and dumbfounded, and did not move at all. Ray couldn't blame him for freezing up, given the nightmarish situation they were all in, but this was his daughter at stake.

Vincent's own niece.

They had only really known the man for ten months, but surely family meant *something* to him?

The demonic entity turned its head towards Vincent, who shrank away under its gaze and took a few steps back.

'Leave... leave her alone.'

In response, the monster uttered a kind of chattering noise that, to Ray, sounded something like a chuckle. The demon clearly didn't see Vincent as any kind of threat. And why should it?

It took a step towards the man, and Vincent again backed up in kind. However, Ray was beginning to get his bearings again, and his vision had cleared. His head still throbbed, but Ray was at least now steady on his feet.

'Get away from me!' Vincent cried out.

In a flash, however, the monster was on him, moving with a speed that was almost impossible to comprehend. It suddenly had him in its grasp, and the long claws of one hand wrapped around his throat. Vincent wheezed, struggling for air, and his eyes went wide.

In that moment, Ray saw an opportunity. He quickly sprinted over to Chloe and scooped her up, holding his daughter in both arms. Though he was still a little wobbly, her light weight was easy to bear. She was breathing, and the relief he felt at her not being dead was overwhelming.

He knew he couldn't just leave Vincent. Not after the man had distracted the demon and allowed Ray to collect his daughter. But... what could he possibly do?

As it turned out, Ray didn't need to do anything.

The monster lifted Vincent from the floor, and his legs kicked wildly beneath him. Then, just as the demon's mouth opened and those sharp, spindly teeth moved closer to Vincent's terrified face, there was another thundering noise that boomed all around them. It was forceful enough that the vibrations ran through the floor beneath them. Ray even felt them run up his legs and into his gut.

There was another crashing sound, and the very walls around them shook. The demon, in turn, looked around in what Ray assumed was fright. The inhuman features actually appeared... scared.

Is it afraid of the house?

The creature looked like it was listening, though Ray had no idea to what. Another booming sound rang out and the walls shook again. The demon screeched, and dropped Vincent to the floor. The man began coughing and spluttering, rubbing at his neck as he sucked in desperate breaths.

He scuttled away while the ground beneath the demon's taloned feet started to discolour. It then changed, just like Ray had seen the walls downstairs change before...

The demonic entity wailed, but inhuman arms slithered free of the leathery skin that was the floor. They grabbed the shrieking demon. It fought against the monstrous arms, which were lined with bubbling black and red flesh, but the demon was overpowered. It was then dragged down into the ground beneath it. After letting out a final, hideous scream, the demon was pulled fully into the floor, the flesh swallowing it whole.

Ray's mind spun, unable to comprehend what had just happened. He, Chloe, and Vincent had just been saved. It was almost like the house itself had pulled the demon away from them, bringing a wild dog to heel.

Ray sprinted over to Vincent, holding Chloe tightly to him. He then helped his brother-in-law up.

'We need to go,' he urged. Vincent coughed and nodded.

Then they ran, all the way back to the entrance lobby. As they moved, it occurred to Ray that the screams around the house were dying out.

Either whatever was happening was drawing to a close, or there weren't many left alive to scream.

55

RITA CLAWED AT MARCUS' back, digging her nails into his skin. She bit his lip as they kissed, and their tongues thrust against each other in a wild dance.

She was getting close.

'Keep going,' she said, panting. Their sweat mingled and intertwined just like their bodies.

The whole room was cold, but that just added to the sensations, and it helped give everything a sharpness. Her skin felt like it was on fire.

Through blurred vision, Rita looked up over Marcus' thrusting shoulder, and noticed shadows move about, seeing the forms of people floating close to her and looking down.

Watching.

She blinked the sweat away so that her vision cleared. What she saw there should have terrified her. But it didn't.

There *was* an audience of curious and pale faces. Milky eyes. Decayed flesh.

This is madness! Run!

Rita shook her head, trying to silence the voice that threatened to ruin everything for her.

'Keep going,' she repeated, pulling Marcus down into her. 'Harder!'

56

Vincent ran along behind Ray, who carried Chloe while they navigated the stairs. They then fled out through the entrance door and into the night, their escape unhindered.

It was cold out, and Chloe—still unmoving—was only in a t-shirt and pyjama bottoms.

However, the more they ran, the more Vincent's stomach churned, and a fiery pain started to prickle over his skin. It became worse the farther away he got from the house.

In addition, his throat still burned from the icy-cold grip of the demon. Breathing was difficult, made worse by a panic that still ebbed inside of him; it had spiked earlier when Pazuzu had grabbed his throat.

Vincent had thought he was going to die back there at the hands of that vile, demonic entity—one that had been a constant tormentor to him in Perron Manor. However, the house had stopped it, and seen fit to spare Vincent's life.

That meant it still had a purpose for him.

He had an idea what that might be, but second-guessing the house was futile.

It seemed to perceive things in a different way, one he

wasn't privy to. The plan to have Rita fall pregnant could not be a certainty, given the complications of conceiving.

Yet it had all fallen into place.

And the *Ianua Diaboli* had found its way to the house when the Blackwaters had taken ownership.

Marcus had met Vincent, who in turn had brought his sister to the house. She had then fallen pregnant exactly when she had needed to.

The right people at the right place at the right time, all bringing everything together. Just how far did the hellish tendrils from the house stretch? And how far into the future could it see in order to move its pawns on the chessboard as needed?

Was the future therefore set in stone, or could things be changed?

'Hold her,' Ray said after they stopped midway down the drive. He thrust Chloe into Vincent's arms and slipped off his jacket.

Ray then wrapped it around his daughter to give her some extra warmth before taking her back and checking her over. Vincent could see that the girl was breathing, so he hoped she was just unconscious with no serious injuries.

'Is she okay?' he asked.

'I hope so,' Ray replied. Vincent could hear the worry and anxiety in the man's voice. Ray then gently shook Chloe and started to stroke her hair as he cradled her to him. 'Wake up, kiddo,' he whispered.

Chloe remained unresponsive, and Vincent had a horrible feeling that she may be more hurt than he first thought. However, after a little more prompting from Ray, the young girl's eyes slowly flickered open.

'Daddy?' she asked, looking up at her father, clearly confused.

'It's okay, sweetie,' he said, hugging her tightly. Chloe winced and brought a hand up to the back of her head. 'Are you okay?' Ray asked.

'My head hurts,' she groaned. 'What happened?'

'You just had a little tumble, that's all,' he said. 'But you're fine.' Ray then turned to Vincent. 'Rita is still inside,' he whispered.

Vincent nodded. Surely she would still be safe? The house wanted her. *Needed* her. And though it was clear the spirits and demons inside could act on their own if left unchecked, Vincent didn't doubt that Rita would be protected.

Wouldn't she?

'I have to go back,' Ray added.

Better you than me, Vincent thought, knowing the house had no use for him, only his wife. While Vincent didn't want his sister to die, he himself didn't have the strength or bravery to go back inside to get her.

Not yet. Though when things calmed down, Vincent knew he'd be spending the rest of his life in that house. He couldn't get away. He'd fled this far, but the very thought of going any farther filled him with nausea.

Perron Manor still owned him.

Back inside, Pazuzu had clearly wanted Chloe, but the house had allowed Vincent enough freedom to save her. Maybe it was because she was inconsequential, or perhaps there was another reason. Regardless, it had protected him and saved his life. So there was no way it would let him leave.

'I'll take Chloe,' Vincent said, holding out his arms. Ray looked down at his daughter, then over to Vincent. Vincent could see deliberation on his brother-in-law's face. Eventually, Ray relented and handed Chloe over.

'What's happening?' Chloe groggily asked.

'Nothing,' Ray said as Vincent took hold of her. 'You just need to wait out here with Uncle Vincent for a little while, okay?' I'm just going to get your mother.' Ray then ran a loving hand over her hair and gently kissed her on the forehead. 'I'll be as quick as I can.' Ray then looked to Vincent. 'Keep her safe,' he instructed.

Vincent nodded. 'I will.'

Ray gave one last look to his daughter, then turned and ran back towards the house.

57

HE COULD HOLD out no longer; the building pleasure was just too great.

Marcus shuddered and let out an involuntary cry as he spilt his orgasm inside of the host. Finally, he flopped forward on top of her—completely spent and gasping for breath.

He had seen the 'others' gather in the room during the act, which had confused him. They shouldn't have been nearby, given Vincent had put the protective seals in place.

Don't worry about it. Your ascension is now.

With a satisfied smile, Marcus rocked back onto his heels and pulled himself free of Rita.

The cries of pain around the hotel had long stopped, so he hoped the house had had its fill. If so, some of the house's power should have been infused into Marcus during the Ritual, which in turn would have spread into the host. The life growing inside of her would now be tainted. More than that, it would be *clavis*—the key. And it would usher in something terrible to the world.

But the power Marcus had been blessed with still

lingered, and it should stay with him long enough to cross over. He would gain eternal life, but at the same time keep his own free will. He would not be an eternal puppet like the other souls in the house, but an actual force in the dark and mirrored reality, possessing the ability to cross over at will.

Rita pushed herself up to her elbows. 'That was great,' she said. Her cheeks were flushed, and her smile was one of satisfaction.

But Marcus didn't care. She was just a means to an end. The house had gotten what it wanted—she would stay here now and birth its child.

And Marcus would get what he wanted as well.

After starting down the path his grandfather had been too fearful to tread, he was going to become more than a man. He would stand alongside demonic forces of the underworld.

Excitement filled him.

Rita then looked about at the silent entities watching them, all eerily motionless. However, she did not seem frightened, which was yet more evidence that the house still had its hold on her.

'What now?' she asked.

Marcus just smiled and pushed her from the pentagram. Rita backed up out of the symbol with a look of confusion on her face.

'Now' he began, 'I take the final step.' Marcus looked around for the knife he had used earlier. It surprised him that one of the gathered spirits—a small child with no eyes —stepped forward and held the blade out, offering it to Marcus.

He took it.

'Thank you, young one.'

The expression of the boy was as empty as his eye sockets.

Marcus then brought the knife up to his neck, ready to draw the edge over his throat. And he would do so under his own free will. Which was critical.

The metal sank into his skin, drawing blood. Rita gasped as Marcus felt the warm liquid dribble down to his chest. Pain spread like liquid fire and he yanked the blade horizontally.

Flicking his eyes down, Marcus saw other hands on the handle as well, covering his own. The child that had given him the knife was now standing behind him, and had reached around to take hold of the weapon. He felt the child's coldness and smelled its stench.

Why was the spirit helping him?

No matter, there was no reason to stop now. Marcus pulled harder and screamed in agony as he was forced to saw and slice at the tendons and thyroid cartilage. But he knew pain was only temporary.

The prior trickle of warm blood was now a stream, and it spilled from the gaping wound in his neck, wetting and warming his chest completely. He coughed, spraying the crimson liquid to the ground beneath him. His body instinctively fought and struggled for air, and he heard wheezing, gurgling sounds come from his open throat.

Marcus fell as the strength to hold his body up vanished. He slumped to the floor, and the dead in the room gathered around him.

Come see me die, he thought to himself. *I will soon rise up and control you all.*

Something was wrong. The souls that watched him die all started to smile.

It was only then that Marcus realised the truth. For his

plan to succeed, he needed to carry out the ritual under his own agency, and not under the possession of the house.

Now, however, it became immediately clear that was *not* the case. He had no doubt Perron Manor had allowed him to realise that in his final moments, blowing away the veil of lies.

He had been a puppet of the house all along. And would continue so in eternal death.

58

RAY WAS WALKING through the remnants of a massacre. Bodies of the dead littered the ground, and the floor was damp with blood.

But it was quiet. Horribly quiet. Ray's sloshing footsteps were the only thing to break the intense silence.

He was terrified—more scared than he could ever remember being. The things he'd witnessed only minutes before had been almost impossible to believe, yet he had seen them for himself. Having one's worldview completely shattered like that, on top of the horrific violence itself, was not something he was prepared to handle.

And to top it all off, there was a worry growing in the pit of his gut about Rita.

If any of the people inside had survived what happened, then surely they would have fled outside, just as Ray had.

To him, that meant no one else had survived.

Ray tried to push the thought from his mind, because he wouldn't stop searching until he either found her or found proof she was dead.

But it was hard not to think that he'd lost her, and keeping a lid on that realisation was difficult.

He carefully navigated the ground floor as quietly as possible, checking every room. Though the unexplainable activity had apparently now ceased, Ray was still on edge, certain that *something* still remained here. He knew it could simply be waiting to pounce.

However, the longer he searched without incident, the more he began to feel safer... relatively speaking. Eventually, he began to call out for his wife.

'Rita!'

But he got no response, and that made his worry grow. Surely there was no reason not to reply.

If the worst had happened, then Chloe would be without a mother, and he would have lost the only woman he'd ever loved. Their recent troubles suddenly seemed irrelevant, and an enormous surge of guilt came over him. He knew he should have done more to fix things between them before...

Ray began to quicken the pace and screamed her name again.

'Rita!'

She might still be here. She can't be dead. Can't be.

Cold logic was replaced with desperation, and Ray sprinted upstairs, searching that floor as well.

'Rita!'

Don't be dead. Don't be dead.

It had occurred to him that his wife could well be among the mushy, torn-up remains he'd already seen, or that she had been sucked into the house itself. If that was the case, he might not be able to find any physical proof of her death.

'Rita!'

With only one more storey to search, he turned the

corner to the stairs—and immediately jumped. There was a figure standing at the top.

Ray braced himself, ready for the madness to start all over again.

But when the individual didn't leap down and attack him, and Ray's initial shock wore off, he realised just who it was that stood at the head of the stairs.

'Rita!'

She was alive.

'Ray?' she asked softly, sounding confused. Her eyes were wide with fear, and she looked as fragile as Ray had ever seen her.

He rushed up the stairs towards her as relief flooded through him.

~

Rita's legs felt like they were about to give out, and she was immediately thankful when Ray took her in his arms and pulled her into his chest. She cried into him.

'What happened?' she asked in between sobs.

'I have no fucking idea,' he replied, squeezing her tightly. 'But I'm so glad you're alive. I... I didn't think I'd find you.'

'What about Chloe?' she asked, pulling away from Ray. She was desperate to find out where her daughter was, but terrified of what he would say.

'She's safe,' Ray told her. Rita's tears flowed again, but this time she cried with utter relief.

The confusion that filled her was overwhelming. After seeing Marcus cut his own throat, it was as if a fog had been lifted from her eyes. She had stood motionless for a while, watching him cough and splutter as the life faded from his eyes. The strange entities around Marcus had then slowly dissipated away to nothing.

And then she was alone. And scared. And suddenly ashamed for all that she had done recently: ignoring her family, cheating on her husband, giving herself over so completely to Marcus, a man who had initially made her skin crawl.

When she then looked at his dead body—throat cut into a gaping yawn—similar feelings of revulsion quickly returned.

What have I done?

She'd run from the room, out into the hallway, and was met with a horrific sight.

Bodies were strewn around the corridor, though none were whole. A leg. An arm. Even a jaw.

'I'm so sorry,' she wailed, clutching Ray again. 'I don't understand why... how...' But she couldn't finish. She wanted to tell him that it was almost like someone else was controlling her, making her do those things. She even remembered screaming internally as she had flirted with Marcus before fucking him.

She realised that Ray was crying too. 'It's okay,' he said. 'It wasn't you.'

'What do you mean?' She looked up into his wet eyes.

'It was this place,' he replied. 'This *house*.'

Rita wasn't following, but it seemed there was no time to explain.

'Come on,' he said, taking her hand. 'We need to get out of here and back to Chloe. Let's go.'

Rita followed, desperate to see her daughter again. At the same time, she was ashamed at the prospect of facing her.

'CHLOE!' Rita yelled and ran over to her daughter.

Ray watched, feeling something approaching happiness —as much as he could muster knowing there were many people dead back inside the house.

Rita seemed different. She reminded Ray of how she'd been a month ago, that one night where he thought he'd broken through to her, before she'd fallen back into whatever stupor that was controlling her.

But now, as she hugged Chloe as tightly as Ray had seen, and with such desperate love, he knew he was in the presence of his wife again.

That meant whatever had just happened in the house, Rita was now free of its pull.

Ray just hoped the change was permanent.

It was all so clear to him now. Perhaps he'd broken free of his own haze, but he was suddenly angry with himself for not seeing what had really been going on earlier. Hell, even his wife's *physical* appearance had changed.

Though, could he really blame himself for not realising

that his wife had somehow become possessed by a haunted fucking house? It was insane to even think of.

'What's going on, Mum?' Chloe asked, still wrapped up in Ray's jacket.

Rita looked over to Ray with uncertain eyes.

'There was an accident,' Ray told his daughter. 'We have to leave here now.'

Chloe frowned. 'Will we be coming back?'

Ray paused for a moment, knowing how much the answer might upset her. But it wasn't something he could lie to her about. 'No, sweetie,' he said, as gently as he could. 'We're never coming back here.'

I MONTH LATER.

'Good news,' the lady on the other end of the phone said. 'The result is positive. You're pregnant. Congratulations!'

'Thank you,' Rita replied, feeling deflated. She then set down the receiver. That wasn't the result she'd been hoping for, though it was the one she had been expecting. She'd been late, and—worried about what it could mean—had gone to the doctor for a sample bottle so she could test for pregnancy. After returning the bottle, the five-day wait until she could make the call had been excruciating.

Now she had to tell Ray.

Rita pulled her coat tighter around herself and left the phonebox she was in. It was a short walk back to the hotel the family was staying in, but she planned to take her time. Chloe was at school, which was the only thing Rita could be thankful for at the moment.

How would she break it to Ray?

The issue of her cheating—if that was the word for it—was still raw. More so for her than for him, as Ray insisted he didn't blame Rita at all for what had happened. In his head, he was convinced she had been possessed by a supernatural presence, which was still something Rita was struggling to come to terms with.

But at the end of their time in Perron Manor, when Marcus had died, Rita had *seen* those spirits for herself. So it had to be true.

Regardless of how understanding Ray was being, however, and even if Rita wasn't to blame, the infidelity had still happened. And now there was a further repercussion to deal with.

Even though she dragged out the walk back as much as she could, Rita still reached the door to the hotel room far sooner than she'd wanted to. She took a breath and stepped inside.

Ray was lying on the bed, reading a magazine. He smiled upon seeing her and sat up. 'Hey, how was your walk?'

'Fine,' she said and closed the door behind her. She then slipped out of her coat and hung it up.

She felt nauseous.

Rita turned to him. There was no putting it off any longer... she had to get this over with.

'Ray,' she began. 'There's something we need to talk about.'

He sat up, and a frown crossed his face, no doubt mirroring the one Rita was wearing herself. 'What is it?'

She slowly padded over to the bed and sat near him, shaking, struggling to control her nerves.

She took a breath.

'I'm... pregnant.'

Ray's eyes widened. She could see him doing the mental arithmetic, something she had already done weeks ago.

Since getting out of the house, Ray had been patient

with her, letting Rita try to recover both emotionally and physically from what had happened. For the first week after leaving she had done nothing but sleep and eat, and it had helped her body return to a healthier state. It was only in the past week that she had felt comfortable enough to again give herself over to her husband physically. Prior to that, however, the last time she had slept with Ray was months ago.

She saw the realisation quickly dawn on him, and Ray was unable to hide the expression of pain. The news hit him like a physical blow.

'I'm so sorry,' she whispered. Ray sat in silence for a while, and Rita was braced for him to explode—to scream at her for ruining their family.

But he didn't.

Instead, he reached out his hand and placed it on hers. 'It isn't your fault,' he said. 'I keep telling you that.'

'But... I'm pregnant,' she said again. 'With *his* baby.'

Ray shook his head. 'No. The baby is ours.'

Rita swivelled her body to fully face her husband. She was stunned. But a sliver of joy sprouted up from her gut like the green shoot of a plant breaking through the heavy, dark soil of her fear.

'Are you sure?' she asked.

He nodded and gave her the most genuine smile she had ever seen. 'You're damn right I am. That house nearly ruined us. Nearly *killed* us. But we beat it, and we got out. This isn't a setback, Rita, it's a blessing. And, if you agree, we'll have this baby together. Then Chloe will get a little brother or sister.'

Rita didn't know what to say. She'd been terrified of how Ray was going to react, especially since the idea of not keeping the unborn child was one that made her feel physically sick. It wasn't an option for her to do anything but keep it. But she had been scared of where that would leave the family unit.

So, hearing Ray understand the situation, and more than that, actually *want* to bring the baby into their family and love it like he did Chloe made her burst with joy.

She started to cry. She couldn't help it. The whole situation was just too overwhelming. 'I want that, too,' she said.

Ray smiled, tearing up himself. He brought her towards him and hugged her. 'Then this is a good thing—we're going to have another baby together. But promise me this: no matter what, we never tell either child what happened in that fucking house.'

Rita let out a small laugh. 'I *definitely* agree with that.'

∽

Vincent lay on his bed in the foetal position. He rocked and pulled at his hair.

It had just gone three in the morning. He hadn't slept in what felt like weeks. The room was ice cold and the dead surrounded him. They *always* surrounded him now. Everywhere he went in the house, they were there watching him. And with them was Pazuzu.

It wasn't the only demon in the house, but was by far the most evil. It had decided to torment Vincent relentlessly since that night.

Pazuzu couldn't kill him. It wasn't allowed to. His job as the warden of the house was far too important.

But his comfort and sanity were not.

The demon stood over him, looking down on Vincent with that twisted and horrific face. It reached out a black talon as Vincent cowered and mewled. He then felt a sharp claw rake down his cheek, drawing blood. He screamed.

'Leave me alone! Please. Just leave me alone!'

But it wouldn't. This was his life now. The demon was angry at Vincent, and now it would have years of revenge on his mind and soul.

Even when Vincent was allowed to leave the house for a brief respite, to shop and gather basic supplies, he always had to return. Staying outside of the walls triggered an ever-rising pain and burning within him, which became unbearable after only a few hours.

Even if that were not the case, Pazuzu itself had said it would come for him if needed, no matter where he ran. And then, it wouldn't need to hold back.

Vincent almost wished that, after the night of Halloween, he had been arrested and forcefully taken from the house. Even if it had killed him, at least he would have been free of all this.

But that wasn't what had happened. The police investigated, and certainly suspected Vincent, Ray, and Rita, but could prove nothing. So, they were all set free, and Vincent was forced to return back to this hell.

Vincent knew that when the house was finally finished with him, and the time was right, Pazuzu would take his life... and Perron Manor would claim his soul.

Then, at long last, the unholy child created within these walls would be called home.

THE END

HAUNTED: PURGATORY

THE DEAD ARE SUFFERING...

Haunted: Purgatory
Book 3 in the Haunted Series.

Picking up immediately after the shocking climax of Haunted: Perron Manor, a paranormal research team is hired to help gather evidence and prove beyond a shadow of a doubt that Perron Manor is haunted.

The owner of the house needs the Church to sanction an exorcism. It is the only way to free the souls of the dead who are trapped there and suffering in eternal torment.

But the Church will not act without proof.

However, the team soon discover that they are ill-equipped to handle the notorious house, or what it really is.

Truths emerge that impact not only their fight for survival, but the very world around them.

Can the team survive long enough to free the dead from Perron Manor, or will their souls be forfeit as well?

Buy now to find out how the story of Perron Manor finishes. However... this is not the end. More horror lies outside of those walls.

Buy Haunted: Purgatory now.

INSIDE: PERRON MANOR

Sign up to my mailing list to get the FREE prequel...

In 2014 a group of paranormal researchers conducted a weekend-long investigation at the notorious Perron Manor. The events that took place during that weekend were incredible and terrifying in equal measure. This is the full, documented story.

In addition, the author dives into the long and bloody history of the house, starting with its origins as a monastery back in the 1200s, covering its ownership under the Grey and Perron families, and even detailing the horrific events that took place on Halloween in 1982.

No stone is left unturned in what is now the definitive work regarding the most haunted house in Britain.

The novella, as mentioned in Haunted: Perron Manor, can be yours for FREE by joining my mailing list.

Sign up now.

www.leemountford.com

OTHER BOOKS BY LEE MOUNTFORD

The Supernatural Horror Collection
The Demonic
The Mark
Forest of the Damned

The Extreme Horror Collection
Horror in the Woods
Tormented
The Netherwell Horror

Haunted Series
Inside Perron Manor (Book 0)
Haunted: Perron Manor (Book 1)
Haunted: Purgatory (Book 3)
Haunted: Possession (Book 4)
Haunted: Mother Death (Book 5)
Haunted: Asylum (Book 6)

ABOUT THE AUTHOR

Lee Mountford is a horror author from the North-East of England. His first book, Horror in the Woods, was published in May 2017 to fantastic reviews, and his follow-up book, The Demonic, achieved Best Seller status in both Occult Horror and British Horror categories on Amazon.

He is a lifelong horror fan, much to the dismay of his amazing wife, Michelle, and his work is available in ebook, print and audiobook formats.

In August 2017 he and his wife welcomed their first daughter, Ella, into the world. In May 2019, their second daughter, Sophie, came along. Michelle is hoping the girls don't inherit their father's love of horror, but Lee has other ideas...

For more information
www.leemountford.com
leemountford01@googlemail.com

ACKNOWLEDGMENTS

Thanks first to my amazing Beta Reader Team, who have greatly helped me polish and hone this book:

James Bacon

Christine Brlevic

John Brooks

Carrie-Lynn Cantwell

Karen Day

Doreene Fernandes

Jenn Freitag

Ursula Gillam

Clayton Hall

Tammy Harris

Emily Haynes

Dorie Heriot

Lemmy Howells

Lucy Hughes

Marie K

Dawn Keate

Diane McCarty

Megan McCarty

Valerie Palmer
Leanne Pert
Justin Read
Nicola Jayne Smith
Sara Walker
Sharon Watret

Also, thanks to my editor, Josiah Davis (http://www.jdbookservices.com) for such an amazing job as always.

The cover was supplied by Debbie at The Cover Collection. (http://www.thecovercollection.com). I cannot recommend their work enough.

And the last thank you, as always, is the most important—to my amazing family. My wife, Michelle, and my daughters, Ella and Sophie: thank you for everything. You three are my world.

Made in the USA
Coppell, TX
23 June 2023

18445819R00192